D1407843

praise for *BONK'S BAR*

"Putkowski brings the gritty, gristly northeast Philadelphia nether-world into delightfully vivid life like no author since *roman noir* grandmaster David Goodis. In less than 300 action-packed pages ... alternately heart-warming and bone-chilling ... *Bonk's Bar* shows that there's more to Philadelphia than just cheese steaks and the *Rocky* franchise." — PETER CHOMKO, *THE TEMPLE NEWS*

"From an industry perspective, *Bonk's Bar* works on so many levels. The nuances of the nightlife game seep through every chapter, as Tom Bonk's fiscal learning curve and the evolution of his manage-ment style reflect the one notion that every tavern owner knows: The experience inside the bar mirrors the experience within the per-son. Putkowski's depictions of the internal struggles and rewards, magnified by the extroverted nature of the bar business, make *Bonk's Bar* a great read for not only bar owners — who will recognize every character along the way — but for anyone who wants to know just how personally affecting this roller coaster of a profession can be."

— CHRIS YTUARTE, EDITOR-IN-CHIEF, *BAR BUSINESS MAGAZINE*

BONK'S BAR

also by DANIEL PUTKOWSKI

An Island Away

BONK'S BAR

a novel

DANIEL PUTKOWSKI

HAWSER
PRESS

This book is a work of fiction. Names, characters, places and incidents are products
of the author's imagination or are used fictitiously. Any resemblance to actual
events or locales or persons, living or dead, is entirely coincidental.

BONK'S BAR Copyright © 2009 by Daniel Putkowski
All rights reserved. Printed in the United States of America.

No part of this book may be used or reproduced in any manner whatsoever without
written permission except in the case of brief quotations embodied in critical
articles or reviews. For information, contact publicity@hawserpress.com.

The scanning, uploading, and distribution of this book via the Internet or via any
other means without the permission of the publisher is illegal and punishable by
law. Please purchase only authorized electronic editions, and do not participate
in or encourage electronic piracy of copyrighted materials. Your support of the
author's rights is appreciated.

ISBN 978-0-9815959-1-7

FIRST HAWSER PRESS TRADE PAPERBACK EDITION JUNE 2009
10   9   8   7   6   5   4   3   2   1

danielputkowski.com

This book is dedicated to John Bonk, Jr. and his fellow Marines who gave their lives in service to our nation.

1 ♣ ♥

I NEVER WANTED TO BE A BARTENDER. I wanted to finish college, to become a professional with letters behind my name. But my brother got himself killed, and I got stuck behind the bar, wiping up other people's drinks, listening to their bullshit, and wondering what my life would have been like.

It wasn't my brother's fault, and I don't blame him. He was always a big, tough kid, and he wanted to be even tougher. The only way to do that was to join the United States Marine Corps, the toughest of them all. He enlisted before he graduated high school. He was a natural at basic training and mastered all the skills of a good soldier. When the graduation ceremony was held at Parris Island, his drill sergeant spoke to our father and me personally. The sergeant was a powerfully built redneck with a Georgia accent and a pair of sledgehammers at the end of his arms. He told us that John Bonk was the best recruit he'd ever trained and that the United States of America would be a safer place if more men like him joined the Corps.

After a few years, John was promoted to corporal and then buck sergeant. He sent home photos of himself with his men. They looked like a merry bunch, five guys holding machine guns and grinning. The pictures came from far off places like Colombia, Brazil, and the Philippines. Then the shit hit the fan in the Middle East for the one hundred twenty-second time in a century. John shipped out to keep the peace, to guard vital U.S. interests, to keep the savages on their side of an imaginary line in the desert.

Mrs. Kirzner, the neighborhood know-it-all, called that afternoon. She wanted to know if I'd heard. Heard what? I wanted to know. I was in my room, studying for an upcoming final exam. It didn't take me long to figure it out when I saw the news. There was a solemn broadcaster, hiding his speech impediment behind therapy-perfected words even as he struggled to pronounce the name of some cluster of mud bricks that doubled for a town. He reported that there had been a firefight between some insurgents and the Marines guarding a convoy of relief supplies. Several Marines had been killed. I knew John was dead before the official car pulled to the curb.

It was my job to accept the bad news. Our father, John, Sr., was at one of the new casinos in Atlantic City, one that would still give him credit. A tall man wearing his dress uniform explained that my brother, John Bonk, Sergeant, United States Marine Corps, had died in action. His remains were coming home with those of fifteen others who died with him. They would arrive at Dover Air Force Base where they could be claimed. The man expressed his formal condolences and the thanks of the American people for my brother's service to the nation. My first thought was back to the drill sergeant. I wondered how he felt about his legendary recruit getting killed by a bunch of guys who didn't so much as wear uniforms.

I learned from the newspaper that the relief convoy that John and his men had been guarding was first hit by bombs buried under the road. The terrorists, or insurgents as some people called them, rushed the stopped vehicles. The attending Marines held them off for more than half an hour. This was quite a feat given that they were surrounded, outnumbered, and the lead vehicles were on fire. By the time helicopters and reinforcements arrived, there was no one left to save.

My brother died in battle like the Marines who stormed the islands of the Pacific, like the ones who marched to the shores of Tripoli. I imagined him firing his machine gun, shouting orders, urging his men to hold fast even as the rocket-propelled grenades exploded around them. Still, I doubted some movie star would be immortalizing John. There would be no Sands of Iwo Jima to show the public a fantasy that was supposed to be his reality. Hollywood didn't like what was going on over there. *The Philadelphia Inquirer* managed a photo of John on page 8 and a list of the dead at the end of a short article that did as much to question America's motives as it did to explain what happened to my brother. That had me boiling, but I kept it to myself. Who would listen anyway?

My college semester ended a couple of days later. It was the day our father got back from the casino. He was broke and hung over. I told him what happened, that his oldest son was not coming home alive. He grabbed the baseball bat kept behind the bar and ran into the street. I heard him scream he would kill any Arab he saw. There weren't any Arabs living in Port Richmond, our Philadelphia neighborhood. He didn't come back for two weeks. I had guessed it would take him a week to exorcise his demons, but it took him another seven days to run out of money, and I had some bruises that needed to heal.

I opened the bar that afternoon and every one thereafter. Growing up with the stink of alcohol in everything, the talk of beer and liquor was never far away. I knew how to work the taps and mix the simple drinks liked by people who patronized the place. Recipes and ritual soaked into my brain by osmosis.

That first week, everyone from the neighborhood came by to offer condolences and sniff for a free drink. "John was a hero," they would say, expecting me to pour them a drink in his honor and on the house. I loved my brother, and he was a hero. He died doing the right thing no matter what half of Congress said. Therefore, I accepted sad words with a silent nod but poured nothing for free. Instead, I went back to cleaning glasses, dreaming of an important job and just how high above street level my new apartment might be if only I landed a position in the coveted corner office.

On the night my father returned, I had lit a fresh pipe of tobacco and was watching the smoke curl up to the ceiling. It was a habit taken up sometime between high school and college and only done when I was alone. It was my private vice, something that smelled better than old beer. I sat in a ratty recliner, which had been mine since I learned to climb into it as a toddler. The sounds of my father coming up the stairs interrupted thoughts of John's funeral.

My father was piss drunk, full of melancholy, and oblivious to my black and blue eye sockets. He lectured me on the evils of the government, his hatred for the Arabs, how stupid the whole world was, and how nothing was fair. If my mother hadn't died giving birth to me, he would have had a decent wife to look after him. If John hadn't died, the bar would have been his. But since mom was gone, and John, too, it was about time I gave up dreams of all that bullshit they were teaching me in college and learn how to run a bar. At this point, I figured he would have seen my bruises but it wasn't to be. His lack of sympathy didn't annoy me, neither did his belated advice regarding the bar's operation. I was already on my way to re-shaping the place to my vision.

"And get rid of that pipe," he finished. "If you're going to smoke, smoke cigarettes. Be the Marlboro Man or something."

"I'm not trying to be anybody," I replied.

"Ah, sure you are. Borrowing money to go to college, playing the piano, keeping your nose in the air, people think you're an asshole. You're not fooling anyone. It's enough to make your mother roll in her grave."

He rambled on about my mother. If only she hadn't died giving birth to me, life would have been different. A familiar refrain, it was his explanation for everything that was wrong with the world. She was a saint who missed her calling. She was the only one who understood what it was like to be married to a man like him. He was right about that. The grass hadn't grown over my mother's grave before he ran through a parade of floozies and bimbos who thought a bar was a good business and that the man who owned it would be worth some money. They were more disappointed in him than he was in them. The mutual loathing manifested itself into a series of arguments that ended in shouted curses, slammed doors, and broken heels on the steps leading downstairs. One woman threw a bottle at him. It hit a window, went through the glass, and landed on someone's car in the street below. A piece of plywood still covered the hole.

I took all this from my father without saying a word. I knew my father was a degenerate gambler, a moderate drinker, and sometimes a fool. Arguing was a waste of time. Long ago, about the time I conquered the recliner, I learned to ignore his deficiencies and focus on the future.

I took an interest in schoolwork from the first grade and earned high marks from all my teachers. They encouraged me to go to college, and I won a few small scholarships. There was hope for me to escape the nature of my birth. No money or support came from the bar. With the casinos such a good investment, my father couldn't understand why I spent money listening to some former hippie teach me worthless shit. I worked various jobs, although never in the bar, and borrowed the rest. Four semesters later, things were going anywhere but toward a career behind the taps.

Then that first truck in my brother's convoy exploded. The terrorists killed my brother and destroyed a piece of my future. I knew it, my father knew it, and there was nothing I could do about it. Maybe there was a chance for me to walk away, to finish school, to stay on the right track. For a few nights, I imagined my brother telling me to do just that, to walk away from the bar and be my own man. But that's not how it went.

I wasn't a victim. I was a willing participant, a volunteer just like my brother who signed up for the United States Marine Corps. I took on a challenge to prove I could do anything the way my brother proved the same thing to that drill sergeant.

And I did, too. I turned that bar into a source of pride. I made friends and money and stood up to people who needed to be put down. I screwed married women, committed burglary, and murdered a scumbag who deserved worse than death. It wasn't the best of times, but it was never boring.

THE ACTION BEGAN ON MY FIRST DAY, though I didn't know it at the time because it got off to a slow start.

There was an upright piano in the far corner of the dining room. This my father bought for me when he hit it big at the blackjack table. What a surprise it was to find some burly guys rolling the old one onto a truck! I was in fourth grade and had been playing that old thing for a little more than a year. My feet hardly reached the floor. When I saw it going into the back of the truck, I ran down the block, arriving on the scene with tears ready to spill. One of the guys looked down and smiled. He pointed at the door to the bar. I spun to the left and saw the new piano sitting where the old one had been. It was a handsome upright that became my anchor to a place that otherwise held no fascination.

For the next eight years, I took lessons from my elementary school teacher. She was a nice lady with plenty of patience for all the wrong notes and kind words for the right ones. Music came to me naturally, the way hitting a baseball came to other kids. I could play by ear, and after she taught me to read music, it was easy to pick up most anything. I practiced mornings and Sundays when no one was around. Later, I took to playing Doors songs because I liked the honky-tonk, backbeat, retro-culture aspect of them.

I was knocking around the keys when my first customer came in. He was Matt, the manager of the tire shop down the street from the bar. I'd seen him from time to time. He sat near the dining room end of the bar, ordered a beer, and promptly lit a cigarette.

"Sorry about your brother," he said. "I didn't know him, but it's still a shame."

"Yeah, thanks," I muttered.

"I guess Diane's not feeling well," he noted.

Diane, my father's regular bartender, was off sick, which is why I was standing there by myself. She called to let me know she just couldn't make it.

"How's college life?" Matt asked.

At this point I was still enrolled, so I said, "Good." College was good. I enjoyed learning, and there were students from different parts of the country as well as the rest of the world. Group projects were a drag, but they gave me the chance to meet outsiders, as in people other than those from Port Richmond. I divided my acquaintances into two groups: natives and foreigners. The natives were usually from the suburbs of Philadelphia and found the city a great place to hang out. The foreigners fell into another pair of categories. The first hated the United States and were enrolled because their parents wanted them to get an American education, whatever that was. They pontificated at length about the U.S. being no different than the Imperial Empire in *Star Wars*. They jumped me when I told them my brother was a Marine, but their criticism was so much bullshit because I knew John wasn't stabbing babies with his bayonet or standing guard duty for an oil company. The second gang had educational visas and wasn't going home no matter what happened. Who could blame them? They came from places like Guyana, Senegal, and Bolivia. At any rate, they were all different from me, a guy trying to launch himself out of a lower-middle class saga and into the big time.

Through the open door, Matt and I watched a tractor-trailer turn onto Tioga Street. The trailer was stacked with giant tires headed for the P.J. Dooling Tire Co., the shop where Matt worked.

"Those are the biggest tires I've ever seen," I said to Matt.

"Some of them weigh several tons," Matt informed me. "They sell for ten grand a piece."

I thought about my student loans and figured that if I stole four of those tires and managed to sell them to somebody I would be debt free. There might even be something left for a party.

"See you later," Matt said and tossed three dollars on the bar.

I rang up the sale in the ancient cash register that had been installed by my grandfather. The drawer popped open. On the left side of the tray was a snapshot of my brother. It was the one taken on the day he graduated from boot camp. I smiled reflexively. My brother and I, unlike so many other siblings in this world, always got along. He was a bruiser; I was a runt. No one got between us. No one so much as made fun of me for playing the piano or being the last one picked for an intramural game. They knew I was John Bonk's brother, which was all the protection I needed. I eased the drawer closed and faced the bar.

A few of the regulars straggled in. They all drank beer, one of the four brands on tap, among which Yuengling Lager was the most popular. I gave them a freshly chilled glass with each new pour. It was something my father never did, but to me it was necessary. In the first place, warming beer stank of the molded grain it really was. Ice-cold brew, on the other hand, had the fragrance of fresh-cut fruit. So I served it that way. Furthermore, shuttling glasses between the dishwater and the fridge kept me moving and my mind off grandiose ideas about expensive cars, penthouse apartments, lingerie-clad women, and a career that paid for it all.

Most of these guys worked night jobs or collected unemployment. They talked to each other or mumbled at the television. I stared into space when I wasn't dreaming of my future profession. It was a struggle to defend my sanity against the endless patter of injustice from the customers. They lamented the cuts in Social Security payments. They harbored plenty of anger for rich people. And no one thought the unemployment checks were sent out on the right day. Sometimes they came on the weekend, and the poor bastards had to go two days without any money.

Right about this time I snapped out of my daze. Someone was calling me, a female voice this time, which was startling for its rarity.

"Yo, Tom! How about a six-pack of Bud?"

I spotted Ally, a neighborhood girl standing at the bar. She wore old jeans and a tight shirt, unbuttoned to reveal her bra.

She was a familiar face from my high school days but was several years younger than me. More recently, I had seen her around Port Richmond, walking with a guy who looked like he smoked butts from the gutter.

"You have I.D.?" I asked her without moving away from my post. Being only twenty-two myself, I figured she couldn't be more than eighteen or nineteen.

"Come on," she pleaded. "Your dad always gave me a six-pack when I wanted it."

"So do us a favor and go find him," I said.

I knew she wasn't old enough to drink legally. Selling her a six-pack wasn't worth a fine or the risk of being closed down for a week by the Pennsylvania Liquor Control Board. My father might have taken that chance. Not me. I wanted to tread water and not run afoul of the government or anyone else until Diane came back to work or the next semester began, whichever came first.

Ally wasn't used to people denying her requests. She looked around the room for support but the regulars weren't volunteering, although one managed a shrug. At last she kneeled on one of the stools, leaned over the bar far enough to show me the best part of her tits, and said, "Tom, can I please have a six-pack?"

Everyone was waiting to see what I would do. It was more than just a question of whether or not I would sell her the beer. They wanted to know what Bonk's kid, the younger one, the smug little prick, was going to be like behind the bar. They knew my father was gone and were sizing me up. Most of them thought I was a college punk, too good to work a real man's job. From time to time I heard them through the floorboards asking my father where that college kid of his was. His only response was, "Where do you think?" He meant they shouldn't bust his balls about his younger son, the one too small to be a soldier but maybe smart enough to get a seat at the boardroom table. This occasional mockery came from a bunch of guys who looked upon their bartender as a hero. He was someone who put up with their stupid jokes, who gave lots of free marriage counseling, and who had a few tips about horses and ball games and where an available woman could be bought. Their bartender was part of the crowd, yet a little above it.

"When you have I.D., I'll sell it to you," I said to Ally. "Button up your shirt on your way out."

"Are you some kind of faggot?" she retorted.

The guys laughed into their beers.

"Are you some kind of whore?" I asked.

"Kiss my ass, Tom! I hope you go broke."

At that point, it was too early in my tenure for anyone, including me, to know how wrong she was. But in that quip she had presaged a scary reality that the bar was going to be mine to win or lose. And the tone had been set. There was going to be a lot of shouting across the bar, and some fighting, too. Ally would be involved and her age would not be a factor.

When the door slammed behind her, one of the regulars, Tony, said, "Your father always sold her a six." He was still watching the space through which Ally had walked. Her body was worth a look, except that when a man Tony's age looked at a girl like her it gave me the creeps.

"Good for him," I said.

Tony, and the rest of the bunch for that matter, now knew I had my own rules. The first one was that I didn't take advice from that side of the bar. After another shrug, Tony went back to the television.

About an hour later, Matt returned with two other guys. They were Doolings, Greg and Paul, who owned the tire business that bore their father's initials. The three of them ordered bottled beer and took a table against the wall.

Unexpectedly, Diane showed up as I brought the Dooling boys their second round. She looked terrible, as if someone had rubbed sandpaper around the corners of her eyes and nose. Still, she had spruced herself up with a clip in her hair and a necklace that caught the light. She was somewhere around middle age but still had the spark that had been snuffed out in most of the other women in the neighborhood. Then again, I wasn't the best judge. I had a crush on her from the time I was five until I got laid for the first time in junior high school. My earliest memories were of her keeping an eye on me when my father was away at the casinos. She used to doze off on the couch and I would watch whatever I wanted on television. She was a stickler about my homework, coming upstairs to check on me at least three or four times during the afternoon. I credited her with keeping me on a straight course to higher education.

"I wanted to see how you were doing," Diane said.

"No problem," I told her. "Go home and get some rest."

She looked around the bar. "I could get plenty of rest here."

The Doolings waved to her. She smiled back and my crush flashed for a second. Diane had never given me any shit about wanting to better myself, nor had she tried to take advantage of my father. She could have robbed him blind when he was on one of his benders. The cash drawer always added up. The inventory correlated to the till. She took her salary in cash and thanked my father when he paid her. He frequently said she was too young for him, too old for me, and just right to work the bar. She usually gave me a pat on the shoulder, or a hug, or reminded me to double-check my essays before she went out the door. It may not seem like much, but it meant a lot to a kid with no mother.

"Your father should do something," she said looking around the room.

"Like what?" I asked.

"I guess he was waiting for your brother to get out of the Marines," she answered.

It was never a secret that my father wanted the bar to be John's, which was why I never invested any time or effort into it. My plans were my own.

"Anything would be an improvement," Diane added.

"You're right," I said. At the time, I had no great ideas for making the place into a first-rate establishment, but it wouldn't be long before some dramatic improvements took hold.

Diane seemed to feel that she was treating me badly. "I'm sorry, Tom," she said. "I've had this cold for more than a week. It's making me grouchy."

"Don't worry about it. I'll be here until you get better." It was the least I could do for her, and myself for that matter.

She left and, soon after, so did the Doolings. It took another hour for the regulars to blow their budgets and find the door. When I was alone, I switched off all the lights in the bar and took a seat at the piano. Of course it was a Doors' song that came to mind. Depending on whom you talked to, it was called *Whiskey Bar* or *Alabama Song*. The notes rattled out of the piano and bounced around the empty room like pebbles tossed against a plate glass window. The song was appropriate for the moment. Ally had cursed my future. Diane had reckoned my past. And I thought I was just passing the time until the next semester began. I might have done just that, but I heard the door open and in walked a guy who would be one of several who kept me from my original goals. I should have played *Riders on the Storm*. It would have been apropos for what came to pass.

"We're closed," I said getting up from the piano.

"I want not to drink," the guy said in an accent I recognized as Russian. There were a good number of immigrants from the old Soviet Socialist Republic living around the northern edge of the neighborhood. They had displaced some of the Polish and Irish, who were either dying off or moving out.

"We don't have anything else, so I'm going to have to ask you to leave," I informed him politely.

We met at the threshold that divided the dining room from the barroom. In the dim light I saw that he was as big as my brother and more ominous than a funnel cloud in Kansas.

"Where is Bonk?" he asked.

"Which one?"

"John Bonk."

"Junior is dead. Senior is probably at a casino in Atlantic City."

"You know this fact?"

"I grew up with them both. I know it better than anyone."

He nodded his head. "Ah, you are the other one. The boy."

I thought of myself as a man but didn't relay that to him. "Who are you?" I asked.

"Sergei. I leave message. You give to your father."

"Sure," I replied.

He hit me square in the face, right between the eyes. I landed flat on my ass with stars over my head.

"You not forget, no?" he said.

Hitting back was out of the question. I could only moan.

"I collect from Bonk on Monday. Today is Monday."

He helped himself to the cash register then returned to my side.

"This is not interest on what he owes. Where is rest?"

"I don't know."

"You the son. You know where he hide money."

As far as I knew, my father never held on to money long enough to hide it.

"Go get it!" Sergei yelled.

"Listen, I ..."

"You tell me to listen? I have not ears to hear but eyes to see no money. What is line from movie? 'Show me money!'"

"There isn't any," I said, sitting up.

He took a second to digest that I was not a threat and that I was telling the truth. "Probably you stupid boy," he said.

The money from the register landed on my lap.

"This is nothing, stupid boy. How can I accept nothing? To me, to you, is insult. I come back. Talk to man. Is best not to waste time with children. That is job for woman."

With that he walked out the door.

My first thought was of my fellow college students who watched too many episodes of *Cheers* and thought owning a bar was a great way of life. To them it was a never-ending stream of witty jokes, impossible love affairs, and plenty of cash to support it all. Maybe there were places in Philadelphia that were like that. Bonk's Bar wasn't. I used to fall asleep to pointless arguments about baseball and hockey. There were fights that spilled into the street and lasted half an hour. Frequently, someone honored the bathroom with a pile of puke. You had to be a masochist or insane to want a life like that.

And yet, the one hundred twenty-eight dollars on my lap was seed money for my brush with truculence and mental disorder.

AS I EXPECTED, MY PUFFY EYES gave me credibility with the regulars. They already thought of me as a conceited little wiseguy, but the black and blue flesh left them guessing. I overheard their musings. They were confused as to whether or not I had taken a beating or dished one out. There wasn't enough damage to confirm it one way or the other. The final word was that even if I was an uppity asshole, I was still John Bonk's little brother, and John Bonk was one tough son of a bitch. It took a hundred towelheads to get him and not before he stained the desert with a good amount of their blood. By Thursday night, I was getting occasional thanks for the cold glasses and fewer pleas for free drinks.

On Friday afternoon, the phone rang just as I was about to unlock the door. It was Diane.

"I hate to bother you, Tom," she said, "but can you pick up me."

"Sure," I replied, eager to spend a few minutes alone with a former crush and a woman I generally liked.

"It's a little far, but I'm at the Food Distribution Center, you know, by the stadiums. I was covering for a friend who works down here and the bus won't get me back in time."

"No problem," I said.

We agreed to meet at the corner of Third and Pattison. My car was a mid-90's Cadillac Sedan de Ville. It was a ridiculous choice given the price of gasoline, but I bought it cheap from an old man who had to give it up to go into a nursing home. The cut-rate insurance fit my budget, too.

The drive down Richmond Street depressed me. The renaissance that had renewed other neighborhoods had yet to flower here. Buildings on both sides of the street leaned shoulder to shoulder. Pairs of vacant stores slept behind faded going out of business signs. Some residents tried to keep their places up with fresh paint and clean windows. But there was usually a plastic bag stuck in the foliage or empty beer bottles standing on the stoops.

Port Richmond had once been a solid working-class neighborhood, full of Polacks and Irishers who worked at the shipyards. There were social halls named for noble soldiers who had died before my brother lost his life in a nameless conflict. These people walked to work and, afterward on the way home, stopped at the bar my grandfather had put his name upon all those years ago. They supported him and my father and would have supported my brother if he had lived to overcome our father's mistakes. The area was changing, not necessarily for the worse, but not for the better either. The new immigrants, Russians, Chinese, Mexicans, and some Vietnamese, had nothing in common but low-income jobs.

Farther south, on Delaware Avenue, I passed through a strip of nightclubs and waterfront condominiums that celebrated the Philadelphia renewal that the mayor-turned-governor liked to brag about. I had been in a few of those clubs and dated a girl whose father had bought one of the condos at the pre-construction price. There was a lot to be said for an eight-dollar shot of whiskey and a five-hundred-dollar-a-month maintenance fee. The whiskey tasted the same, but the view was a hell of a lot better than the one from my bedroom window.

After the clubs and a dozen blocks of no-man's land came the marine terminals. Shipping containers, stacked seven high and in all the primary colors, looked like some abstract artist's idea of a multimillion-dollar installation. Then it was the Food Distribution Center, which the same mayor-then-governor managed to keep in town despite a wicked attempt by New Jersey to lure it across the river.

I rounded the end of Delaware Avenue, which turned into Pattison at this point. Diane stood on the corner by a lunch wagon. She waved with a big smile. I pulled up and she hauled open the door. She didn't so much as blink at my bruised face.

Before I pulled out, she asked, "Do you like seafood?"

"Lobster," I answered.

"How about crabs?"

"Crab cakes are good."

"Well, there's a guy up at Silva's who is throwing away two huge boxes of crabs."

Perplexed, I said, "Maybe they're spoiled or something."

"Nah. He was cursing his head off about how he brought in these special crabs for a customer at one of the big restaurants and the chef changed his mind. I'd never throw something like that away."

Too bad, I thought. Life is full of disappointments. I wheeled into the parking lot, past a few tractor-trailers, in search of a place to turn around.

Diane pointed to a huge metal bin parked at the end of the warehouse. "There he is!" she shouted.

A beefy guy carrying a pair of cardboard boxes hustled up to the side of the dumpster. He set both boxes on the ground then took the top one and hefted it onto his shoulder. There was no doubt about it. Those crabs were headed for the landfill.

I don't know why, maybe because I thought it would make Diane happy, I slammed on the horn and the gas at the same time. The guy turned, shifted the box on his shoulder, and gave me the finger. The Cadillac crossed the lot like an angry bear. I hit the brakes just in time for Diane to hop out and stop him from heaving the box over the side.

"Who the hell are you?" he asked Diane. "The seafood police?"

"I'll buy those crabs," Diane told him.

"You work for that shithead at Two Rainbows?"

"I work for him," Diane replied pointing her thumb at me.

"Who's he?"

"Tom Bonk."

"Yeah? You have a crab fest or something planned for tonight?" he asked me.

"No."

"Then what else would you do with two bushels of the best crabs money can buy? Wait. Don't answer. You could take them up to Two Rainbows and serve them there."

Two Rainbows was no restaurant I had ever heard of and I told him that.

"You're going to throw them away," Diane pleaded. "What do you care?"

"I care about the price, lady. I ain't getting duped into giving them away. I'd rather throw them out just to teach that shithead a lesson."

"Forget it," I said to Diane. "Let's go."

"Fifty bucks," Diane said to him.

"Fifty bucks for two bushels of crabs? You need your head examined."

"You're right," she said. "Put them in the trash and get nothing."

He looked at the box of crabs, at the dumpster, at me, and finally at my car. The machinery of his brain grinded out the only conclusion that made sense: the black-and-blue-eyed wheelman of a '95 Cadillac had nothing to do with a trendy restaurant. That and fifty dollars was better than nothing.

"Let's see the money," he said.

Diane put her hand out to me. "Do you have fifty bucks, Tom?"

I did and I gave it to her. The guy double-checked the count before shoving the boxes toward Diane with the toe of his shoe.

"There you are," he said. "Cook 'em all tonight. They'll be spoiled tomorrow."

With the crabs in the trunk, we rolled up Delaware Avenue.

"I take it you know how to make crabs," I said when we stopped for the light at Washington Avenue.

"I don't have a clue," Diane admitted.

"I just spent fifty bucks, Diane."

She was nonplussed. "How could you go wrong for that price?"

"They'll spoil and the fifty will be down the drain."

"Sell them at the bar, Tom." This she said as if it was so obvious that I should never have asked.

Driving again, I decided not to take any chances. At Dock Street, I cut into the city.

"Where are we going?"

"To get the rest of what we need."

"Great!" she beamed.

I parked on Walnut, a few blocks from a popular bookstore. Diane waited in the car while I perused the stacks. There were dozens of cookbooks on the shelves. It took me fifteen minutes to settle on *Seafood Delights of the Stars*. A huge book, it was spiral bound and featured celebrity photos beside their favorite seafood recipes, of which there were several for crabs.

Diane squealed upon seeing the book. She sat with it across her lap and read off the contents.

"This sounds really good: Crabs with Special Hot Sauce. That would go great with beer, just like down the shore. I'll bet we can sell all of them tonight."

Her optimism was contagious. I found myself daydreaming about the good times I'd had at the Jersey Shore with my brother. Shortly after he got his driver's license he bought a junker that became our ride to and from the beach towns. We slept Friday and Saturday nights in the thing, showering in the ocean or somebody's rental. Soon I was back to reality. Who was going to cook this magic potion and would the people who patronized Bonk's Bar appreciate the taste? If they did, would they pay for it?

"Don't worry," Diane said, "Lizzie can cook anything."

"Who's Lizzie?"

"The lady from my church. She does all the cooking," she explained. "You get the bar open. I'll pick her up and get whatever else we need."

At the bar, I gave her the last of my ready cash. She slid behind the wheel, waved with her fingers, and when I had the two boxes of crabs at the door, pulled away.

Inside, I opened the top box. The crabs were ugly creatures. It was a mystery to me what parts were edible. I decided that I was willing to sell them, but there was no way I was going to eat them. When they were packed away in the cooler, I roamed through the kitchen to see if I could get things ready. The space was clean, as it hadn't been used since my father's last cook quit about a year earlier. Since I didn't know my way around that end of the business I left for the dining room.

The dining room itself occupied half of the first floor. The other half consisted of the bar, which was also wide enough to host several tables. Most of the tables and chairs were older than I was. Some of them needed to be repaired. Some of them needed to go the way the rescued crabs nearly went. The window onto the street was cracked in one corner. A piece of peeling duct tape patched the wound. The place was depressing, except for the piano. It needed a tuning, but the action was snappy. I sat down and played a reprise of *Whiskey Bar*. The music cheered up the room.

I heard the side door open, expecting Diane and Lizzie. Instead, Ally stood in the doorway.

"I didn't know you played the piano," she said. "What kind of music is that?"

"The Doors," I answered.

"Yeah, cool, like hippie music."

It seemed she wasn't holding a grudge against me for not serving her.

"Is Diane around?" she asked.

"Went to get Lizzie," I said. "She'll be back in a couple of minutes."

"Mind if I wait?"

"No," I said, hoping she wouldn't ask me to sell her beer.

Playing for other people was not something I did, so I pushed a broom around the floor.

"What's Lizzie going to cook?" Ally asked.

It seemed that everyone knew Lizzie's profession but me. "Crabs," I said.

"No way!" she cheered with her hands on her hips, striking a stunning pose backlit by the fractured window. If she was a few years older and a few pounds heavier I would have bought her a few drinks and tried to get her upstairs before my father came home. As it was, she was scrawny, needed some help with her makeup, and below the minimum age for the rides at Tom Bonk's private amusement park.

"One time, Craig and I were down the shore and had crabs. They were the best! But they cost a lot for what you get."

"How much?" I asked.

"Two bucks for the tiny ones, three-fifty for mediums and six bucks for the giant suckers."

The prices sounded low to me, but I was thinking of those fancy clubs. I wondered what Two Rainbows intended to charge for the crab special. Still, the guys at the bar might spring for them. I thought there must be people around the neighborhood who had also eaten crabs at the shore. I put my education and my former sparring partner to work.

"How about making me a sign?" I asked Ally. "And if you give Lizzie a hand, I'll pay you a few bucks."

"You have a picture of a crab? Something I can work from?"

"On the box in the freezer," I said.

She went to the kitchen and returned with a piece of the box in her hand. On the way out the door, she said over her shoulder, "I'll scrounge up a board, some paint, and put it out on the corner. Okay?"

Diane and Lizzie arrived a while later. They toted four sacks of groceries through the bar and into the kitchen, which was located beyond a swinging door. It wasn't but a few minutes before Diane came out. She unlocked the front door and propped it open. I saw the lights flicker in the bar and heard water running as she filled the basins for washing the glasses. After an hour or so, I heard her laughing.

"Look at that sign," Diane said, pointing through the open door.

It was the type of art that might have been on the front of a World War II bomber. A smiling crab tugged at the bikini bottom of a buxom woman. Ally leaned over the sign with a brush. "Bonk's Crabs," she painted.

"How much do I owe you for the wood and paint?" I asked.

"Nothing. I got it down at Masgai Demolition. They're always throwing away truckloads of stuff. If I had more time this would look a little better. Anyway, I'm going home to clean up and then I'll come back to help Lizzie."

Soon after Ally left, the smell of hot peppers drifted out of the kitchen. It was strong enough to drive out eight decades of stench.

Diane carried a plate loaded with crabs up to the bar. "Try one," she said.

I stared down at the boiled and sauced aliens. They looked a little better cooked than in the box. Still, there was no way I was going to eat one, but I didn't want to hurt my celebrity chef's feelings. I dipped a finger into the sauce and licked it.

"That's good," I said.

"You're not going to try the crab?"

My face betrayed the answer.

"Fine," she pouted. "Another one to sell."

"Those things look disgusting," I said.

"They look like good eating, Tom. You have to expand your tastes." She cracked open a leg and sucked the juice out of it.

"I was thinking about selling a crab and a beer for five bucks."

Diane nodded her head as she wiped sauce from her chin. "That sounds like a good deal, and you're the boss."

I wasn't the boss. My father was. But I was there and he wasn't, so things just ran along as if the big decisions were mine to make.

The regulars came in, noticed the smell, and despite Ally's sign didn't know what to make of it until she showed up.

"Did you guys have a crab?" she asked them as if they should have known better.

No one answered that they had.

She went to the kitchen and returned with a giant Tupperware basin of crabs stewing in the hot sauce. She tore off a leg and did a repeat performance of Diane's move. I didn't know whether it was the smell or the sight of Ally sucking on the leg that did the trick. Either way, Tony and another guy said they would try one.

"Five bucks for a crab and a beer," I said.

"Let's have it," Tony said and the other guy nodded.

Ally brought out plates, put a crab on each one, and slid them across the bar. I tapped two beers and waited for a reaction. Both of them knew how to eat crabs and did so without regard to the mess they were making. I noticed they quaffed their beers like camels at an oasis.

"Give me another of both," Tony said. Not to be out done, the other guy asked for the same.

After Ally changed their plates, I pulled her on the side and asked her how many crabs were back there.

"I don't know, maybe a hundred," she answered.

I couldn't help but smile. If I managed to sell a third of them it would be a good night for a guy with no experience at running either a bar or a restaurant. Then I remembered I would have to pay Lizzie and Ally. I dodged into the kitchen to do my own count.

Lizzie stood beside the huge gas range in the back corner. She was a large, middle-aged woman who whispered Psalms while she cooked. When I asked her about the crab count, she said there were usually between seventy and eighty jumbo crabs in a bushel. These were a little bigger than jumbos, she informed me, so there were probably a few less.

"Thanks, Lizzie," I said, "What do I owe you for coming in?"

"I used to get sixty bucks for a half day at the diner," she replied. "That was a while ago, but I wasn't doing anything tonight so I'd be happy with that."

"Alright," I told her. "See me before you leave." I hustled back to the bar to see how things were going. The pressure was on the sales department to meet my recently increased overhead.

As it turned out, I had nothing to worry about. The Dooling boys showed up, and with them were Matt and a few guys from the shop.

"You got crabs, and you don't call us?" Greg yelled at me. "For Christ's sake, Tom, we're neighbors!"

Ally rescued me and served them at their regular table. They mowed down a pair of crabs each and thereby put me very close to the break-even point.

A few locals drifted in, scoped the pan of crabs, but didn't bite. An argument among the regulars fired up over whether the fishing was better in the Chesapeake Bay or the Delaware. I could see these guys making it down the river, but the Chesapeake was beyond their theater of operations. I let them ramble on for a while before smacking a shot glass on the bar and asking them to keep it down.

Just then a good-looking guy wearing an expensive sport coat came through the door. It was Lottery Joe, the luckiest guy to graduate two years ahead of my brother. He hit six numbers for a small seven-figure payout. He and his jacket were as out of place as a tutu on a Pit Bull. Before he made it across the room, Ally was all over him. I should have seen this as a clue to the future, but I was too busy thinking about money to concentrate on what was really important.

"You came for the crabs, didn't you?" she asked.

He smiled, looked past her, and said, "That and other things."

Greg got up from his table and waved him over. "Take a seat, Joe. She'll bring you a crab and some beer."

"How about a martini?" Joe asked.

Greg belly-laughed.

Joe caught Ally's hand, brought it up to his lips, and gazed into her eyes. He said, "A vodka rocks, a tall glass of water, and one of these crabs Greg is talking about. Can you remember all that?"

"If you can remember my number," she replied.

He winked and made his way to Greg's table.

Seeing this exchange left me feeling like a pimp, which was about the strangest feeling in my life to date. There were other odd emotions to come. First, there was the telephone, which was ringing. I forgot about Ally and answered it. The caller wanted to know about the crabs. I told him the deal and he asked about take-out.

"In that case," I said, "they're five bucks each and bring your own container."

To my surprise, he showed up looking for ten crabs. I took his money while Diane shoveled the crabs into his covered pan. The parade began in earnest after he left. I was busy answering the phone and tapping beer while Ally shuttled crabs from the kitchen to the dining room and Diane served them to the bar patrons and take-out customers.

Who knew the crabs were going to be my trademark, that they would become a pillar on which I'd build a successful business? Not me. It was a fluke, something I did because I thought it would make Diane happy.

I should have known, especially after the last crab was sold around nine-thirty and people were asking why I didn't have more. They were disappointed at having missed the crabs but hung around the bar for a beer or two, which put some extra money in the cash register.

It wasn't until I'd closed the bar and counted the money

that I realized Ally had left at some point. Pimp or not, she skipped out, which had me fuming. Now I owed someone money, which made me angry because, other than my college loans, I lived a debt-free life. Or so I thought.

AS A KID, I NEVER WATCHED Saturday morning car-
toons. I should have. An upright-walking coyote has as much
to teach as any tenured professor. The residential quarters of
Bonk's Bar were only equipped with basic cable, so the more
intelligent channels were not an option either. At any rate, I
was busy with my homework and the piano and trying to be
smarter than everyone around me. It was that kind of arrogance that made me the guy who would turn Bonk's Bar into
a landmark. It also got me into trouble with the law, my father's bookie, and someone's husband. Before all that, I had
to deal with the fundamentals of running a neighborhood
taproom.

Luckily, my father slapped a magnet bearing his beer dis-
tributor's number on the cooler. After Friday night's crab fest
and a decent Saturday, the supplies of the beloved Yuengling
and other beers were running low. Diane did me the favor

of putting together a list of things I was to order on Monday morning. The money from the weekend gave me the confidence to make the call without fear.

A man named Marty answered on the second ring.

"This is Tom Bonk calling," I informed him.

"Who?"

"Tom Bonk."

"Oh, yeah, John Bonk's other kid."

"That's me," I said and rattled off my order.

"No problem, small order," he said when I was finished. "So look Tom, I got to get the money when my guy delivers this stuff. You understand?"

"I do. How much?"

"Well, your old man is into me for like five thousand and change. I spare him the interest."

The only thing that surprised me was that it wasn't more.

Marty was saying, "Give the driver eight fifty and that will take a hundred off the old number."

As if I had a choice, I said, "Okay, Marty. I'll be looking for your guy."

"He'll be there, and by the way, give my guy cash. I don't want no checks. Sorry to hear about your brother."

After hanging up, I took out one of the order pads left over from the time when the dining room functioned regularly. Five thousand and change? I estimated that to mean five thousand two hundred fifty dollars, or the price I had paid for a pair of courses at my university.

Knowing less than nothing about running a business and thinking about the cash I'd made over the weekend, five grand and change didn't seem like a big debt to overcome. Besides, I didn't have a gambling habit, I wasn't a drunk, and I wasn't involved with any expensive women. I hadn't forgotten about the guy who knocked me on my ass. That was between him and my father. I mean it should have been.

Before Sergei returned to drag me up the learning curve, I had a visit from another form of vermin. Again, I didn't suspect a thing because I was too stupid to know how stupid I was.

The mail came and my grades, as always, were stellar. I celebrated by cranking out a few hits on the piano. Heading up the stairs for my pipe, I heard someone knocking on the door and figured it was Marty's delivery guy. I jogged to the side door, pulled it open, and found a dapper gentleman on the other side.

"Who are you?" I asked with all the congeniality of a medieval jailer.

"Sy Kranick," he said and pointed a business card at me.

I took his card, saw attorney at law embossed on it, and was glad I hadn't bothered to shower. Breaking out in a sweat, I asked him what he wanted.

"Let's find a seat inside so we can talk," he suggested.

This was the last time I let anyone in the bar with those credentials. Someone else would break in, but there was nothing I could do about that.

Sy took a seat at a table in the center of the room. His clean-shaven face was narrow, angular, with eyes like a wicked priest.

"You must be Thomas Bonk," he began.

"Good guess. And you are?"

"Sy Kranick," he repeated. "I'm the managing partner of Factor Associates."

"Congratulations," I said.

He managed a smile for me, but it didn't last. "Is your

father here?"

"No," I replied.

"Do you know when he will be?"

"Don't have a clue," I said. The way the guy sat in the chair, stiff as a board, asking questions like I was a four-year-old, rubbed me the wrong way. Because of this and the fact that some of my arrogance was peeking through, I said, "I'm running things until he gets back."

Now Kranick offered a braggart's grin and started moving with all the alacrity of a spider monkey. He yanked out a stack of papers, made a show of going through them, then turned a page for me to study. School wasn't in session so I ignored it.

"Literature isn't my major," I said. "Just tell me."

"The short version is that Factor Associates has acquired your father's debt from the Marina Casino Corporation of Atlantic City. The net total is one hundred twenty-five thousand dollars. Your father signed a note, collateralizing the debt with these premises. He has thirty days to pay the interest, which accrues beginning today at a rate of twenty-one percent per annum. If he fails to pay the interest, we'll foreclose and sell the real estate at auction to recover our investment."

If only college had gone so quickly, I would have had a doctorate in business and life and avoided all the nonsense in between.

"Would you like a copy?" Kranick asked triumphantly.

I got the sense that he liked going out on these little terror missions, threatening the foolish and the unlucky. It irked me that he had lumped me in with that crowd. After all, I had two years of college under my belt and was the brother of John Bonk, Junior, the toughest recruit that one drill sergeant had ever seen. Just the same, my father was Polish, my mother Irish, and as the old joke went, that made me too stupid to know when to leave a bar. Actually, it was my high opinion of myself that got me in trouble. I would learn that later, after I discovered what success really was and had some perspective on who I had been before I figured out how to operate like a professional.

And then Kranick made a critical mistake. Apparently, his message of doom was not enough to satisfy his own ego. He had to pile on some insult to the injury. He said, "I don't know you from Adam, but I suggest you give these papers to your father and find another place to live."

He might have mocked my deceased mother while he was at it, or called my brother a baby-killer. The fact was that this room held my piano, and at the moment, I had nowhere else to put it. In addition, I slept upstairs, sat in that old recliner with my pipe, and shared the occasional meal with dear old gambling dad at the kitchen table. Despite his faults, my father put that roof over my head, scored the piano without me asking, and had promised the bar to his other son. I wasn't ready to give any of that up just yet, especially to a guy with a smirk and a fancy pen that he used like a rapier.

"You'll get your money," I said standing up.

He failed to suppress a chuckle, put his papers away, and headed for the door. Before leaving he looked at me and asked, "For the record, what was your major?"

"Music," I told him though I had not yet decided.

He grinned one last time then hustled out to his car, which I noticed was a jet-black Mercedes, the kind of car driven by big shots the world over.

A smarter guy would have taken Kranick's advice. I did

think about putting my bad attitude back in the closet, finding a job for the summer, and an apartment to go with it. However, I had a few things to prove. Besides, in the worst case, I would be looking for that job and apartment in three months instead of this afternoon. Therefore, it was full speed ahead.

I forgot about my pipe and sat down at the piano. Not half a song later I heard a twang from inside the case. In my fourteen years of piano playing, I'd never heard a string break but I knew that's what happened. I lifted the lid, saw the curled end sticking up from the tuning peg and couldn't help but laugh. A more sane person would have taken the broken string as a bad omen. Not me. I figured the worst was over.

Before I had a chance to call someone to fix the piano, Sergei walked in. I cursed at the ceiling and steeled myself for a clubbing.

For whatever reason, Sergei was in a good mood. Maybe the guy he harassed before me had paid him or his girlfriend had healed up from her boob-job. I didn't know why, but he was smiling and his hands were in his pockets, which meant I had a chance to run away before he popped me again.

"The boy here again," he began. "Bonk, where is he?"

"Haven't seen him."

"Is bad, you know? He should come out like man, not hide like girl. No?"

"You're right," I said, which was how I felt. "How much does he owe you, Sergei?"

"Fifty thousand for sport book," the thug replied as he pulled his hands out of his pockets and held them palms up. "I don't know why he bet on Eagles every time. Should take other side for change."

"You sure about that?" I dared to ask.

"Curiosity, you know? It kill cats," he replied.

So does not paying your bookie and loan shark, I almost blurted.

"Now I need payment. I have boss, too. Man who must be paid. So I take some money from you, what you have, because I want not punch to face like give you last week."

I gave him the eight hundred fifty dollars I was going to pay for the bar's supplies.

He counted it with a grin. "Is good. Is week's interest. Thank you, young Bonk. I start like you."

With that he was out the door. Before I could lock it, I saw Marty's truck backing up to the curb.

OF THE BAD THINGS I HAD DONE and would do, breaking my word was not one of them. While Marty's driver humped the barrels and cases of beer into the cooler, I darted upstairs, found my cookie jar full of cash, and paged off eight hundred fifty dollars from one of the rolls. This was money I'd saved for college expenses, but I wasn't about to follow in my father's footsteps, at least not as far as finances were concerned. I wasn't gambling it away; I was investing it.

As soon as I handed that dough to Marty's guy, I knew I was in for the penny, the pound, and all the wrong reasons. It wasn't that I wanted to honor my brother's memory or to impress my father. I handed over my savings because I was a greedy bastard who thought he could make more hustling in his old man's bar than he could doing anything else.

It was the crabs. Selling them, watching people gobble them up, seeing the money stuffed in the register, it went to my head.

I had visions of glory that included a golden altar in my bedroom, festooned with hundred-dollar bills folded to look like swans. It didn't matter to me that my father was in hock for nearly two hundred grand, a big chunk of which was owed to the Russian Mob. I didn't care about the fact that the place was not mine, nor who might be affected by the decisions I made. I would deal with that later, if at all. I had three months before the cock crowed and was determined to make the most of it.

To celebrate my deal well done, I played the piano, broken string and all, until Diane showed up. She noticed my mood, gave me a look usually reserved for the recently institutionalized, and set about doing her job. When the first batch of regulars showed up, I closed the lid over the keys and joined her behind the bar.

"We have to get more crabs," I told her.

She gave me a more encouraging look this time and said, "You think your father will go along with that?"

"I didn't ask him," I replied. "I haven't seen him in a week, and there are bills to pay around here."

"Speaking of which, did you take care of Marty?"

"No problem. What about Lizzie?"

"You paid her already."

"Yeah, and I'll need her to cook the crabs again."

"I can ask her," Diane said.

"Call her as soon as you can. I'm thinking about making the crabs a Friday and Saturday night feature."

The shine in her eyes confirmed that Diane was part of the team. There wasn't time for her to express the sentiment, however. A cop walked in and brought the room to a dead stop.

"Please," the cop, who wore a white cap, began, "as you were."

Like kids taking a supervised exam, the guys at the bar put their heads down over their beers.

"I've never seen you behind the bar," the cop said, sticking his hand out to me. "I'm Sergeant Larsen."

"Tom Bonk," I replied shaking his hand. He had the build of a pro football player gone to pot. His complexion was flushed, like a guy who spent too much time in the sun.

"I know who you are," Larsen said. "Please accept my condolences for the loss of your brother."

"Thanks," I told him.

After looking around the room, he said, "Seems different in here. I don't know what it is."

The smell of crabs and money I wanted to tell him, but kept my mouth shut, which was a sign that I had recently learned something.

"Well, your brother was a hero, Tom, and the city suffers his loss. That's why I'm here with Mr. Kern. Have you met him before?"

"No," I said looking at the other guy who seemed nervous. He was too short for his suit and too wide for his shoes. I shook his hand to show I wasn't a bad guy. Before my tenure ended, I'd find out he had a streak of decency, too.

"Mr. Kern is the civilian liaison for the precinct, part of our community policing effort," Larsen explained. "He also oversees a scholarship fund for the children of officers killed in the line of duty."

Kern held a book of tickets in his other hand. Larsen took it and fanned the pages out on the bar. "Five dollars, a chance to win a brand new motorcycle," he said, addressing everyone. "It's a Harley, too. Made here in America, the way everything should be. You have a better chance than in the slot parlors they're going to build down there on the waterfront. All this money goes to kids who lost their moms or dads in the line of duty. It honors these fine people who have served us, just like Tom's brother."

This got the attention of the guys at the bar. They perked up, stared at the tickets, and waited for someone to go first.

"Let's have a word," Larsen said to me.

We met in the dining room, where my broken piano waited for the guy I called to fix the string.

"I know I can count on you to buy forty of those tickets," Larsen said with a hand on my arm. "That's two hundred dollars' worth."

Having recently lost my brother, I appreciated the cause, but for two hundred dollars, I could buy a lot of crabs. "Things are tough around here," I said.

"Of course! You are mourning your brother. I understand. Still, your father always made the commitment to support those in need. Where is he by the way?"

"Out," I said not wanting to tarnish the old man in front of a stranger.

Larsen let go of my arm, reached into his jacket pocket, and pulled out another book of tickets. He tore the stubs off in a single motion, demonstrating that his strength was not to be underestimated.

"Come on, Tom," he said, handing the stubs to me. "Make your brother proud. The kids are counting on you."

Not only was Larsen a bully, he seemed clairvoyant. I wondered if he already knew who was going to win the motorcycle. To keep the peace, I gave him the two hundred, which he kept in his hand until he joined Kern in the bar.

It was my turn to make demands. Mimicking his move, I

took his arm and stopped him in his tracks. He glanced at my hand then at my eyes, telepathically informing me he didn't like to be touched.

"What do you know about the mob in this neighborhood," I asked.

"Hey there, Tom, watching too much cable television?"

"No," I answered, putting my face a little closer to his. My bruised eyes were fading but still a clear reminder of Sergei's first visit.

Larsen ignored my colored flesh. He said, "We have a tip line. They take anonymous calls. Maybe you should make one."

His psychic powers no longer impressed me. "Thanks," I said and let go of his sleeve.

In the bar, good Sergeant Larsen made a point of thanking everyone for their support and urged them not to drink and drive. Kern nodded and followed him out the door.

"How many tickets did he sell?" I asked Diane.

She grinned then said, "I bought one."

Scanning the bar, I didn't see any ticket stubs beside the ashtrays or beer glasses. My chances of winning the Harley were looking good, but I would have preferred the odds on selling another two bushels of crabs.

I took the phone into the dining room and started calling seafood wholesalers. Not knowing the difference between a blue crab or a stone crab, a jimmie or a sook, they figured me for an idiot making a prank call. It took the better part of my day to gain enough knowledge to get an accurate price, which was far above the fifty bucks I'd paid for the first two bushels. If I bought four bushels or more, some places would deliver them for the current price of one hundred seventy five dollars the bushel. Everyone was quick to tell me that the price changed everyday, sometimes a couple times per day. The only way to guarantee the price was to make a firm order. Since they didn't know me from the mayor, they needed a credit card to assure payment. I decided to wait to make a commitment until Diane had talked to Lizzie.

By the time I hung up the phone, the bar had emptied out. Diane waved at the vacant stools.

"It's Monday, Tom, what do you expect?"

She was right, but I was greedy, out two hundred dollars on the tickets plus the money I'd paid Marty, and in denial of reality. I wanted people lined up at the bar, the way I'd seen them at the places downtown. Without a large and steady clientele, there was no way to make my fortune.

After half an hour of bullshitting, Diane found the television remote and put on her favorite program. I could only handle five minutes of celebrity gossip and decided to survey my newly adopted domain.

The bar was long enough to face fifteen stools. Behind them was enough space for five two-person tables. The bathroom, there was only one, was a minor disaster. The sink tilted away from the wall and the toilet was the kind with the tank above eye level. In the dining room, I counted six doubles and eight tables for four. There was a door in the back wall that led into the two-car garage where my sedan sat beside an empty space reserved for my father. The kitchen where Lizzie had cooked the crabs shared a side wall with the dining room. Every square inch lingered under years of nicotine stains and grit.

To complete the tour, I went outside. This was the corner of Tioga and Richmond, the latter being one of the busiest streets in the area. Corner properties were supposed to be good for business. Mini-markets were always on corners, as were gas stations. But Bonk's Bar, a red brick building that looked like a combination of the leaning tower of Pisa and a faded licorice twist, was anything but lively.

Since it was getting dark, I went back inside. Diane had her feet up on a stool as she watched the end of her show.

"Lizzie says she can work Friday and Saturday nights," she told me. "You have to let her know by Wednesday."

"Good," I said then asked, "What do you normally do on Monday nights?"

"Watch TV, read a book sometimes," she answered. "Have any ideas?"

I did but they involved her and me committing sordid acts from my adolescent fantasies. I had more respect for her than that so I decided to put myself to work.

While I scrubbed the dining room from top to bottom, Diane sold a total of four glasses of beer and two shots. In between, she asked if I wanted help. As filthy as the place was, it embarrassed me to have her anywhere near it. The funny part was that when I put the mop, rags, and bucket away, it hardly looked any better. It needed paint, new tables, better lighting, and customers. After a week on the job, I was an expert and cataloged a mental list of next-steps.

"We might as well close," I said to Diane.

"Your father has me stay until midnight," she said.

"It's not worth the electricity," I replied and started switching things off.

Diane gave me a hug, gathered her things, and left. Having been taught a lesson two weeks in a row, I locked the door. Anyone who needed to get inside had a key, including my father, whose schedule was unreliable at best.

I wasn't halfway up the stairs when I heard someone

knocking on the door I had just locked. Like the know-it-all I was, I ignored it and headed for the living room where my pipe waited next to my favorite chair. Besides, unannounced visitors had a habit of taking my money even when they didn't blacken my eyes.

Upstairs, just as I was about to pack my pipe with Special Blend No. 4, the small window in the living room shattered, and a rock landed on the threadbare carpet. Red-face angry, I crossed the room, looked down, and started cursing a blue streak until Ally looked up at me. She covered her face with her hands and sat down on the stoop amidst a few pieces of freshly broken glass.

"I'm sorry, Tom. I'm sorry. Really, I'm sorry," she said when I pulled open the door.

"Why'd you break the window?" I asked.

"I didn't mean to," she replied.

"What did you think was going to happen when you threw the rock?"

"I said I was sorry. Can we drop it?"

Shaking my head, I asked her what she wanted in the first place. She said she forgot her purse last week. She made a show of looking for it but there was as much chance of her purse showing up as my father forgoing the blackjack table or the sports book. No woman went a weekend without her purse. Even I knew that.

"What do you want?" I asked her when she came into the dining room empty-handed.

"Do you have a number for Joe?"

"No, and why didn't you just ask me for his number instead of breaking my window and acting like you forgot your purse?"

"You're an asshole, Tom. You know that?" She barged out the door and left me to put the second piece of plywood in an upstairs window frame by myself.

The trouble was, I didn't have any plywood, so several layers of duct-taped cardboard had to do. To make a good job of it, I swept up the glass both inside and out, and then settled into my chair.

The world around me had never been so interesting. At school, there weren't any tiffs with psycho chicks or gangster beatings or scores on cheap crabs. I was used to organized classes, condescending professors, and fellow students who talked about nothing worse than the pot they bought in North Philly.

Sitting there with clouds of smoke — the legal kind that caused cancer but didn't get me high — swirling around my head, I thought that the summer was looking like more fun than it had been since John and I ventured to Ocean City, Maryland, the week after I graduated from high school. He only had a weekend pass. We made the most of it by rolling south, to a beach we'd never seen before. Not in town three hours, we stood between a pair of girls willing to share drinks and more. Those forty-eight hours passed like a sappy movie: close dancing, innocence lost and found in bed, and sweet kisses good-bye. Promises to stay in touch were made to be instantly broken.

There were tears in my eyes before my pipe went cold, and if someone had seen them, I wouldn't have been the least bit ashamed. There were plenty of mother's sons out there with lesser brothers than mine.

I WOKE UP ANNOYED AND DISAPPOINTED, mostly because I didn't have a woman looking for my number, maybe a woman like Ally or Diane or someone in between. There were nagging doubts, too. Who was I kidding to think that I could turn my old man's bar into a cash machine? Truth be told, only myself — and possibly my brother's ghost — but I stuck to it by launching myself into another frenzy of cleaning.

It was the basement this time. Rolling hills of junk filled the two rooms down there. I started at the bottom of the stairs where there were heaps of old newspapers and magazines. Using string, I bundled these into hefty packages and stacked them against the wall. Moving on, I found old beer lights that advertised brands I remembered from my childhood. The lights were atop wooden crates that might have held milk or beer; it was difficult to tell which. I gathered them together by name and placed them in a neat pile.

At this point I realized that simply organizing the junk wouldn't do any good. I had to remove it in order to make further progress. Fortunately, Tuesday was trash day, which saved me the cost of a dumpster from Masgai. Up the stairs and out the door went the newspapers and magazines.

After my last trip, I took a break on the stoop. As if on cue, a faded Toyota station wagon slowed to a stop and a squirrelly looking guy climbed out. A slip of paper was in his hand. He glanced at the sign hanging from the corner of the building, back at the paper, and then at me.

"Yeah, this is Bonk's Bar," I said to him in case he was still in doubt.

"I'm from Jacob's Music."

"This way," I told him with a wave.

"Nice," he said looking at the piano. "Mason and Hamlin upright. Decent shape."

"Except for the G above middle C. Broken string. I'm Tom Bonk by the way," I informed him.

"Kyle," he said and shook my hand.

"I'd like to have that string fixed and tune it."

"No problem." He sat down, banged out a few chords, and then opened his bag of tools.

I watched a few minutes before deciding he knew what he was doing. Just the same, I didn't want someone to come in, punch him out, or curse him up and down so I stuck to the bar. I risked a life-threatening infection by cleansing the bathroom. When I was done, I threw my rubber gloves in the trash and washed myself from the elbows down and the neck up. I'd had enough therapy for one day.

By this time, Kyle had finished and wanted me to give the piano a try. I played the backbeat chorus of *Love Me Two Times*.

The piano never sounded so good, and I told him as much.

"The Doors. Nice," Kyle said when I stopped. "Don't hear them much. Mostly I'm working for old geezers who're lucky to crank out a little Mozart."

To show him I was a guy who knew his stuff, I slipped into *People Are Strange*. He bobbed his head and danced a little jig around the room.

"Man, that's cool. You should play with us sometime."

"Who's us?"

"My band," Kyle said. "We play gigs at clubs on Delaware Ave, sometimes down the shore, the Poconos if they pay the travel expenses."

"What kind of music?" I asked him.

"Whatever. Mostly contemporary stuff, but we go back as far as the sixties for a few hits everyone knows."

"I never played with a band," I remarked.

"It's a blast, man. I play bass guitar and some keyboard, you know, just to fill out the sound."

"My repertoire is fairly limited," I informed him.

He looked around the room and asked, "You ever have music here?"

"Just me keeping myself entertained," I answered.

"Think about it. People love live music. Charge a five-dollar cover. Split that with the band and keep all the money from the bar. It's a good deal."

Now he had my attention. "You think this room is big enough?"

"Not really, but when I was starting out, I played coffee houses and dinky bars. It didn't matter. People care about the sound, man. You have to have it. If you don't, it doesn't matter if you're in Carnegie Hall."

"And you have it?" I wondered aloud.

He smirked. "Give us a try," he said and reached for his bag.

"Maybe I will," I told him.

After I paid him the hundred and fifty bucks for his services, he gave me a card, which I put in my back pocket. He was out of there, and I was alone again with a cluttered basement. The trash truck arrived early, so there was no point to hauling any more crap outside. Still, I tried to gather it into an orderly mess.

"You down there, Tom?" Diane called.

I really needed to remember to lock the door. Thank God it was Diane and not a debt collector.

"What are you doing?" she asked when I reached the top of the stairs.

"Cleaning up," I said. "Next week I'm calling Masgai for a dumpster."

"Be careful," she warned.

"He'll rip me off?"

"No," she said. "You don't want to throw away stuff that's valuable."

"Valuable? It's all junk to me," I assured her.

"Let's take a look."

We ventured into the forbidden zone for a second opinion. She poked at my piles, clucked her tongue, picked up a few things, held them to the light, and then put her hands on her hips.

"I'll bet you have a grand worth of stuff here," she said.

"A grand?" I asked incredulously.

"If you sell it on eBay, you'll probably get more, but you don't have the patience for that. Take it to the outdoor market at Tasker Street on Sunday. It'll sell there."

My brain overheated at the possibility of making a grand in a day.

"You better ask your dad. He might want some of this," Diane warned.

I wasn't about to ask him a damn thing. He was in hock up to his eyeballs. It was time to liquidate unnecessary assets to repay debt. Of course, a grand wasn't one percent of what he owed, but it was significantly more than nothing.

Since I never heard of this outdoor market, I offered Diane ten percent of whatever sold if she would go with me.

"You're on," she said. "We have to get there early, about seven. That way, we'll have a good spot. A corner."

There was the corner again. Destiny hadn't caught up with Tioga and Richmond just yet, but I was confident that it would. Thus, I went upstairs, picked up the phone, and ordered four bushels of crabs.

Having completed my duties for the day, I strolled down the street to Dooling Tire. The place reeked of new rubber, which was slightly better than old beer. Matt sat before an institutional-grade metal desk with two phones over his shoulders. He nodded for me to take a seat on the only other chair in the room while he cleared his calls.

"Do you happen to have a number for Joe?" I asked when he finally hung up.

"Lottery Joe?" Matt asked.

"Yeah. There's a chick looking for it."

"One of many, but I'll bet it's Ally."

"Yeah. She broke my window last night."

"No shit?"

"No shit. I can't afford any more."

Matt flipped his Rolodex, found the number, and jotted

it on a message pad. "They left together that night," he said, handing me the number.

"None of my business," I told him, adding, "There'll be crabs on Friday and Saturday."

"We'll be there."

He was, along with Greg, Paul, and a few guys from the shop. The neighborhood showed its support by lining up for take-out and sit-down meals. Lizzie brought along several giant bags of frozen sweet potato french fries, which gave me the opportunity to raise prices by a dollar. Ally did her part by not breaking anything. She hustled through the bar, full of smiles, helpful as ever, picking up tips that she stuffed in her jeans. More than a few lechers drooled into their beers at the sight of her ass in those jeans. Like I told Matt, that was none of my business.

By eight o'clock Saturday night, the crabs had sold out. There were people in the bar like never before. It wasn't packed, not like the places Kyle had mentioned, but there were strange faces, people I might have seen on the street, and people I didn't know from the governor. They ate the crab special, lingered over glasses of beer, and bullshitted the night away. What really made me smile was that I nearly ran out of beer, which meant that the cash register was loaded like a pack mule coming down from the Klondike. I locked the door on a record night, and it was only my second week in the game.

Back in my favorite chair, I loaded my pipe in anticipation of a relaxing hour relishing the sweet smell of success. Before I struck the first match, I heard my father's loping gait on the stairs. His two-week bender had ended. He wasted no time beginning his lecture. He got through the stuff about the Arabs, my mother, and my college dream rather quickly. When he'd run out of steam and flopped onto the couch, I scratched an Ohio Blue Tip and lit off the Special Blend No. 4. He made his wicked comment about me being the Marlboro Man and then ran out of inspiration.

It was my turn. I gave it to him straight, the way my brother used to talk to me about sports. "You're too small," John once said. "You play football, you'll get crippled. You play basketball, they'll laugh you off the court. Wrestling? Forget it. Use your head. Get a college degree and a good job where you can wear a suit. Keep your hands off your secretary and find a nice girl to marry."

I looked across the room at my father and said, "You're into some Russian gangster for fifty grand."

"Screw him," he said.

"He punched me in the face," I retorted with a gesture toward my discolored eye sockets.

"Maybe he knocked some sense into you."

"A little," I admitted.

"Good."

"There was a lawyer who stopped by. His company bought your debt from the casino, another hundred twenty-five grand. You have to make the first payment on July 10 or they're going to foreclose."

"They won't."

"I bet they will," I told him pointing at the papers on the end table.

He didn't have a clever comeback for me.

My pipe had gone out. I took a few moments to relight it, puffed a blue cloud, and focused again on the man who had brought me into the world. Although I didn't know my mother, I couldn't imagine what she had seen in him. It must have been something; she bore him two children. Maybe he was luckier back then.

"What if John hadn't died?" I asked.

"He's dead," my father replied. "No one can change that."

"You promised him the bar. What were you going to tell him when he came home from the Marines and the place was in hock to the ceiling or worse?"

He flushed bright enough to give me pause. "I win more than I lose," he said. "Your brother knew that. He also knew that you don't let a lawyer scare you into pissing your pants over a stack of papers."

"I didn't piss my pants," I said defensively.

He held his nose as if I did. "I saw someone at the casino," he continued. "They told me you were selling crabs. I never thought you wanted anything to do with the bar."

"Only because you always said that it was going to be John's."

"You didn't waste any time taking his place," he said.

That was a cheap shot. I did what I had to do, which happened to be the right thing. What would have happened had I not stepped up to the plate? The bar would be closed and the two of us would soon be looking for another place to live. I kept these facts to myself. What sense did it make to point out the obvious to the oblivious?

I said, "The bar has a lot of potential, dad. I'm serious."

"John always said you were the smart one," he put in.

This comment left me wondering about the conversations they might have had about me. Whenever my brother called from his far off postings, he typically spoke to my father at length. Every once in a while my father would look over his shoulder at me and say something like, "Yeah, he's here studying."

My father got to his feet. He wobbled a little but remained upright. He said, "I'm a little behind right now, Tom, but what happened to your brother is a sign the worst is over."

"Come on, dad," I said, trying my best not to beg. "This crab thing is going to work better than you could ever imagine. The beer nearly ran out tonight. We'll make enough money to pay off those bastards."

Maybe it was what I wanted to believe, or my enthusiasm-clouded judgment, but I swear the look on his face was the same as the day my brother completed boot camp. He had as much confidence in me as he had in John. I wished he would have left it at that and took his leave without another word. Yet, we shared more personality traits than either of us cared to admit, including the need to announce our intentions.

"You think you know how to run a bar, how to make money?" he asked.

"Yeah, I do," I said, thinking that I had already demonstrated my aptitude.

"Good, because that casino is gonna give me back what they took this week," he replied. "I never let them keep it all. Ask Diane. She'll tell you."

This question I would never ask Diane because, contrary to his claim, the evidence showed that he did let them keep it all.

"And since you're doing so well," he went on, "I won't get in the way. When I come back we can compare notes and see how things turned out. What do you say to that?"

If I had it to do over again, I would have tackled him at the door, implored him to honor John's memory by working with me at the bar. But my brother always told me the game was held on Sunday afternoon, not Monday morning. Therefore, I lost this one to the silence of a play not made. More than that, I was hell bent on showing my father that his older son was right about his little brother, the smart one.

From the window that wasn't broken, I saw him get into his car. He drove down Tioga Street and out of sight, which suited me just fine. Although he and I shared the genetics of addiction, I had a different variety. For me, the love of money was satisfied through the application of intelligent investing and serious labor. It seemed he didn't appreciate the necessity of doing things that way when it was much easier to draw the best cards or pick the right team with or without the points. And it was true that he did win often enough to reinforce his theory.

He bought me that piano, didn't he?

7 ♣ ♥

WITH DIANE'S HELP, I LOADED JUNK from the basement into the Cadillac. She prioritized it by perceived value, and I didn't second-guess her wisdom. We rolled south, the trunk and back seat full to the brim. My thoughts were less on the market than on the conversation with my father. It made no sense to wager money at a casino where the odds were against him when he could be working in his own place and win a little every day. However, what bothered me most was that he might have inadvertently screwed my brother out of the bar. Maybe that was why John joined the Marines in the first place. It was his Plan B since Plan A was never going to happen. He might have thought our father was incapable of following through, or maybe I had it all wrong. Maybe my dad would hit the number the way Lottery Joe did and everything would work out.

Whatever the case, Diane and I arrived at Tasker Street,

where a guy with four gold front teeth assigned us a corner spot. Diane smiled as I switched off the car. She put her hand on my shoulder and told me how much fun this was going to be. I had my doubts but kept them to myself because I was too lightheaded from her touching me.

We spread our swag over the ground, atop the trunk lid, and on the roof of the car. There were vendors around us who seemed to be regulars. They owned panel trucks, tables, and showcases in which they displayed their wares. There were average citizens like us, too, selling everything from black and white TV sets to children's clothes. Diane volunteered to watch the stuff while I went for coffee.

A row of food service vehicles bordered the one end of the market. Like a good businessman, I studied the competition. Most of it was uninspiring. None of them sold crabs, but everything else could be had for a reasonable price. The usual Philly cheesesteak dominated the menu boards. A group of Amish in straw hats sold molasses pies. Some guys advertised roast pork sandwiches to die for. I stuck to my mission, returning to Diane with a large black coffee, the same way I liked it.

We downed barely half our dose of caffeine before the first customer arrived. The market hadn't officially opened, but some vendors ventured from spot to spot buying or offering to sell what they could. A guy towing a hand truck looked at the wooden crates and stuck out a ten-dollar bill.

"Ten for the crates," he said.

Diane stepped up. "Get out of here," she said.

"That's a gift," he said.

"For you, pal," she replied. "Get lost."

Not knowing exactly how the market worked, I hung back. Still, I would have taken the ten and been happy for it.

Diane held her ground, getting angrier by the minute as if the guy had called her a thief. Finally the guy left.

"He'll be back," Diane said.

"I hope so."

The general public arrived a short time later. They brought their change purses, canvas sacks, and bargaining skills. The place was an economic free-for-all. Buyers and sellers haggled and traded. Two fights broke out, someone lost their kid, and I sold five beer lights to a bunch of college kids seeking decorations for their fraternity house. They hardly looked twenty-one, but I mentioned my bar to them. They said they would check it out, not that I believed them.

"How much did you get?" Diane asked me when they were out of earshot.

"Fifty bucks a piece."

She punched my shoulder. "Told you."

After a lull in the action another surge of people rolled through the aisles. A well-dressed couple stuck their noses up at my remaining beer signs, but the female half pointed at the wooden crates and asked how much.

"Fifty each," Diane told her, adding, "The bottles are extra."

"Twenty and throw in the bottles."

"Forty-five and the bottles are fifty cents each."

I counted twelve bottles when I heard the lady say, "Thirty each and nothing for the bottles."

"Next!" Diane moaned and waved her on.

Since there were twelve crates, Diane was passing up three hundred sixty bucks. I raised my hand to catch the lady's attention.

Like a demanding schoolmarm, Diane slapped it away. "Don't worry," she whispered to me, "I won't take less than forty. Those are antiques, Tom, and they know it."

Our buyer looked to her husband who gave her the nod. "Forty each, bottles included."

"Sold!" Diane announced, saving me from heart failure.

I bought us lunch. The pork sandwiches were good, but not to die for. The molasses pie tasted fantastic.

By the afternoon, only some old glasses and a few beer lights remained. The crowd bustled through the aisles without pausing to gaze upon our merchandise. Their attitude mattered not one bit to me. I had more than eight hundred dollars instead of an invoice from Masgai.

"Let's go," I told Diane.

"Yeah," she agreed. "We have nothing to draw them in."

Like the gentleman I sometimes was, I drove Diane to her door.

"You owe me eighty-two bucks," she said putting out her palm.

I handed her a hundred and thanked her for showing me how to earn it.

She folded the money and kissed me on the cheek.

"What are you doing for dinner?" I asked.

"Larry and I are eating in," she replied.

"Okay," I said, a little too dejected.

She cupped the side of my face and giggled. "Larry's my cat."

I blushed like a preteen thrilled by his first kiss.

"You're welcome if you don't mind a cat who sits on the table while we eat."

"Doesn't bother me. Seven?"

"Perfect," she said and got out of the car.

A real gentleman would have escorted her to the door. My

skills were rusty in that department, and more important, I didn't want to risk mauling her, at least not this early in the game. I smiled when she waved and motored off to a cold shower.

Like a fool, I thought I might find my father at home. He wasn't there, nor was anyone else. This I knew because I took the time to check. As I closed the apartment door behind me, I thought about changing all the locks as a message to my father that he needed to show me some respect and earn his way into the fold. I wanted to compare what he'd won or lost to the money from the flea market. But this was petty nonsense in view of the big picture. Winner or loser, he'd be back, and once he saw the bar doing well, he'd certainly prefer a sure bet to one that might go bad.

I added the flea market cash to what remained in the cookie jar. No doubt it would come out to pay Marty again. Just the same, it felt good to make a deposit rather than a withdrawal from the personal bank of Tom Bonk. Then I remembered the take from Friday and Saturday nights, which was almost three thousand dollars. This I left in an envelope beneath a book on my nightstand because, neat freak that I was, I had spread it out on my bed to organize the bills.

After my shower and shave, I took a minute to put myself in the right frame of mind. For all my filthy thoughts about Diane, I wasn't seriously interested in having sex with her. She was my first friend in the world. She treated me better than anyone else and deserved the same. However, had I a real bottle of wine, I would have taken it with me. It might have changed my mind or hers or both.

It turned out to be a casual dinner among pals, including Larry who sprawled on the far side of the table. She served up a beautiful pair of broiled filets with mashed potatoes and glazed carrots. While we ate, Diane related funny childhood stories about my brother and me, most of which I remembered. We shared a quiet moment after that as we both realized John's body would soon be landing at Dover Air Force Base. It occurred to me that my family had never belonged to a church and that I was in no position to organize a funeral or burial. I thought maybe he could be interred at Arlington.

"Your father is always good to me," she remarked with a slight smile.

Did my gut clench with chivalrous jealousy at that comment? It did. I couldn't help but wonder if my father had bedded her at some point along my childhood or more recently. At the same time, I couldn't recall seeing any looks between them that would have betrayed such a relationship. My memories of her as the perfect doting female remained intact. Only my piano teacher had been as kind or spent as much time with me.

"He never questions me about the drawer," Diane was saying.

"That's because you're not a thief," I said authoritatively.

"I know, but bosses can be a pain in the ass about stuff like that."

"They can," I agreed, relieved to hear her speak well of my father, who did have a way of charming some people and enraging others.

"One time, when you were maybe six or seven, he had a good run at the tables. You know what he did?"

I shook my head.

"He treated me and a whole bunch of people to the best dinner out. There were steaks, lobster, bottles of wine, everything you could imagine. When he told me where we were going I was so nervous. I didn't have anything to wear."

"I'm sure you looked great," I heard myself say as an image of a Diane fifteen years younger filled my head.

"A lucky woman is going to marry you, Tommy," she said.

The subtlety of her comment was not lost on me. It was her way of marking the boundaries and setting goals. Just as she used to assure me I'd get an A on my algebra test, so she let me know that I would find a great woman to be my wife. I'd sooner take a beating than disappoint her.

After washing the dishes we retired to the television, where like a typical married couple, we promptly dozed off to some non-reality reality show. I woke up at quarter past eleven with Larry atop my chest staring straight at me. He sighed, I yawned, and we both got up. I kissed Diane's cheek and let myself out to her murmuring that I should be careful driving.

The drive lasted five minutes only because the traffic lights on Richmond Street ran a different schedule after eleven. I parked the Cadillac and entered the bar from the garage. No sooner had the door closed than someone called my name.

"Tom?"

Cocking my fist, I listened closely. This time I was going to get a lick or two in before going down. Then it dawned on me that it had been a female voice, not one of my male tormentors.

"Tom?"

"Ally?"

"Yeah," she answered.

I found the light switch and a second later saw Ally hunched over one of the dining tables. She had her head down on her folded arms.

"What's up?" I asked her.

"Can I stay here tonight?" she asked.

"How did you get in?" I wanted to know before committing to any acts of charity.

"I know how," she replied. "I'll stay down here."

"Come on," I said, "I'll take you home."

"No!" she screeched.

Startled, I stood there, trying to make sense of what was happening. She had broken into the bar, wanted to stay the night, and was on the verge of hysteria. What I had to do with all that was a mystery. Didn't I just tell Matt and myself that this was none of my business?

"Listen," she said in a barely controlled way. "I don't want to go anywhere right now. I want to stay here. I'll be gone in the morning. It won't cost you anything."

For the first time in recent memory, I wasn't worried about the money. I was concerned that people could get into my place without keys and that they came for reasons that only brought me misery.

"You can stay if you tell me why," I said, figuring there was no way she would explain and I could therefore kick her out with good reason.

"I'll show you," she said, taking a seat, "but I don't want to talk about it. Deal?"

Like an idiot, I answered, "Deal."

She sat back in the chair, caught the bottom of her shirt and pulled it over her head. The only thing she wore underneath was a set of bruises that made my black eyes seem like pin pricks.

WHOEVER BEAT THE HELL OUT OF ALLY did a thorough, professional job. Her face and neck were untouched. Not a mark was visible beyond the borders of her shirt. However, she had an ugly handprint on her right breast that made me wince. The left side of her ribcage sported a trio of lumps that hinted of brass knuckles or a hand hardened by street fighting.

Upstairs, I made her an icepack, which wasn't much good because the damage was spread out. After giving her a couple of aspirin, I escorted her into John's old room. She sat on the bed, shirtless and teary-eyed.

On the far side of the room, John's poster of the ideal Marine, the one in his dress blues, sword braced against his shoulder, stared down at us. That had been my brother, and I felt his eyes on me.

"If you need anything," I told Ally, "my room is at the

end of the hall."

"Thanks, Tom."

"Semper fi," I said and retreated to the living room.

Sleeping was out of the question so I read every word of Sy Kranick's paperwork. Most of it was legal boilerplate. The rest was simple math. Factor Associates charged twenty-one percent interest, which meant $2,395.84 was due in less than three weeks. This figure did not include the principal. Assuming the crabs continued to sell and I put a thousand a month against the base amount, it would take ten years to pay off the debt. Then there was the fifty grand Dear Old Dad owed Sergei.

I packed the pipe with Special No. 4 and puffed away. My mind went blank as I gazed at the swirls of smoke. When the tobacco ran out, I cleaned the bowl and checked on my guest. That she could fall asleep in a strange place with those wounds amazed me, but she dozed under the covers without a twitch.

Haunted by questions about Ally and my own decisions concerning the future, I was less comfortable than she appeared to be. My father had thrown down the gauntlet, and I had promptly accepted the challenge. Just the same, I owed him nothing. If I'd wanted to, I could have walked out with my college savings, got a job, and moved on with my life. I probably should have done that.

Probably; then again, maybe not.

My father was the only living relative I knew. Was I prepared to abandon him and everything that had been my life to that point? Was I going to throw him to the debt-collecting wolves, strike out on my own, and disavow the past? How could I ever visit Diane without her wagging the finger of shame at me? I could hear her saying, "Your father bought you that piano, Tom, and when he won he shared with the rest of us, too."

I wasn't as tough as my brother, not physically. Neither was I a coward. Walking out was the loser's choice, and although winning wasn't everything, I hated to lose. In light of my early success, why surrender when it appeared the battle was going to be won? Even if there were setbacks to come, momentum was on my side.

I managed a few hours of sleep before taking the plunge. By sunrise, I had my order ready for Marty and Enright's Seafood, both larger than before. Beside them sat a list of calls to make, including one to Kyle. The last piece of paper contained a bunch of notes that would have made any business professor proud.

"I need another sign," I told Ally when she padded into the kitchen wearing one of my brother's old T-shirts.

She brightened up at this request. "Sure. I'll see what I can find at Masgai's tonight."

"I'll go with you," I said.

She eyed me across the table then scanned the papers lying before me. "Making plans?" she asked.

"Yeah. What're you doing for the Fourth of July?"

"I don't know."

"You want to make some money?"

"Uh ... yeah."

She helped herself to a glass of orange juice while I fired the shot heard round the neighborhood.

"It's going to be a block party," I said.

She was less than impressed.

"We'll serve the crabs, steak sandwiches, fries, and whatever anybody wants to drink. I'm going to see if I can line up a band for a few hours, too."

"Fireworks?"

"I don't think so."

"I love fireworks," she said.

"What do you think about the block party?" I asked.

"Whatever you want to do, Tom. It's your place."

It wasn't my place, not yet, but I was acting like it was. In order to pull this off, I needed help. By the looks of things, Ally needed a place where no one would lay an angry hand on her. I resisted the temptation to ask her what had happened.

"You'll be there?"

"I got nowhere else to be," she said, gulping the last of her orange juice.

"How about Wednesday through Saturday? Can you work those nights, too?"

"Cash?"

"Cash," I affirmed. An official payroll was something I didn't want to deal with.

"Okay."

"You hungry?" I asked.

She looked at her bare feet then up at me. "No," she answered. "I'm gonna go."

She refused my offer of a ride home. At the door, I remembered that I had Joe's number. She took the slip of paper without looking at it and descended the stairs. Again I was at the living room window, looking down at the street, wondering who had given her the beating. Yeah, it was none of my business. My business was running my old man's bar, and I was about to show him just how well I could do that.

Marty took my order, commenting that it was a hell of a lot easier dealing with me than with my old man. "No hard feelings, Tom," he said, "but since it sounds like you're getting on your feet, how about an extra five hundred on the past due balance?"

"I can swing that," I said. "I'll be making a bigger order for the Fourth of July, too."

"Like how big?"

"I'll let you know," I said and told him I would be waiting, cash in hand, for his driver.

My father had no history with Enright's Seafood so there was no need to kiss ass. They actually tried to kiss mine, offering me coconut shrimp, ready for the fryer, at a twenty percent discount for orders over thirty pounds. I told them maybe next week and inquired as to where I could buy french fries, chipped steak, cheese by the case, and rolls. I jotted down their suggestions before moving on to new territory. There were companies that rented all sorts of food service equipment. I needed a couple of buffet carts, the kind with steaming water that heated the pans of food above. As I collected the information in my former college notebook, Diane arrived.

"That's a lot of work," she sighed when I finished filling her in on my plans.

"I want to have crabs every week, Wednesday through Saturday. Ally says she can work those days. I'm hoping Lizzie is up for it and that she can find a helper or two."

She wasn't looking at me when she said, "It sounds like you know what you're doing."

Without hesitation, I answered, "Yeah, I think I do."

She took a deep breath, smiled at me, and said, "Okay, Tom."

It was an awkward moment, one that should have ended with a hug to celebrate our future. We had a future all right, one full of heartbreak, but that was several months off. Taking the lead, I put my hand on her shoulder.

"You're going to need help behind the bar. Any ideas?"

"I can ask around."

"Please do," I said.

Sergei walked in, looked at the empty bar, and stiffened as he saw me coming straight at him. I tamped down my anger and nodded for him to meet me in the dining room. He entered warily, his eyes darting around, no doubt looking for a trap.

"What's the interest rate on this loan?" I asked him.

"Ten percent," he said, adding, "Per week."

"So that's more than five hundred percent per year?"

"American schools not so good. Is more like six hundred. I can show you. Was good in mathematics."

"Spare me," I told him. "Basically my father owes you five hundred a week on the fifty thousand?"

"You show intelligence now. For simple things."

"Thanks. Why did you take eight hundred last week?" I prodded him.

"You insult me. I take money. Now is forgiven."

I held my smirk and placed an envelope on the table that separated us. He picked it up, counted the money, and stuffed it into his pocket.

"Maybe you smart like American rocket scientist. Eh? New career. You work on star war project."

It was the kind of thing my father should have been saying to me. To show I was part of the program, I stuck out my hand. He shook it with a grip weaker than I would have expected. My brother had warned me about guys who shook hands like girls. They would let you down, he said. Now wasn't the time to prove the point.

"Next time," I said to Sergei, "we'll share a shot of vodka."

"Yes. Cultural exchange."

"If I pay on the principal, the interest goes down, right?" I pressed him.

He gave me an iron smile. "Is not bank this thing I have. You pay all principal then no interest."

I didn't understand and told him so.

"Now you disappoint. Maybe not rocket scientist. Is easy. You pay all interest until you have all principal. Yes?"

At this point it was clear. "I get it. You want the fifty grand in one lump sum."

"Good student! Get star on homework. One lump sum, no lumps on head. Yes?"

"Yes," I said and let him find his way to the door. My courteous side had expired.

I expected Ally to show up at the bar sometime after dark. When she didn't, I started pacing and Diane pretended not to notice my anxiety. Ally wasn't my girlfriend, but on a human level, it pained me to imagine her getting another beating. My attempts at distraction failed until I banished myself to the basement. Down there I rearranged what junk remained, finding old toys, clothes, and stuff that definitely qualified for the trash haul of fame. The garbage I put in beer boxes while the other stuff awaited Diane's appraisal.

A pair of doors mounted in the far wall sported an ancient pad lock that had long ago rusted fast. I was looking around for a pry bar or something to break the hasp when I heard my name. The treasures within would have to wait.

"You ready?" Ally called down the stairs.

"Here I come."

We stole down the street like a couple of commandoes. Actually, we were more like two kids looking for a dark corner in which to conduct some heavy petting. Masgai's yard was just past the elevated portion of Interstate 95 that carved the neighborhood in two. Steel containers big enough to hold my Cadillac lined the fence. Most of them were empty. A few overflowed with demolition debris.

I followed Ally to a spot where she pulled the fence off the ground and waved me under.

"Move it, Tom," she said. "You're slower than Craig."

"Who's Craig?" I asked sliding through the gap.

"The guy who usually does this with me," she answered.

I didn't push the issue. Holding the fence for her, I noted the pain her bruises caused as she wiggled to my side.

She knew her way around and swiftly crawled up the side of the first loaded container. "All bricks and stuff," she whispered.

I met her atop the next one and peered into the pile. The mess was a jumble of wood, plaster, broken glass, and lengths of wire and pipe.

"Damn," Ally said. "I should have brought my cutters. We could have grabbed that wire."

"What for?"

"The copper, Tom. Craig and I burn the plastic off then take it to the junkyard."

"Let's get what we came for," I advised. I didn't know Masgai but taking something worth more than trash was a crime I didn't want to commit.

In the fourth dumpster we found some plywood and a trio of two-by-fours. These we carried to the fence, then shoved them under before both of us did the same. On the other side we stacked our booty into a makeshift litter and carried it up to the bar.

Diane didn't say a word as we laid everything on the floor of the dining room; nor did anyone else because the place was empty.

"What's this sign for?" Ally asked.

"The John Bonk Memorial Bash," I explained. "Fourth of July. Crabs. Steaks. Beer. One to whenever."

Ally gave me a high-five, mentioning that Craig would come by with a saw to cut the wood to size. "Give him a few bucks for paint, okay?"

"I'll give it to you," I said since she had spent the night and Craig was a complete stranger.

After Ally left, I asked Diane to take a look at the stuff in the basement. She came up the stairs beaming like a pirate who found where X marks the spot.

"Old toys," she said. "Good as gold."

Two days later, I reached into the cookie jar to cover my bill with Enright's. Between Sergei, Marty, and some incidental expenses, my previous week's earnings had been used up. The good news was that Lizzie and her pals were on board to do the cooking. Ally's new sign stood beside the one for crabs. People wanted details, which Diane provided. She also gave me numbers to call for additional bartenders.

Wednesday and Thursday were not as busy as the weekend, but I netted enough to make it worthwhile. The frat boys who bought the beer signs didn't show up. Still, there was a smattering of new faces. Most important, the number of customers continued to increase. At one point, Tony lost his seat to a guy who slipped into it when he went to the bathroom.

"Hey," Tony protested. "I been coming here since the first

time Rizzo was mayor."

The guy vacated the stool with an apology.

Running through Diane's list of bartenders proved a chore. Too many of them wanted benefits or odd hours or more than I was willing to pay. One young lady, who answered on the first ring, wanted to start that night.

Having heard her accent, I asked if she was Russian.

"I'm better than any Russian dog!" she snapped.

"Sorry," I replied. "I know a Russian guy and you sound a little like him."

"Hah! A little. I am Polish," she said. "Thank God for our hero, the Pope, or I would have been raped by Russians like my grandmother."

Not one for politics, I asked her if she could come in on Monday.

"This I can do. Is okay with you, I bring my sister, Magda. She needs job, too."

"No promises," I said. "I need help for the Fourth of July, but after that, I may not." Soon I would need all the help I could get, but I was thinking small at the moment.

"I understand. Magda will understand."

Of the many things I did and did not understand, the Polish-Russian relationship was one that I would come to thoroughly comprehend. For the time being, I was satisfied that I had a potential candidate (actually two if Magda was counted) lined up to assist Diane.

The weekend passed marvelously. The crabs sold out, not until ten this time, which made for more happy patrons, not to mention a thicker envelope on my Sunday morning nightstand. Diane and I trekked to the Tasker Street Market where we cleared six hundred dollars for another load of junk. For dinner, we ate pork chops and split a bottle of cheap red, which only put us to sleep early without affecting our judgment. I woke up with a headache, my honor intact, and found no visitors in the bar when I arrived just past midnight.

On the way to my room, I caught sight of that Marine hanging on my brother's wall.

"Semper fi," I told him one more time and saluted the way I'd seen my brother do it as he passed by the grandstand at Parris Island.

STACY AND MAGDA SILENCED THE BAR. I might have been hallucinating, but I swear even the TV went dead for a few seconds. They stood as tall as me, which put them at five-ten, and that was in flat shoes. Both blue-eyed and blonde, they might have stepped out of the beer calendar that Marty's guy left that afternoon.

Being the professional that I was, I looked them in the eye, rather than at their cleavage, and asked if they had green cards. Since they did, I told them what I expected and that Diane was going to be their boss. This was news to Diane but she took it in stride, though I sensed she found the pair threatening. With me, she had nothing to worry about, as I would rather have Sunday dinner with her than a roll in the hay with these two. Okay, had I been gay that would have been true, but I knew business and pleasure only mixed in small doses.

Down the bar I noticed Phil, one of the regulars, take up

his cell phone and make a call. He stared at Stacy and Magda while he talked. Only minutes after Diane had shown them the tap room, where the liquor was stored, and the price sheet, two new guys walked in and sat on either side of Phil. They nudged each other at the sight of my trainee and her sister.

The tour concluded, Diane brought Stacy and Magda back to me. "What's next?" she asked.

"On-the-job training," I said to Stacy, "starting tonight."

"Thank you!" she gushed. "Magda, too?"

Although there were two more guys in the bar, which put the paying population at exactly six, I couldn't afford three people watching television. This wasn't a cruise ship where the personnel to guest ratio was a published statistic.

"I don't have enough business," I said. "Only for the day on the Fourth."

"I stay, you know, in the back. You don't pay me. Then I go home with my sister," Magda suggested.

"Okay," I said warily. "But I only need one person now."

"Sure. Sure. No problem."

Diane stood at the end of the bar while Stacy started tapping beer and pouring drinks. It took me fifteen minutes to detect the pain I'd caused my favorite person. I asked her to meet me in the basement.

"There's not much good stuff left," she said looking around at my piles and avoiding her feelings.

Boldly, I put my hands on her shoulders and made her look at me. "Don't worry," I said carefully. "They're not going to replace you."

"I hope not," she replied, tears ready to spill. "I've been here a long time, Tom. You may not believe me, but I like this place."

"I believe you," I told her.

She sucked in a shaky breath and let it out slowly. I pulled her close, letting her wipe her eyes on my shirt.

"I always thought your brother would come home and do something," she said.

Rubbing my hands over her back, I replied, "Yeah, he would have." I left out the part about how my father might have lost it to the casino or the mob before John decided to come home. It incensed me that he risked not only the bricks and mortar, but the people like Diane, too. No matter, we had the chance to put off disaster if not eliminate it entirely.

"I guess it's up to you now," she said finally.

"It's your fault," I remarked.

"My fault?" she asked pulling back.

"Yeah. You said those crabs were such a good deal."

"They were a good deal!"

She held me tight, the way only a happy woman can, the way I had always wanted her to.

"If I find out you're sleeping with one of them, I'm going to get really mad," she warned.

"Not my type," I said.

"I heard that before."

They really weren't my type, but I left it at that, satisfied that Diane believed in me.

"We usually don't gig on the Fourth," Kyle explained. "Something stupid always happens."

Baffled, I asked him to explain, but he only gave me a shrug. He walked around the bar, took stock of the dining room, and then wanted to know where the door in the wall led.

"To the garage," I replied.

"You need to blow out that wall. It'll give you room for a

band, some more seats, space to make money."

"Great idea, Kyle, but how about the Fourth?"

"How are you going to charge a cover when we're out in the street?"

"I'm not. I'll make it up on the food and drinks," I answered.

"I'll let you know," he said and got into his squirrel mobile.

He left me at the curb, wondering what a block party would be like without music. I thought about setting up a stereo system but that sounded half-assed. To date, I was doing things right, and the John Bonk Memorial Bash deserved the best. Didn't I have a movie star's recipe for the crabs? Yeah, and one hot chick behind the bar and her sister reading magazines in the distance. The menu had grown to crabs, coconut shrimp, sweet potato french fries, and two new beers on tap, which Marty let me test for him at cost.

Wednesday afternoon, shortly after Diane opened the bar, Sergeant Larsen strutted in with his left-hand man, Mr. Kern. Kern produced a sheet of paper listing the winners of the previous raffle in type big enough to read from out in the street. My name wasn't there.

"Hey, maybe next time, Tom," Larsen offered.

Consolation prizes gave me no satisfaction. I was an all or nothing guy, something Larsen would eventually find out.

"That's a good thing you're doing for your brother," Larsen said next. "I hope the money goes to a worthy cause."

"It will," I assured him.

"Just in case, I'll send a few patrol cars over to make sure everything stays under control." He raised his finger. "No fireworks. Leave that to the professionals."

"Yes, sir," I said, thinking that the budget was hinging on Kyle and his band. If he took the job, there might be nothing left unless a big crowd materialized.

With Kyle's proposed renovation in mind, I drew a crude diagram of what the bar would look like if I followed his suggestion. As I sketched where the stage would go, Matt came in, ordered a beer and took stock of the result.

"The way this place is growing, you're going to need the space," he said.

"I worked construction a couple of summers," I said. "I was thinking about doing it myself."

He took a long pull from his beer and rolled his shoulders. "You're too busy for that," he said.

Like a good student, I let his words sink in. This was a guy who worked for a business that survived through three generations of ownership, a world war, probably family squabbles that made mine look like an episode of *Mister Roger's Neighborhood,* and a city that liked to tax everything from wages to widgets.

Hedging, I said, "It's only been a few weeks."

"About a month, Tom. Ride it while you can."

For this piece of advice I granted him a free beer, which in light of my generally miserly behavior, was a resounding note of thanks.

Sipping from his free bottle, he informed me how the offices inside their warehouse had been built in a single weekend. The contractor was a friend of the family who normally built suburban houses. Prefabricated pieces rolled in on the back of a truck one Friday afternoon, and by Monday morning, they were plugging in the new computers.

"Think about it," Matt advised.

"Get me his number," I said, visions of a full house in my head.

"I'll bring it up tomorrow," he offered then emptied his beer and headed for home.

Diane and Stacy seemed to have things under control. Ally had yet to appear but she had a few minutes before she was officially late. I remembered those doors in the basement, the ones with the rusty lock, and forgot about my employees for a second. There might be something worth selling on the other side. Why else would it be locked?

I found a claw hammer among my father's tools. I wedged it behind the hasp and pulled with all my weight. After bouncing on the handle several times, the screws yanked free of the wood, and I was into the unknown.

The space turned out to be dark as a tomb, which wasn't comical in light of my brother's recent death. I hadn't figured out what I was going to do with his body but it was on my list. Despite that, I retrieved my flashlight and ventured over the threshold. The first thing I noticed was a pair of narrow railroad tracks embedded in the floor. There was plenty of headroom for a person, but hardly enough clearance for any type of train to move. I followed the tracks, which led straight ahead, on what seemed like a slight angle. The solid brick walls showed no signs of buckling or damage. They were in better condition than the ones that held up the bar.

I arrived at the opposite end of what I now considered to be a tunnel. There was a brick staircase there, which ended at a flat steel door, also locked, where the ceiling should have been. Still curious, I jogged back for the hack saw I spotted in the box with the hammer. It took ten minutes, but I cut the lock, pressed my back against the door, and heaved it open.

I smelled new rubber wafting down on me and knew instantly that I had traveled under the street behind the bar, across the length of Dooling's shop, and ended up in the far eastern corner of it. To be sure, I poked my head up, saw a bunch of giant tires, and crawled out. I was in their shop, trespassing to be sure, but with no ill intent. I stole a quick look at their offices, which appeared to be well-built if a bit industrial, and then retreated through the tunnel, leaving all doors as I'd found them aside of the cut and smashed locks.

I'd heard once that Dooling's shop had been a boiler works more than a century ago. Part of that business must have occupied the area where the bar now stood. Perhaps there was a system to shuttle heavy parts back and forth through the tunnel to avoid problems at street level. Whatever the case, it was clearly something left behind with no current purpose.

"Are you deaf?" Diane called down the stairs.

"Coming!" I hollered.

"Are you digging for China down there?" she asked when I appeared at the top of the stairs.

"Just exploring," I admitted.

She pointed at the phone. "There's a guy wants to talk to you."

It was Kyle. He was willing to play the John Bonk Memorial Bash, admitting that his band might be two members short.

"I told you something always happens on the Fourth," he said.

Thrilled at having live music, I replied, "Give me a chance on a few songs."

"Yeah, okay. There'll be four of us. We'll set up around three, start at four, and quit when we run out of steam."

"Perfect," I said. Man was it ever.

KYLE'S BAND, THE EXECUTIVES, put me over the top. Until they started playing, I was losing my ass. But Kyle and three other guys unloaded their gear from a panel truck, piquing everyone's curiosity. By sound check, people strolled in from every direction.

Lucky for me they did. The block party was a praise-the-lord-pass-the-ammunition event. I gambled all the money I earned to date as well as several hundred from the cookie jar, too. My goal was to make enough to pay Factor Associates, Sergei, and finance the continued operation of the bar, which I believed was capable of supporting me in the lifestyle I deserved. Being my own boss was as addictive as crack cocaine. There was no going back to dead-end summer jobs or dreaded no-pay internships that upper classmen liked to tout on their resumés.

I almost didn't make it. The first couple of hours barely

put a dent in the food and booze. Stacy and Magda muttered to each other in Polish, no doubt about the loser they worked for. Diane smiled, but in a comforting way. Then Kyle lit off the first song. Suddenly people needed another beer, which could only be purchased at the bar, conveniently located past the food. They decided a steak sandwich was a good idea, with fries of course, and a paper basket of coconut shrimp wouldn't hurt either. Lizzie and her kitchen crew sliced more steak, stacked rolls, and refreshed the steamer trays as needed. Ally handed out foil-wrapped meals and took money, which was passed to Diane who controlled the register.

Kyle and his bandmates came in the bar between sets. He introduced them to me, but I could only remember the singer/lead guitar player. He was Dillon, "One name, like Elvis."

"Tom Bonk," I said to him. "Two names, like everyone else."

They laughed at that, drank a beer, and soaked up the crowd's adoration.

"You going to play a set?" Kyle asked me.

"Maybe later," I said. "I've got my hands full." Between switching kegs, stacking fresh bottles in the coolers, and dumping trash, I had to hurry when I pissed.

Ally caught me in the middle of a trash run. "Did Joe call?" she wanted to know.

"I haven't touched the phone all day," I answered.

"Let me know if he does," she said hopefully. "He said he was going to stop by."

I nodded affirmatively but with no intention of slowing down to answer the phone. One look outside revealed a crowd in the thrall of The Executives and their own revelry. No one said a word about my dead brother or the fact that my father wasn't there. They were enjoying themselves, having a good time on artery-plugging food and blood-thinning booze. They pressed up against the curb that separated them from the band and mouthed the words they knew. Four guys carried a pair of kiddie pools to the other side of the street. One of them helped himself to my hose and filled the pools while his buddies went for beer. Minutes later, they were all soaking wet, singing along, and splashing anyone who dared approach their spot.

"Next set in ten minutes!" Kyle shouted into the microphone. "Tom Bonk plays The Doors!"

The crowd clapped enthusiastically and darted in to line up for refills.

The last thing I wanted to do was leave more work for Diane and the others, but I was feeling proud, emboldened by the cash I had dumped into a box and locked behind the door to my apartment. So it was with little encouragement that I took the stage.

Kyle's keyboard featured a myriad of buttons and knobs. He pressed a few, and when I touched the keys, the sound of a genuine honky-tonk piano burst from the speakers. He caught Dillon's eye then started the bass riff to *Roadhouse*. The crowd went crazy, waving their arms back and forth, sloshing their beer on one another. The guys in the pools stood up and started jogging around in a circle. A bunch of girls jumped in and formed a tidal pool conga line. A couple hundred people joined Dillon singing the lyrics.

In the crowd, a woman grabbed my attention. She was about Diane's age, which put her in the low forties. She stared at me and no one else, not even looking once at Dillon, who ruled the females like a roughshod Prince Charming. I smiled for her and concentrated on the keys.

Kyle and the band gave me no time to sneak away. They rolled into *L.A. Woman*, which gave me a chance to show off for my fan. It was kind of creepy to have someone focused on me like that but a big turn-on, too. I forgot about my father, my brother, my undeclared major, and banged out the music as if my life depended on it. Of the few things that thrilled me in life, nothing had set my synapses on fire like this.

Kyle noticed my groupie and winked at me. We wrapped the set with *Touch Me*, during which I thought about the different ways this broad could run her fingers over my body and vice versa. I'd get what I wanted but not just then. First, I battled with a dolt who parked his sedan up against the trashcans I had placed to block the street. He got out, scanned the scene, and started asking anyone coherent enough to reply to a question that was universally answered with a finger pointed in my direction. I stepped off the stage and met the newcomer.

"You got a permit for this?" he asked, waving a hand at the goings-on in the street.

I didn't need to see a badge or official I.D. to know this clown was a born and bred bureaucrat empowered by the City of Philadelphia to piss on my parade. I asked for credentials anyway. After all, if he was going to ruin the party, I was entitled to make him do it right.

He pulled out his wallet in a way TV cops rehearse every week. "Dirkus," he said. "Licenses and Inspections."

"Bonk," I replied, "Tom. Brother of John, recently killed on the other side of the world."

"Yeah, good for you. We don't close streets, serve alcohol, and have live performances on this side of the planet without an approved application, also known as a permit."

"It was sort of spontaneous," I lied with a nod toward the guys in the kiddie pools. At that moment one of them puked over the edge then plopped back into the water.

"You want me to fine you another grand for lack of proper sanitation or just have the cops lock you up for disorderly conduct along with that jerk?"

A witty diatribe almost left my mouth. The sight of a police cruiser interrupted my self-destruction. Dirkus and I shared the revelation that Sergeant Larsen was in the passenger seat. The Sergeant spotted us, got out, and strolled up with his uniform looking spiffy for so late on a hot afternoon in July.

"Mr. Dirkus," Larsen greeted my uninvited guest. "Everything under control?"

"You tell me," Dirkus answered. "This Bonk punk has violated at least sixteen ordinances, and I haven't had a look around."

Chuckling at Dirkus's appraisal, Larsen said, "Now then, Tom here is a decent young man. He's lost his brother and the proceeds of the festivities here are no doubt going to a worthy cause."

"Don't pluck the heartstrings," Dirkus groaned. "I heard it all before."

"Let's not be hasty, Mr. Dirkus," Larsen continued. "Just a couple of weeks ago, Tom donated two hundred dollars to our Blue Line Scholarship Fund."

"Doesn't mean anything to me," Dirkus said.

"I understand, but maybe you didn't know that Mr. Kern is on his way here just now because Tom promised him a thousand dollars for the Kerry Outreach at Children's Hospital."

Wisely, I let Dirkus have the next word.

"Yeah?" he questioned.

"Certainly," Larsen told him. "Now Tom isn't without fault. I had a couple of noise complaints which I'm going to discuss with him right now if you'll excuse us for a minute."

Dirkus took a step back. "You go first," he said. "Then I have a few things to tell him."

Larsen led me toward the bar. Inside, he took off his hat, nodded to Diane and Stacy, and then dropped it back on his head. Most everyone found a reason to exit the room, except for Tony, who was face down over his folded arms.

"Dirkus has a boy with birth defects," Larsen explained. "The Kerry Outreach Program treats kids like his, genetics or something. That's his pet cause. He goes easy on people who share his sympathies."

"I understand," I said.

"Maybe you don't," Larsen countered. "You should have got a permit, Tom. It's a little paperwork, and if they give you trouble you call me and I call them and it all goes away."

"Are you sure Mr. Kern delivers all that cash to the right account?" I almost asked. Instead I admitted that he was right.

"I'm glad you see the logic. Dirkus will stick around until you make the donation. In the meantime, send Ally and the rest of your crew out there to clean up. Got it?"

"Yes, sir," I snapped like a new recruit.

"You're not screwing Ally are you?"

I looked at him for a second then said, "No."

"In case you are, you might want to know that she used to work the street once in a while. Let her loose before you catch something." He swatted me out of the way before having a chat with Dirkus.

Larsen's short visit drove out the most rambunctious

revelers. A collective moan rose up from the crowd after Kyle announced the band was done for the day. People gathered into their cliques and drifted away. The loiterers soon followed when my team, armed with trash bags and work gloves, began to gather the debris.

I avoided Dirkus for the better part of an hour. Eager to prolong my stage glory, I helped Kyle and the band pack up their gear. My groupie sat on the stoop, her back against the locked door to the bar. She caught me checking her out and made no attempt to hide her lust. Her face and figure fit the bill. What type of person she was, I had no idea, and at the time, wasn't overly concerned to know. I had to escape Dirkus first.

"Give me a minute to get your money," I said to Kyle.

"Deal with that jerk from the city," he said. "I'll come by next week."

Pinched between the anticipation of my first groupie encounter and the sting of a potential fine, I said, "Good idea," and left him with his cases.

Mr. Kern showed up in casual dress and with a manila folder under his arm. I shook his hand and steered him up the stairs, past my groupie who looked about ready to eat me alive. Dirkus came in behind us, apparently unmolested as well.

Kern put his folder on the bar, opened it, and took out a stiff envelope.

"Normally only checks are accepted," he said.

"Sorry, but my balance is low," I replied, which was the truth.

"Mr. Dirkus can serve as witness," Kern put in.

I turned to the register where I pulled out a wad of the largest bills. My brother's picture accidentally came with them.

I gently returned it to the place of honor then started count-ing the money. It turned out to be quite a stack because it was mostly twenties and tens.

At the bar, I double-checked the count. Kern held the envelope open for me. He closed it and sealed the flap with-out ever touching the contents. Dirkus took a deep breath, shook Kern's hand, and thanked him for the good work he did around the city.

"I'm sure the kids appreciate it," I added for effect.

Kern took his leave, and suddenly I was alone with Dirkus.

"This is your warning," he said. "Don't pull shit in my district. And make sure that kitchen is spotless, the measur-ing shot is honest, and none of that booze is watered down. I find so much as the smell of a rat's ass in any corner and you're gonna be shut down for a month."

"Won't happen here," I assured him.

"We'll see," he said and stomped out of the bar.

Following him out, I spotted a silver BMW coupe parked at the end of the block. Ally leaned in the window, speaking to the driver. I heard her giggle as she hot-footed around the car, hopped in the passenger seat, and closed the door. It was still none of my business. Who was I to talk when on the opposite corner sat a chick who might be waiting to carve me up with a kitchen knife she had tucked in the back of her shorts?

Satisfied that the street was cleaner than when the party began, aside of two guys passed out, each in a kiddie pool of his own, I took my crew inside to settle their wages. Lizzie and her pals went first. They rolled up their cash and headed for the bingo parlor. Then came Stacy who took both her pay as well as Magda's. She almost begged me to give Magda a full-time job, and it was hard to resist, but drunk with success as

I was, it was better to count the chickens that hatched before making any assumptions.

Only Diane remained. She sat in the dining room where more food had been sold in a single afternoon than any week during my father's tenure. Her face showed her exhaustion. I figured she was used to the casual evenings of serving regulars and catching up on her TV shows. Still, she smiled as I put an extra fifty dollars atop what she normally received.

"Thanks," I said. "Don't forget it was you and the crabs that got this started."

She rose slowly, stretched her back, and gave me an opportunity to offer her a ride home.

"I think you'll be busy," she said and saw herself out.

I was busy, but not the way she assumed. I bolted to the cash register, emptied it into a beer case, and carried it to the basement. I spread out the money from both boxes, separating the bills by denomination. Once there was four thousand dollars in a single pile I scooped up the remaining stacks and stuffed them back into the nearest box.

It was party time.

11♣♥

MY GROUPIE SPORTED A TWICE-CUT Cesarean scar, hair that hung off the edge of the bed, and the sexual appetite of a spring rabbit. She must have had her fill because she didn't stir when I slipped down the hall at six o'clock the next morning. No two-hour sexercise class was keeping me from that box of cash.

Not having a proper place, such as a safe or even a drawer with a sturdy lock, I hid the previous night's earnings among a half-dozen other empty cases of beer that were jumbled in the corner of the basement. They looked like so much trash as compared to the neat piles of real junk, which were better organized yet worth comparatively little. After finding the box, I counted the money. The woman upstairs, whose name was Tina, could never have put a smile on my face the way the ten thousand four hundred twenty-three dollars in that box did. Had I been smart enough to get a permit, whichever one it was, another thousand would have been in there.

I tore the flap off the box, scrounged up a pencil, and calculated my net. Payroll had been made the night before so it was only the cost of the food and booze. I roughed it out, making some assumptions but always against the net instead of in favor of it. Subtracting a few extra bucks for electricity, water in the kiddie pools, and wear and tear, I figured I cleared an honest six grand. Paying Factor Associates and Sergei the loan shark was nothing more than a cost of doing business. I put them where they belonged, in line behind Marty, Enright's Seafood, and PECO Energy. I couldn't help but wonder how my father was doing at the casino. Did he have six large in his pocket?

Just for the fun of it, I counted the money a second time, bundled it according to denomination, and carried it upstairs. As soon as my guest was out of the building, I would find a more appropriate hiding place. For the time being, I loaded it into a crock pot I'd never seen used. The odds of my father showing up, cooking us a stew, and reminiscing about the old days were slim to none. Of course, if he knew I had money in the house he might be back like a bolt of lightning over a golf course.

I resisted the urge to burn an hour's worth of Special No. 4. Maybe Tina was a nonsmoker. To stay busy, I pulled out my notes, reviewed the events of the previous day, and started working on my plan for the rest of the summer. If I played it right, I'd make enough to keep my father's debt at bay, pay a year's tuition, and have a blast cranking out tunes with The Executives and scoring chicks like Tina. Then again, I thought, why not let the bar pay my way through the next two years of college? The potential was there. I proved that. All it took was some effective management and the absence of a gambler's temptation. Hopefully the old man would find renewed interest in the business that had more potential than the wrong side of a blackjack table.

Speaking of temptation, Tina came out of the bathroom wearing nothing but her hair, which was strategically draped over her breasts.

"Tom," she said, "do you have any more condoms?"

"A couple," I said.

"I was hoping you would say that."

It was a proud moment when I dropped a cashier's check on the receptionist's desk at Factor Associates. The date was July 9 and I wanted to be sure the account was properly credited. Factor Associates hosted their activities on the thirty-seventh floor of a building on J.F.K. Boulevard, not far from City Hall. I was the only guy in the elevator not wearing a jacket and tie, and I was proud of it. I knew how to make money without pulling the yoke for the man.

"We don't accept payments here," the secretary said. She had a couple of years and twenty pounds on Tina.

I was ready for this answer. "It says in the contract that payments can be made in certified funds, which that check is, at this address."

"Let me call my supervisor."

"Do that," I said and ranged atop the plush carpet, scoping the high-style art but not availing myself of the ultra-mod chairs that looked as comfortable as a pile of bricks.

"Mr. Bonk?" called the receptionist.

"That's me," I replied.

"Mr. Kranick will see you."

Kranick held court in a corner office with a view of the northeast swath of the city. His furniture was more traditional than the lobby, including a pair of chairs, one of which held my ass about four inches lower than it should have. Picking up on the game, I got to my feet and leaned over his desk.

"Is that check acceptable payment, or do I need to find a bank and get the cash?" I asked, perturbed at the silliness of people like Kranick who wasted their time calculating how to lower a chair for that extra measure of intimidation.

"This is perfectly acceptable. Can I get you a cup of coffee?"

"Gives me bad breath," I answered.

"How's your father?" he asked next.

"Good," I said. This was a reasonable assumption given no one from the coroner's office had called.

"And the bar?"

"Better than ever," I said.

"I'll have to come by and see for myself."

"Bring cash," I remarked.

He unleashed his lizard smile and said offhandedly, "Looking forward to getting back to school?"

"I'm transferring to the University of Pennsylvania in the spring," I said, which was my biggest lie to date.

"Maybe we'll have a job for you when you graduate."

"Maybe," I said and walked out.

He probably knew I was lying about Penn. So what? Regardless of the fact that one payment was hardly my ticket to the big time, I had fired the shot heard round the neighborhood and hit a Red Coat right between the eyes. Two, in fact, had been neutralized as Sergei had collected his interest also.

Now that the war had begun, I protected myself from

any sneak attacks. Dirkus frightened me more than Sergei and Kranick combined. He had the power to pull the plug on my hard won progress. To keep the juice flowing, I hired the second half of the Polish power team. Magda and I bonded through a four-day cleaning session that began in the kitchen and ended on the front stoop. Diane and Stacy handled the bar, which percolated with the aroma of money, beer, and spicy crabs.

Perhaps intentionally, Dirkus had dropped a clue. He mentioned watered-down booze, and after everything had been cleaned, I decided to see if he was on to something. I put two bottles of whiskey next to each other, one from the rack and another that had not yet been opened. After pouring each selection into a water glass, I held them up to the light. They looked more or less the same, smelled that way, too. Then I took a sip of each. One set my throat on fire, the other took a while to make my stomach burn. Was it cut with water or something else or was it just old? No expert, I couldn't be sure. At the same time, could I risk a second encounter with the wrong side of Dirkus or the Liquor Control Board?

Diane saw me steam up to the bar and scan the bottles behind her. She backed out of the way, giving a clear view of the twenty-seven different vessels that my father probably doctored in an effort to milk the bar for a few extra rounds at the blackjack table. My math skills went to work and soon determined that if I wanted to keep on Dirkus's good side, I needed to toss three or four hundred dollars down the drain.

I was about to do that, beginning with the suspect whiskey bottle on the table in the dining room. Then another concept hit me out of the blue, something that satisfied my version of honesty. It was only a temporary patch, good enough to hold until closing time on Saturday. It worked better than I could have hoped.

"Shots and mixed drinks are half price," I told Diane. "Make sure everyone knows."

■ ■ ■

Time was not on my side, and it was more than the summer months that were ticking away. There were things happening around me that would have a dramatic effect on my life and those closest to me. Despite my ignorance of the unknown, I still felt a sense of urgency, a stiff kick in the ass to push forward, to make the bar a place that spit money like a slot machine.

That's why I was sitting across the dining table from Brett McNally, the guy who built Dooling Tire's offices in a weekend. McNally spent a couple of hours taking measurements, studying my crude drawings, and figuring with a pencil in his notebook. His job was to come up with a price to do what Kyle had suggested, which was to blow out the back wall, expand the dining room into the garage, and make room for a stage where live music would draw the kind of crowd that gathered for the John Bonk Fourth of July Memorial Bash.

McNally's artistic skills exceeded mine. He drew to scale, in perspective, and with a confident hand. Most impressive was his price, he wanted eight thousand five hundred dollars to tear out the wall, install a steel beam to support the floor above, brace it with columns all the way to the basement, and then create a riser for the entertainment over the spot where my father's car was sometimes parked. A partial upgrade to the electrical service was included. An option for a pair of two-stall bathrooms, men's and women's, was another five thousand.

"These prices include Dirkus and his permits," McNally said.

"You know him?" I asked.

"Yeah. He thought he was going to bust my balls down at Dooling's shop, but I ran circles around him."

"The Kerry Outreach?"

McNally coughed. "Call it what you want," he said.

"How long will it take you?"

"We'll do the work in the basement first, electrical, plumbing, that stuff. Then the demo and rebuild might take a week. It depends on what we find."

"What you find?"

"This place is older than both of us combined. You never know what's behind the walls."

I thought of the tunnel that led across to Dooling's shop. "I see what you mean," I said.

"Put some money aside for the unknown."

"Give me a couple days to think about this," I said and offered him a free beer.

Of all the things that caused me to spend the money with McNally, the one that I least expected was the return of my father. He strolled into the bar Saturday night, happier than I'd seen him in years. I thought he must have had a great month at the casino while I was breaking my hump paying his debts.

My old man wasn't half way across the room when Tony embraced him like Lazarus back from the dead.

"Jesus Christ!" Tony said. "I thought you were gone forever."

The room awaited my reaction. A beer overflowed under the tap Diane held open. Stacy slipped into the kitchen, no doubt to warn Lizzie. Ally hid in the bathroom. The regulars gawked shamelessly at the two of us.

"How are you, Tom?" my father asked, as if I was a distant cousin he hadn't seen in years.

"Busy," I said.

He looked around the room and saw that most of the stools were filled at the bar, that people were cracking crabs in the dining room, and that the phone was ringing and no one was going to answer it.

He picked up the receiver and said, "Bonk's Bar?" After a few seconds he asked me, "You have crabs?"

"Yeah, but not for long."

"Yeah," he repeated into the phone, "but not for long." He returned the phone to the cradle and set about chatting with his old customers the way he had for time immemorial.

A son with more fire in his belly might have punched his father in the face, or dragged him upstairs for a screaming match, or even stormed out of the bar. Being a slow-burn type of guy, I let him do his thing. He held court with his pals, forcing Diane and Stacy to dodge around his bulk as they served the customers. He seemed to like the fact that other people did the work. He requested a plate of crabs and fries, asked Ally to take the mess away after he tasted it and didn't like it, and glared at Tony who wanted to know how he couldn't love that spicy sauce. I lurked in the shadows, rehearsing the speech that I wanted to deliver when his undivided attention was available.

Something new happened that night. Diane asked me if I was going to make last call. Usually the regulars faded away without prodding. It might have been my father's presence or the general increase in business caused by the improvements I'd made. Either way, there were at least twenty people in the building, not including those who worked there, when the clock struck two.

"Last call!" I shouted.

Tony, by this time a six-pack beyond his limit, looked at me as if I had threatened his life. "Where am I gonna go?" he asked.

"Go home, Tony, and you'll walk if you don't want Sergeant Larsen to write you a personal note," I advised.

He looked to my father who nodded that he should go. By two-thirty the building had evacuated and the fun was about to begin.

After my father took a shower, he helped himself to the fridge, from which he extracted the materials to build a giant ham sandwich. For my part, I loaded my pipe, lit up, and counted the ceiling tiles. I figured he was going to need his strength to survive my onslaught, so I remained quiet until he put his empty plate in the sink.

"How about washing your dishes," I said as he came back to the living room.

"You always were a neat freak," he replied. "You're gonna scare people out of the bar if you keep it as clean as it is."

"I'm expecting Dirkus from Licenses and Inspections any day now," I informed him.

"So what?"

"Did you doctor any of the whiskey?"

His head snapped up in surprise.

"You ever cut it with water or something?"

"I never put water in anything but the toilet," he said.

"You probably took a taste from a bottle that's been sitting there since your grandfather put it on the shelf."

Since I wasn't confident in my analysis I let the issue go by changing the subject. "I made the first payment for what you owed the casino," I told him calmly, "and I've been paying that Russian mobster for a month now."

"We did say we would compare notes when I got back, didn't we?"

His confidence gave me pause. He didn't so much as burp after gnawing on that giant sandwich. Now he sat at the end of the couch with one ankle propped on his knee like a guy without a care in the world.

"You're a smart kid, Tom, but don't take so much credit," he countered. "The bar paid those bills, not you. It was here before you were born."

"This place hasn't sold that much food and booze in years."

He flipped his hands palms up. "How would you know? You were always screwing around on the piano or in class."

"I didn't know, but Marty did. He told me my last order was the biggest one he's had since you started doing business with him. I also paid him about half of what you owe, too."

"You're really proud of yourself, aren't you?" he said, bobbing his head, putting a hand into one of his pockets.

"Yeah, I am," I answered.

"Here's my side of this thing," he said as he drew something from his pants pocket and tossed it at me.

A solid roll of cash landed in my lap.

"Count it," my father ordered.

A hundred-dollar bill faced out of the roll. If it was all hundreds then there was good reason for him to be cocky. He couldn't be too far off what I netted from the block party.

"Just tell me," I said and tossed the money back.

"Five grand even, and that doesn't include what I paid off on my marker."

He deserved credit for doing the right thing this time. However, with his next comment he almost knocked me to the floor the way Sergei had.

The money flew across the room one more time. As it did, he said, "You put that against one of your college loans."

"What?"

"I got more coming," he said, standing up. "Those casinos know I'm hot, and they're going to pay. They changed dealers, closed the table, did everything they could to throw me off my game."

The man was in the midst of an epiphany. I knew the feeling well. I also knew it could evaporate, which is why I gave him something to think about.

I asked, "What about Sergei, dad? This is ten percent of what you owe him."

"That goes to one of those loans you got for college, Tom. When I finish this run, I'll pay Sergei with my pocket change."

This struck me as hilarious. I did my best not to laugh because he didn't deserve the insult.

Seeing my reaction, he asked, "You have a better idea?"

I had nothing but more bad news. "Lieutenant Baxter called today. John's body arrived at Dover. We have to make arrangements for it."

My father seemed to shrink six inches.

"The Spencer Funeral Home quoted sixteen hundred and change to cremate his remains," I informed him. "That includes transportation from Dover and a nice urn for the ashes. I was going to put the urn up on the top shelf behind the bar, along with the picture of him in his dress blues."

"That's a hell of a thing to do," my father said from behind an ugly glare, "trading on your brother's death."

"You always said the bar was going to be his," I told him. "It's as close as I can get for it to be true."

"I hear you have big plans. You're going to knock out a wall, have bands playing. What's that all about?"

Although it was past three in the morning, I gave him the short version without using my notes. He listened more closely than I expected, and after I finished, I couldn't decide if I had been trying to convince him or myself that live music was all Bonk's Bar needed in order to become a fountain of cash.

My father said, "You've made all the right moves so far. Might as well keep it up."

12

THE FIRST PERSON WITH WHOM I MADE A DEAL was myself. Negotiating against my own better judgment was a cinch. I tapped into greed, bitterness, and resentment whenever good sense and prudence seemed to gain the upper hand. Since this was an internal debate, victory and defeat were mine to share. But at this point, the idea of losing anything never entered my mind. So, I reached into my cookie jar and helped myself to a big wad of money to make the biggest investment in my future to date. The cash from my father I kept on the side, as no payments were due on my college loans. If things went horribly wrong, I'd have a safety net.

Truth be told, whole sections of the bigger picture were smeared with emotions triggered by my brother coming home without a handshake or a pat on the back. The last time I'd seen him was when he'd flown home on a spur-of-the-moment furlough. I returned from an afternoon of classes to find him sitting in the living room with his feet up on the end of the couch.

"Hey, Tom," he said. "Let's head out for a couple. See what we find."

It was how he did things, leading by suggestion, using a friendly tone, making me think he had the greatest ideas since Ben Franklin lived in Philadelphia. What's more, while I was forever living in the future, John had dwelled perpetually in the present. The here and now required immediate action. Catching up with the past was a lesser priority and the future would come no matter what. Before I knew it, he was on his feet, reaching for a coat, nodding for me to do the same.

"See what we find," meant see if we can score a few willing women. John's confidence and charm, not to mention a physicality that I'd seen women lust after, afforded him the king's share of concubines. His cast-offs were dream girls for me, and I never complained.

While he was home, I missed half my classes and, looking back, was glad that I had. We rambled through nightclubs, bars, and restaurants, all teeming with single women. Since bringing them back to an apartment above a Port Richmond bar was not an option, we ended up at their places or hotel rooms. It was quite a romp, one that ended as quickly as it had begun. He ate supper with our father and me, packed his bag, and asked me to take him to the airport.

It was a pleasant memory, one I clung to as I stood in the room with his ashes. The Spencer Funeral Home reeked of chemical freshness and tears, but there were none shed for John Bonk, Jr. The Marine Corps sent an officer who issued a final set of condolences and, once more, the thanks of the nation. Having heard that speech before, I left John's remains with my father. It wasn't that I didn't appreciate the effort. I just didn't want to talk about it. Like John, I believed the dirty work of being the greatest country in the world meant that people like him had to go into harm's way. I knew the consequences were sometimes death and that this time his number had been called. Instead, I wondered what he would have said had he come home to a bar filled shoulder to shoulder with people shouting for drinks over a band that commanded a serious cover charge. After all, that's where I was headed, and soon. I wanted to impress him the way he did that Georgia drill sergeant.

A few people from the neighborhood stopped in, including Mrs. Kirzner, the lady who had delivered the original bad news to me. Tony stood beside my father like a sort of wayward best man who had forgotten the speech he was supposed to make. His discomfort spread to several others in the room, all of who lingered without much to say.

One person unaffected by family dysfunction or social dislocation was a reporter from *The Philadelphia Inquirer*. He introduced himself as Fred Persey. He flashed no credentials but did have a notebook and a small digital camera. Since he asked politely for permission to photograph John's urn, I granted it and waited to answer what I figured would be the usual questions about grief and loss. Before I would have my chance, Sergeant Larsen entered the room.

"A sad day, Tom," he said.

Just then, Persey joined us. He and Larsen knew each other, which seemed normal enough to me. Larsen started talking about John as a hero of the neighborhood, how he always looked out for little kids and old ladies, how the Philadelphia

Police Department would have been honored to have such a brave man on the force. Persey dutifully wrote some of this down whenever Larsen took a breath. The second part of the speech surprised me even more than the first. Larsen explained that, like my brother, I was too modest to talk about my own accomplishments and that, in honor of my brother, I was remodeling the family tavern, which now featured some special dishes enjoyed by the entire neighborhood.

"I'll have to give those crabs a try," Persey said to me.

"Call first," I warned. "They sell out early."

He nodded skeptically, listened to Larsen's boast about a soon-to-be broken case, and then took his leave.

Larsen leaned close to me and whispered, "You have permits, right?"

"Yes, sir," I replied.

"Don't forget the Kerry Outreach."

"I won't."

"Mr. Kern and I will be stopping by soon," Larsen said. "Talk to you then." He left me to guess how much his visit was going to cost. I almost laughed at how cheap his indulgence was when compared to the casino and Sergei. Then again, I wasn't exactly sure what I was getting for the money. Larsen ran interference with Dirkus but did nothing more strenuous than turn his head when I mentioned the Russian Mob. He should have let me suffer at the hands of Dirkus, which I deserved to do, and done his job regarding Sergei, a known criminal who exploited me to collect a bad debt.

Terry Masgai interrupted my pondering. "You're fixing up the bar," he said.

Not one nail had been driven and the entire neighborhood seemed to know my every move.

"McNally called for a dumpster," Masgai continued.

The logical connection reassured me that spies weren't sleeping in my camp.

Masgai shifted on his feet and said, "I'll pick you up tomorrow morning, seven o'clock."

"Where are we going?" I asked.

"To look at some stuff," he answered.

I didn't know Masgai any better than Sergeant Larsen, but I felt he was a safe driving companion. "Okay," I said.

The funeral ended with my father carrying John's ashes to Richmond and Tioga where he put them in their place of honor at the top of the back bar. His photo fit nicely beside the tall urn. John gazed down perpetually on the place that was supposed to be his, the place that I was now making my own.

■　■　■

Terry Masgai walked like a dinosaur and drove like a bulldozer. He left his work boots untied, didn't wear his seat belt, and never got within ten miles per hour below the speed limit. A drive that would have taken me fifteen minutes required forty-five given that we coasted most of the way. This test of my patience ended at a shuttered firehouse near the airport. Masgai was under contract to demolish the building and level the ground for a new parking lot.

The building was a post-war, brick fortress complete with all the trappings of institutional living. There was a kitchen bigger than the one I had in the bar, a bunkroom for twenty, and a dining hall equipped for just as many. No brass pole connected the upstairs living quarters to the garage below, but there was a wide staircase with a shiny railing.

"What do you think?" Masgai asked.

"I don't know, Terry," I said, still wondering why he'd brought me down here in the first place.

"Come on, Tom," he said. "Look at all this stuff."

"What stuff?"

"Chairs, tables, eight-inch crown molding," he said, waving at the top of the walls.

"It's nice," I said, still in the dark.

"You're remodeling the bar, and you're gonna let this shit go to the dump?"

Verbal skills were clearly not Masgai's strong suit, but I managed to deduce he was offering me what could be salvaged before he put the wrecking ball to the joint.

"How much?" I asked.

"A grand, cash, for whatever you can haul out of here by Monday morning."

"Throw in the truck and some tools," I countered.

"Deal."

It was the third verbal contract of the several I'd made. The fourth was with my father and Craig, Ally's erstwhile boyfriend. He and my father knew each other, and when I told the old man about Masgai's offer, he rightly noted the two of us would not be enough labor to make it worthwhile. Therefore, Craig was hired by default and at the suggestion of my father.

"The kid has some minor bad habits," my father commented, "but he doesn't mind getting his hands dirty."

The three of us hit that firehouse like a gang of vandals on Halloween. For his size, Craig was a powerful little bastard. After we disconnected the plumbing from one of the toilets, he grasped it by the bowl and pulled it straight up off the wax seal. As if that were not impressive enough, he carried it down the stairs and placed it on the back of the truck with only a final grunt. That feat saved me two hundred dollars, and Craig repeated it four more times. I almost felt guilty about paying him a mere hundred a day for his labor. At the same time, I couldn't help but look at his hands and wonder if one of them had clutched Ally's tit while the other smacked her silly.

We didn't finish until late Sunday night. I gave Masgai his truck keys, a thousand dollars, and a fair amount of thanks. All together, the salvage effort reduced the cost of McNally's work by two grand, and then there were the chairs and tables. The ones from the firehouse needed to be refinished but my father said he and Craig would do that in between other things. Also, there was the molding, a spare stainless steel sink, mirrors, door handles, and miscellaneous other items. In the worst case, I would sell them at the flea market.

To my surprise, the bar was still open when I came in through the soon-to-be removed back door. Normally, the Sunday crowd was home by eight o'clock. Down the length of the room, I saw Stacy standing behind the taps, filling a glass for someone. Dirty and smelling like last week's laundry, I approached slowly, counting the customers and looking for Diane. There were eight occupied stools but not one Diane.

"Where's Diane?" I asked Stacy after she made change.

"She went home. Not feeling good. Ally, too."

"They were both ill?"

"Sorry. Diane was ill. Her stomach I think. A guy came for Ally. Nice suit, nice car."

The man being described could only be Joe. I wondered what Mighty-Man Craig would do when he heard about this.

It wasn't my problem, I reminded myself. Given that it was eleven thirty, a Sunday night, and I was dead-tired, I made last call.

■   ■   ■

A week and three days later, after my father and I parked in the street, McNally blew out the back wall. He had already reinforced the floor from the basement, installed a fair amount of new plumbing and electrical gear, and did not encounter anything that would increase the price. The customers eyed his work through plastic drapes, asking what was going on and then commenting that they were anxious to see the results. So was I. Three quarters of my tuition money was spent, and the return on that investment was my ticket to financial salvation.

For reassurance that it would all work out, I watched food and drink sales continue to increase despite the construction mess. At last, the frat boys (who bought the beer lights) showed up and took no offense when I carded every one of them. They drank fast and hollered into cell phones, no doubt to the kind of girls I saw in class, too. Their eyes roamed over Stacy, Magda, and Ally. My three pros kept them in their place.

Reporter Persey had yet to appear, but he wrote a small piece about John that Diane pointed out to me one afternoon. The article plucked a few heartstrings, which I liked; still, his lyrics centered on whether or not American forces should be in the Middle East as opposed to a local story about a guy who paid the ultimate price. I'd take that up with him someday.

McNally finished one day late, on the Thursday of the

week after he started. Together we inspected the work, flushing toilets, flipping switches, twisting knobs, all in preparation for Dirkus, who no doubt was rubbing his hands with glee at the possibility of finding a defect. The dining room had nearly doubled in size. The one-foot of lift in the former garage didn't exactly tower over the room. Still, it would easily accommodate a five-piece band, and there were enough electrical outlets to plug in the Space Shuttle. I paid McNally the balance due, which he gratefully accepted in cash. He offered to buy me a drink, but I declined. I lived knee-deep in booze.

That night the crowd swelled with nosey types who'd heard about the project and had to see how it turned out. Too busy to play tour guide, I let them gawk and point and make comments, most of which were positive. A few naysayers remarked on how a guy was crazy to think people would actually come to Port Richmond to hang out when there were so many more appealing places downtown and in the suburbs. No sooner than I felt a wave of doubt than Diane informed me that another keg needed to be changed. I went to the taproom to make the switch, and when I returned, noticed Ally coming out of the bathroom sporting fresh makeup and a change of clothes.

"Where are you going?" I asked.

"Joe's picking me up in five minutes," she answered. "He's never late."

"You're scheduled to work until ten."

"Magda can cover. She needs to practice her English anyway."

"This isn't a language school," I retorted. "I need you to stay."

"Well, I need to go," she said. "I'm not passing up a chance to be with a guy like Joe to work in a place like this."

This insult hurt worse than the Polack and Irish jokes people liked to play on John and me when we were kids. Bonk's Bar had just come into its own and deserved a fair shake among its peers, of which there were none within a twenty block radius.

"Look who's talking," I said and headed for the bathroom.

She cornered me there, putting one hand on her hip, using the other to shove me against the wall.

"You're a prick, Tom. You know that?"

"I've been called worse."

"You think you're the only one who can go off to college? You think you're so freaking smart, smarter than everyone else. Look at where you are: right here. Yeah, right here with the rest of us."

I pulled her hand off my shirt and replied, "This place isn't the dump it was two months ago."

"It's still in Port Richmond, and so are you."

"And where are you going, Ally? Downtown with Joe, riding around in his BMW, banging him in the back seat or in his penthouse?"

"Maybe I am," she told me. "And maybe he's getting me into school, too? Did you ever think of that?"

I didn't think Ally actually graduated from high school. I couldn't imagine her going any further in terms of formal education.

Having caught me unaware, she went for the throat. "Go hire a couple more Polacks. You're half their kind to start with."

She was across the dining room and out the door in a

flicker. No one noticed our argument, including the people who happily smashed crabs at most of the tables. I spotted a couple that needed service and moved forward. As I carried their soiled plates to the kitchen, I realized I'd made a brilliant career move by demoting myself to waiter-in-training.

13

SERGEANT LARSEN, MR. KERN, AND DIRKUS stood in the dining room. Dirkus had already passed judgment, almost laughing at the spotless kitchen, the impeccable electrical work McNally had done, and my own eager naïveté. I was too quick to hand Kern envelopes of money, too stupid to act indifferently, and too anxious to get it over with. There were no voices in my head to shout warnings, just a few echoes of my brother's advice. Still, I knew giving money to these people (albeit through known charities) was somehow wrong in the bigger scheme of things. Just the same, I was in business and in a hurry to get rich. I should have known better.

"High quality work, eh?" Larsen said to Dirkus.

Dirkus pursed his lips and tilted his head. He'd seen it all before.

"Good luck, Tom," Larsen said finally. "You're going to do well here. Make us proud the way your brother did."

"I will," I said, feeling awkward and unworthy.

"If you ever want to trade up to the University of Pennsylvania, let me know," Mr. Kern put in. "I have friends there."

Had he heard me lying to Sy Kranick? I wondered for a few seconds before they filed out.

These guys were puppies compared to Sergei. He turned out to be a Pit Bull when provoked, and it wasn't me that taunted him. The following Monday, after an unprecedented moneymaking weekend, I had just opened up when Diane called out sick again, leaving Stacy and I to cover the early shift by ourselves. Sergei made his usual entrance, paused to glance at the recent improvements, then noticed Stacy behind the bar. She caught his eye, looked down, and muttered something. What followed sounded like two bears fighting over mating rights.

It started slow, with Sergei tossing her a comment in Russian or Polish or some other language that's mostly consonants. She replied with an equally but slightly more guttural-sounding form of insult. This must have been sufficient challenge to warrant close combat. He crossed into the bar, moving behind it swiftly so that he stood inches from her. His tone couldn't have been more condescending even as the words roared out of him. For her part, she stood her ground, not flinching, not looking away, and taking his barbs before launching a series of her own.

Then he clamped her right tit in his left hand, and the first thing that crossed my mind was that he was the one who did that to Ally. At this point I was on the move, my eyes focused on Stacy but my mind reeling with Ally's pain. Stacy didn't so much as blink. She clubbed the side of his head with her fist a couple times before he released her to defend himself. He took a step back, spotted my approach, and starting laughing. "You going to be hero? You going to rescue princess?"

"Take your money and go," I told him.

He snorted like a bull about to charge. Thankfully, he wanted the money more than a piece of me. Stacy gave him enough space to open the register, but not an inch more. He scooped out the cash, counted it, and tossed it on the bar.

"Is only two hundred," he said.

I reached into my pocket, felt for the bills there, and took out only a few. They totaled another two hundred, which was still short of his weekly payment.

"Some hero," Sergei commented. "Can't pay ransom for princess."

"I have it," I said, knowing there was more money in my pocket. This I refused to show him out of fear he might steal it all.

"Get it, hero," he ordered.

I backed into the dining room, not wanting to leave him alone with Stacy. Rather than going upstairs, I slipped into the kitchen, emptied my pocket, and gathered the appropriate bills. With five twenties in my hand I returned to the bar.

He took the money from me first then snatched the rest off the bar. In a flash that I would later remember, but at the time saw only as a blur, he backhanded Stacy across the mouth with the force to knock her back three feet and to the floor. I rushed forward several steps only to meet his other hand, which held a gun with a barrel big enough to accommodate my index finger.

"Want to be dead, hero?" he asked.

I didn't. I wanted to be alive and victorious, two things that weren't available at the moment. Therefore, I retreated a few paces, giving him room to put his gun away, laugh at Stacy, and mock me with a sloppy grin.

"See you next week," he said and took his time going through the door.

I filled a clean towel with ice and stooped to help Stacy off the floor. She accepted the towel, holding it to her cheek.

"What were you two arguing about?" I asked.

"He called me a Polish whore. I told him he didn't have the money to buy me. In that case he said he would rape me the way his grandfather raped my grandmother, and I told him he should fuck his sister the way all Russians fuck their sisters when they run out of Polish women to rape."

It took me a second to put her explanation into historical context. Since I paid attention in school, I was able to see the validity of her side. Still, the Cold War was over, the Berlin Wall torn down, and free trade was supposed to bring peace and happiness to all. Of course, the people who killed my brother didn't see it that way, and apparently, neither did Sergei.

"Let's leave politics in the street," I told her. Having heard Sergei ring her bell with that slap, I asked if she wanted to go home.

"And lose a day's pay to him?" She stood up straight, squared her shoulders, and let the ice fall from the towel into the sink. The cheek that took the hit glowed red with a half-inch welt where his ring met her flesh. Other colors would follow, mostly purple and a faded green that surrounds bruised flesh, but I wasn't thinking about that. I remembered that Ally didn't have any matching half-inch welts among her sundry bruises.

Tony interrupted my musings by taking his stool and asking for a Yuengling draft. He barely greeted Stacy and I when he noticed my faded bruises and her fresh one. "I didn't know you were gonna have boxing," he said. "I woulda come early."

■　■　■

There was no boxing at Bonk's Bar, but there was live music that Saturday night. I had five hundred flyers made at a copy shop. Everyone who ordered take-out got one with his or her crabs. I posted a few in the bathrooms as well as around the bar and on the door. I rolled to my campus, put them on the bulletin board, and then drove the Cadillac to every other college in Philadelphia and stapled them up there, too. It was guerilla marketing, which was sufficient given my tight budget.

Kyle and the band set up early in the afternoon, some-thing that also had people buzzing. They saw the van and the instruments being lugged into the bar. Kids on bikes circled a few times then rode off to tell their friends and neighbors. They weren't potential customers, but that didn't matter. It was the fact that something was going on at Bonk's. People were talking about a place that had been previously ignored.

My crew, including my father but minus Ally, hustled like never before. The pile of crab debris overflowed the cans to the point where I made an emergency call to Masgai. He took the cans on the back of his truck to his place and brought them back empty. Beer flowed like the Delaware River, and Diane poured enough shots to drown a school of sharks. I was hop-ing for a younger crowd, that my notices around the city's col-leges might spark some interest among the summer students. However, when The Executives took the stage at nine o'clock, it was mostly people from the block party, people neither old enough to be my father nor young enough to be his children. I had no reason to complain. They paid cash, didn't break anything, and enjoyed themselves without starting any fights.

I did spot the guys who had been in the kiddie pools at the block party. They staked their turf against the wall leading to the bathroom, drinking bottled beer, two at a time. They looked like trouble, but I lost track after the second set when Tina came in. She wore jeans slung low enough that her scar peeked out. Her hair shone like hot glass. A pair of heels gave her four inches of lift, which was enough to put her face to face with me across the bar.

"Are you playing tonight?" she wanted to know.

"It's kind of busy," I replied.

Diane nudged my arm. "Come on, Tom. Everyone loves those songs."

As much as Tina turned me on with her somewhat slutty profile, she was nothing compared to Diane. If Diane told me to drag my naked ass across broken glass and bite the tail off a scorpion, I would have dropped my pants in a heartbeat. Given that all she wanted was a little piano playing, I was happy to oblige her.

"Maybe next set," I said to both of them. "Let me ask Kyle if he can work it in."

Diane went back to serving customers while Tina hovered. I avoided her by changing kegs, pouring booze, and taking out more trash. On the way in I noticed that Lizzie and her pals were cleaning the kitchen. It was only half past ten and the crabs had sold out yet again. I did the math on my way to see Kyle. My cookie jar would soon runneth over.

"Let's do it," Kyle said.

While the rest of the band smoked on the stairs outside the bar, he shifted the gear so the keyboard had a spot farther forward. I noticed that young women tried to talk to him the whole time. He smiled a few times, got a phone number from one, and played the aw-shucks role to the hilt.

I joined him and the band on the steps for a little preshow meeting. The musicians discussed extended solos and things I didn't understand. Kyle's sage advice was to go with the flow, that the drummer would issue cues to end any improvisation that grew tired or boring. I warned them that I hadn't been playing as much as usual given all the work around the bar.

"No problem," Kyle said. "Let's have some fun."

Just as we turned to go inside, two cars full of people showed up. It was the frat boys with their dates, maybe sorority sisters or their real sisters. It was hard to tell. They had money in their pockets. I could smell it through the cigarettes, the beer, and Tina's perfume. It had the mysterious effect of deleting my memories and fears.

14

THE EXECUTIVES, GUEST STARRING TOM BONK on piano, unleashed a legendary performance that Saturday night. The stage may have been twelve inches above the floor, but it felt like the top of the mountain to me. I took my spot at the keyboard and not six feet away stood Tina with another hundred or so people behind her. Beyond them, the bar was full, lined three deep in spots, waiting for Stacy, Magda, Diane, or my old man to hand them a drink. The crowd noise diminished as people noticed we were about to start playing again. I looked to the right, saw the door open to the street, and noticed people peering in at us. I felt the tension build as Kyle and his bandmates slung guitars over their shoulders.

A second later the lead guitar lit off the opening riff of *Roadhouse Blues*. It was to become our signature song. A cheer rose out of the crowd that blistered McNally's fresh paint. Kyle glanced at me, grinned, and added the bass line. I almost missed my entrance, but got my act together on the last beat. Looking up from the keys I saw Tina and the others swaying to the music, clapping their hands over their heads, mouthing the words. I heard myself playing but in an out-of-body way. I saw the packed bar, my old man sliding a glass of beer to one of the frat boys, Stacy touching the back of her hand to her bruised cheek, and Diane gazing across the room at me the way the mother I never knew might have. Not only was I in the money, I was neck-deep in the moment, enjoying the taste of success along with the comfort of what passed for my family.

My solo ran long. I took it up an octave, down two, and even switched keys. Kyle and The Executives played right along. Finally, I got tired and passed the lead off to the guitar player who wound things down with a final reprise of the lead riff. As the drummer rolled his sticks over the edge of the cymbals, the crowd deafened us with their applause, foot stomping, cheers, and whistles. I never did drugs in my life, couldn't imagine getting addicted to something bought from people I wouldn't trust to make me a sandwich, but I was hooked on the thrill of that stage. Those people were shouting for more, clapping, telling their pals how great it was, sloshing beer on each other and laughing about it. It was the kind of good time I never imagined possible in my old man's bar, the place I wanted nothing to do with, the place I had been doing everything to escape from.

We played an extended Doors set. The songs were older than the frat boys and their dates. Just the same, they knew the words and swayed hippie-style to the music. The guys from the kiddie pools bobbed their heads. Tina jockeyed against other women who were lusting after Kyle and the rest of the band. It seemed they had staked out their targets and held the line against any new females with similar ambitions. At one point, Tina and another chick got into a spat that ended in nervous laughter, no doubt when each of them realized they weren't after the same guy. They commenced dancing with each other, grinding their pelvises together in a writhing knot that perked up every male in the joint. I worried they expected a swinging foursome upstairs after the show. One at a time was good enough for me. More than that required the kind of flexibility I dared not risk.

A raft of solos, extended choruses, and the usual delay between tunes led to an hour-long set. When it ended, the clock had struck ten past twelve. There wasn't room for one more body in the place. I bolted for the bathroom, drunk with visions of the money in that cash register and eager to relieve my bladder. Just as I zipped up, Tina shoved her way past two guys waiting their turn. She clutched me around the neck, mashed her lips against mine, and forced her tongue into my mouth. The more I pulled away the tighter she hung on, to the point where she was off the floor. The guys behind me stared wide-eyed at the free show.

"Later," I said, breaking her grip. Rougher than I intended, I shoved her against the wall and surged out the door in pursuit of my cash.

"That was great!" Diane beamed. She patted my shoulder and handed me a towel to wipe my face.

"Thanks," I said. "How're things over here?"

"Busy," she replied. I felt her take my hand and put something in it.

My hand clasped a roll of bills thicker than the business end of a Louisville Slugger. It was my turn to do the hugging and kissing. I put an arm all the way around her shoulders and pulled her close. Then I planted an honest kiss on her cheek, slid my lips back to her ear, and said, "You're getting a raise."

She bent away from me and mouthed, "Promise?"

I spotted a hundred-dollar bill sticking from the roll. This I put down her shirt in a playful way.

"Back to work," I said.

The Executives played two more sets, both without me. I swapped kegs, hauled cases of booze up from the basement, and kept an eye on the register. The whole time, Tina fixed her lustful gaze on me. She pouted at my lack of attention but never left the building. Sometime after two, Kyle announced the last song of the night. Soon thereafter, the crowd managed to find the exits.

I made last call at three, after Kyle and the band had departed. My father had already disappeared. Diane, Stacy, and Magda were dead on their feet. Each of them received their pay in cash. They followed the last four customers out the door. Tina loitered near the stage, pretending to be bored. She waited another fifteen minutes while I did a rough count of the money in the basement.

I wouldn't know until the following afternoon that the take was fifteen thousand three hundred twenty-eight dollars. Since Tina needed attention, I quit counting somewhere above twelve thousand. That was enough to reinforce my self-image as entrepreneurial genius. Since most of my expenses were prepaid, it was almost all net. Only the cost of next week's crabs and booze needed to be subtracted. I estimated that to be about a third.

The calculator in my head crunched the numbers. By the

fall semester, the cookie jar would be full again. Not to mention, the bar would be a cash cow that I could milk for steady money instead of squatting in a cube for some nameless corporation. As for Sergei and Factor Associates, I intended to pay them off as soon as possible. Without those two anvils, my career would surely take off. My father had to know I was in the lead, that he couldn't match my jackpot at the casino of his choice.

This time I put my cardboard box full of money in the tunnel and tossed a bunch of empty cases in front of the doors. It wasn't the best camouflage but good enough for the moment. Besides, my groupie was pacing the floor above me, and who knew what she would do if I didn't soon give her what she wanted.

At some point, I actually passed out in a Tina-induced coma. This I knew only because I awoke startled, confused, and exhausted, which would have been fine, but I also smelled fried eggs. My father never ate eggs and Tina was unconscious beside me. In other words, someone else was in the building.

Having been punched out, threatened with a gun, and harrassed by city officials, I listened for a while before rising to the occasion. Soft sounds and odd smells rose from below, not within the apartment. For a moment, I thought my father was downstairs with his pal, Freddy, or maybe Craig, the bunch of them just back from an all-nighter. Then I heard humming at a pitch that had to be female. Figuring I could take on a chick, I slid away from Tina and found my pants. Just in case I had to run, I put my shoes on, too.

In the dining room/concert hall, I found a single table and

chair in the middle of the floor. A fork and knife bisected a grease-stained plate that sat on the table. A small black purse hung on the chair. I heard a toilet flush and looked across the room at Ally who was drying her hands on her pants.

"Hey, Tom," she greeted me. "You want some eggs?"

"You always break in and make breakfast?" I asked.

Her face went blank with surprise. "It's not like I stole anything, except the butter and some pepper. I brought the eggs and bread myself."

It was then that I noticed a pair of trash bags and a small cardboard box by the door. I never left trash in the open and the box was not one that had previously contained beer or liquor. When I glanced back at Ally she shrugged.

"You look tired," she commented. "Now might not be the best time to discuss this."

"Discuss what?" I growled.

"I got a deal for you."

"I'm not interested in any deals," I informed her.

"Come on, Tom. You're the most money-hungry guy I ever met. Why would you pass up a chance to make a few bucks?"

Thinking of the money in the basement, I said, "I'm making plenty of money."

"Like you don't want more," she put in. "Besides, you haven't even heard what I got for you."

That she had broken in under less-than-dire circumstances infuriated me more than whatever hair-brained idea she was about to propose. Before I could throw her out and get the rest I desperately needed, she fired up her manipulation machine.

"Let me get you a couple aspirin and a glass of water," she said.

These things I welcomed then told her to say her piece in two minutes or less because after that I was going back to bed.

"I'll rent your brother's old room for four hundred a month," she proposed, adding, "and work five nights a week, Sunday through Thursday."

This proposal came from the chick who called me an asshole, who walked off the job on a busy night, and who broke into my place like it was a game we were playing. I was a lot of things, including a decent piano player, an ambitious prick, and a fool once in a while, but I wasn't a complete idiot.

Ally said, "I'm sorry about what happened between us, you know, before, but I need a place to live and a job. I have expenses."

"Don't we all," I reflected.

"Yeah, right, so you understand what it's like. That's why I came to you."

"Ally, I'd love to take your money," I began.

"I knew you would," she interjected.

"But ..."

"Come on, Tom, don't be a hard-ass. My mom is a complete psycho. I can't put up with it anymore, and you and I have some history together."

Was she referring to the one night she stayed over, bruises and all?

Just then Tina appeared in the doorway and asked, "Who's she?" with a finger pointed at my uninvited guest.

"His friend," Ally said quickly.

"Doesn't sound like it," Tina replied. She entered the room looking as bad as me, but wearing all her clothes.

"You were listening in?" Ally shot back.

"Who are you to accuse me of anything?"

"I was here long before you," Ally told her.

They squared off and at that moment I realized I'd had enough. "Whatever you break, you bought," I said and headed for the stairs. Shouted taunts and a few slaps followed me up the stairs. I took another glass of water at the kitchen sink then found my way to bed. Maybe ten minutes passed before I heard a door slam and then silence.

Once again, I think I passed out, or maybe drifted off to sleep. Either way, a female voice woke me.

"Tom," Ally whispered.

"Yeah?"

"I'm gonna put my things in your brother's room, but I won't mess with anything until you say so. Okay?"

I didn't know if my brother was rolling over in his urn or having a laugh as I stuffed my head under the pillow and prayed this was part of a bad dream.

15

THE PHONE RANG AND RANG AND RANG. I refused to answer it. No one I knew owed me money or possessed some critical information on which my life depended. Therefore, it rang itself silent. Besides, the tobacco in my pipe burned perfectly, sending wisps of Special Blend No. 4 into the air.

Ally entered the room, fresh from the shower and half an hour of primping in front of the mirror. She lacked the expensive haircuts, subtle makeup, and latest fashions employed by so many of my female college classmates, but she wasn't ugly, and those other things were easily bought. That said, I wasn't in the mood for another romp. Tina had given me more than enough of a good thing.

"You going to open the bar soon?" she asked.

I ignored the question the way I ignored the phone. She wasn't my boss. In fact, at that moment I was wondering just who was in charge. Tina was bruising my pelvis; Ally invited herself to move in; Sergei was beating me and my employees; Sergeant Larsen and Dirkus were extracting tribute; and my father had flown the coop, for how long I didn't know. All of this was made possible by me, and truth be told, it drove me mad to be carrying the load with neither thanks nor genuine affection.

However, I had a fat wad of cash, which was just enough to keep me thinking about the big picture (i.e., making more money despite the aforementioned obstacles). In that vein, I turned my head to look at Ally, who had taken up my father's position on the sagging couch that any self-respecting tycoon would not have used as a doggie bed. She gazed at me with nervous eyes, probably expecting a tirade or an argument about the rent. I gave her neither.

"You miss one night and you're out of here," I said.

She nodded, blinked, and kept her mouth shut.

"I'm keeping the rent first and paying you second," I continued. "Diane runs the bar. Lizzie is in charge of the kitchen. Stacy is number two. You and Magda are equal but she has seniority."

"What about Tina?" she asked.

"What about her?"

"She thinks we're, you know, getting it on."

"Well, we're not."

"Are you going to tell her that?" Ally wanted to know.

"If she asks and I feel like dealing with it. In the meantime, no drugs, booze, or boyfriends up here or downstairs. You want to shoot up, drink, or screw, you do it somewhere else."

"I got it," she said, looking at the blank television.

Seeing her humbled, I felt like I'd just whipped a stray dog and consequently hated myself for being a confirmed hardass. And yet, it was liberating in a filthy way to tell someone that the rules were mine, created by whim, enforceable without warning. I knew there was more to her moving in than she was telling me, but I really didn't care.

With a gentle tap, I discharged the ashes from my pipe into the freestanding glass ashtray. Then I proceeded to clean the bowl and stem, all the while aware of Ally's tentative curiosity. Satisfied that the pipe would be ready when next I wanted it, I placed it on the edge of the ashtray and rose to my feet.

"Diane will be here in a few minutes," I said. "Give her a hand opening up. I'll be down after I take a shower."

"No problem," Ally said in a previously unheard voice.

In my room, I fanned through the money I had already counted twice. The heft of it impressed me. It was enough to pay for a whole semester with change to spare. For a moment I thought about taxes. Then I realized this was cash, untraceable, unverifiable, and therefore unavailable to Uncle Sam. I couldn't help but smile. Five weekends remained on the calendar before classes started. In that time, I planned on multiplying my stash exponentially in order to pay both my tuition and Sergei. Factor Associates would get their regular payment unless things went spectacularly well, in which case I would give them some extra.

The cookie jar and the crock-pot were not the best hiding places, and Ally was also in the apartment now. I didn't figure her for a thief, a breaking and entering artist maybe, but no sticky fingers. Just the same, why tempt fate? I should have put the money in the bank, but that would have triggered

Uncle Sam's alarm. I remembered reading something about large and frequent cash transactions making banks suspicious about the people who made them. My limited imagination came up with nothing better than the bottom of my closet, where a few pairs of old shoes collected dust. I packed the money into the shoes and took my shower.

Stacy and Ally served the Sunday night regulars. I nodded to them on my way to the basement. It wasn't until I got to the bottom of the stairs that I realized Diane hadn't been in the bar. I went back up and asked the other two where she was. They didn't know.

I dialed her number only to get four rings and her recorded voice telling me to leave a message. I hung up, put my hands in my pockets, and started to worry. The call that I had ignored earlier in the day now haunted me. What if it was Diane? What if something happened and she needed help? The odds were slim, and I thought of myself as a lucky guy. What could have happened on a glorious day such as this one when I had run my greasy mitts over fifteen grand?

Flashbacks of the day Mrs. Kirzner called filled my head. While there was nothing I could do to save John's life, I thought there might be something to be done for Diane. The Cadillac started with a tap of the key, and I was off, leaving Stacy and Ally to mind the bar.

Diane lived about fifteen blocks away. I cruised through a few stop signs and dashed a yellow light to make the trip in record time. Her row house was dark, not a good sign. I knocked anyway, tried to peek in the window, and checked the back door. Not even a neighbor was in sight. Frustrated, I headed back to the bar.

Ally and Stacy reported no calls or visits. They noted my

anxiety and found reasons to avoid me, which was just as well. I was getting angry, with myself mostly, but also at the world, which had a way of dealing shitty cards to good players. I knew the other two behind the bar thought I was overreacting, but it wasn't their substitute mother who was missing.

Watching the clock made me nasty, so I retreated to the basement. I boxed up a few things to sell, put the rest into trash bags, and found myself sweaty, dirty, and no less vicious. This time I muttered about my father, his lack of parenting skills, and his knack for conveniently disappearing. Thoughts of the money upstairs only embittered me as I realized how good things could have been had the old man not been a gambling fool. My brother and I could have had a suburban life where the biggest worry would have been an unintentional pregnancy or beer party raid.

Of course, all of this anger did nothing to solve the riddle of Diane's absence. The only thing left was to wait it out in the basement where I slowly imposed order.

I opened the doors to the tunnel. Musty air greeted me. Using a flashlight as a guide, I traversed it to the other end and poked my head up into Dooling's shop. A row of drowsy pigeons spanned the beam of an overhead crane. One of the massive tires Dooling sold hung from a chain. I wondered why they left them up in the air and decided to ask Matt the next time I saw him.

Back in the tunnel, I examined the walls. The bricks were all tight and even, laid by men who knew what they were doing. Near the middle of the space I found a spot in the ground that must have been a drain of some kind. A metal grate covered it. I gave it a tug and about twenty-five pounds of steel popped up like the lid of a soup can. Examining the space, I found it to be only two feet deep with no pipes leading anywhere. It was literally a hole in the ground. It was also my new safe, the place where I would stash the money I held back from my father's creditors.

The next morning, I had the phone to my ear before the first ring ended. I'd stared at the ceiling most of the night, haunted by what might have happened to Diane, as well as the fact that my father had been gone for over a week. In reality, his absence didn't bother me. It was the idea that he might be doing something that would cost me money.

"Tom?" Diane asked.

"It's me," I said.

"Can you pick me up?"

"Sure. At the food center?"

"No. Jefferson."

"The hospital? Are you okay?"

"Corner of Tenth and Walnut," she answered.

"I'll be there," I told her, already moving off the bed.

The Cadillac didn't like being driven cold, but I wasn't about to let it warm up. I rolled down Interstate 95, took the 676 Exit, jogged around Callowhill Street and powered along Sixth. Turning at Walnut, I didn't spot Diane until I hopped out at Tenth Street and scanned the area. She sat on one of those concrete benches that were good for nothing but collecting pigeon shit. As I approached, she looked up and smiled weakly.

"Just get me home," she breathed.

I helped her into the passenger seat and pretended to be a mute for the drive north. I knew my thousand questions would only make whatever ailed her worse. By the time we arrived at her house, she'd fallen asleep. I hated to wake her.

"We're here," I said, touching her shoulder.

"Larry will be pissed," she said.

A pang of jealousy stabbed my heart as I thought how lucky that cat was to live with her. I switched off the Cadillac and skipped around to her door. She made it out of the car under her own power, but I practically carried her up the front stairs. I took her keys, flipped the lock, and ushered her over the threshold. Diane's house, like every other row home I'd been in, featured a parlor up front, dining room in the middle with a staircase leading to the second floor, and a kitchen in the back. We went to the kitchen, meeting Larry on the way.

"It's okay, Larry," Diane cooed to the feline. "Tom will get you something to eat."

If Diane told me to buy a crate of caviar for her furry housemate I would have flown to Russia and slaughtered a dozen Cossacks to get it. As it was, she told me the cat's food was in the cupboard by the sink. While I reloaded Larry's bowl, Diane helped herself to a glass of water then plopped down at the kitchen table.

I sat against the wall. Larry slinked in, glanced from his bowl to Diane a few times, and decided it was best to sit by the door until something was said. I took my cue from the cat, who I figured knew Diane better than anyone.

"I feel like shit," she said at last. "Yesterday, I went in for some tests and had a bad reaction to the dye or whatever they shot into me. They held me overnight."

"They should have held you for a week," I reflected.

"I can't afford that," she said. "I don't know how I'm going to pay the bills I have already."

It seemed I wasn't the only one with money trouble. I

felt like a scumbag at how proud I'd been when I gave her the extra hundred, like some kind of tycoon who rained hundred-dollar bills on pretty waitresses or lit cigars with them. A hundred bucks was a drop in the bucket of what medical care cost. Even a soon-to-be college junior like me knew that.

Just then, Diane put her head down and started sobbing. Neither Larry nor I knew what to do. We waited again, this time until Diane said, "I have cancer, Tom. I'm not even forty-five years old, and I have cancer."

"Jesus," I said more to myself than to her.

"Yeah, and I prayed to him, too," Diane put in. "You know, your brother was lucky. He died quick. Bang! He was gone. I'm going to suffer for months."

"Come on," I said encouragingly. "This town has the best doctors in the world. They'll fix you right up."

"That's what they said," she added. "You know how they're going to do it? They're going to cut out my girl parts, Tom. Everything. When they get done with that they're going to give me radiation or chemo to make sure it doesn't take hold somewhere else. All my hair's gonna fall out. I'll puke myself silly. I won't be able to work." She started crying again, and Larry showed himself to be braver than me. He hopped on the table and pushed his face against her arm.

"Sorry, buddy," Diane said to him. "Mom's not feeling too good."

Larry rubbed his head against her a few more times then returned to his spot, leaving me to pick up the slack. All I could think about was how I felt when I got the news that John was dead. I was depressed and frustrated and looking for one more escape route to the life that I knew would be better if only I graduate from college and made a lot of money. But again, I was stuck in the middle, this time between Diane and another of life's random tragedies. Yet, in the months since John's death I had grown up a little. His death and Diane's illness had fallen into place as nothing exceptional. Every day millions of people were diagnosed with cancer just as every day soldiers died in wars both declared and not. It was only right that I keep looking to the future, which I was certain would be better than the present, especially if I made some money. Money paid the doctors and the funeral homes, the rent, the utility bills and for the pleasures in life like a meal out, a couple of movie tickets, or a tank of gas to drive on a quiet road.

"You'll get through it," I said.

"Tell me that six months from now," she replied. "If I'm still alive."

"You're tougher than that," I said automatically, just as my brother used to tell me when I whined about something. "The doctors know what they're doing."

"Did you ever look at the door to the doctor's office?" she asked.

"What?"

"You know, on the door to the doctor's office? It says So and So, MD, right?"

"Yeah," I acknowledged.

"Right below that it says, 'Practice Limited to Oncology' or something."

Not getting what she meant I widened my eyes, cueing her to explain.

"Practice, Tom. Medicine is a practice. They practice on you until they get it right, the way you practice the piano until you hit all the right notes."

"They're better than that," I put in. "They have lasers and magnetic scanners and all kinds of stuff we don't even know about."

"We'll see," she groaned.

As if on cue, Larry sighed and put his head down on his paw. I suspected he'd been watching Diane's illness develop for quite a while.

Diane said, "I'm sorry, Tom. You're a good kid. You mean well."

No one called me kid and got away with it — no one but her, anyway.

"Let me go to sleep, okay? Besides, I don't want to puke in front of you and my stomach is doing flips."

"I'll call later," I said, getting up.

"Let me call you, maybe tomorrow."

She didn't lift her head off the table, and Larry didn't move from his spot. Quietly, I walked the length of the house, and left via the front door, making sure it was locked when I pulled it shut.

On my way up the stairs to my apartment I smelled bacon and eggs. It was no surprise that Ally sat at my kitchen table with her breakfast plate.

"You want something?" she asked brightly.

Yeah, I wanted a lot of things, including my brother back from the dead, Diane's cancer to disappear, and a winning lottery ticket. However, Ally was talking about food, so I told her that I wasn't hungry. For the first time in my life, I considered that there were things more important than money — that there were things money really couldn't buy or rent or make up for. And I felt like an asshole because when John had died, money was still at the top of the list. That might have been because I always thought that John could take care of himself. He was among those who trained to fight and who knew they might die at the hands of the enemy. Diane, on the other hand, was a civilian, and the type of person who didn't deserve worse than a broken fingernail. There she was, awaiting the knife and chemicals or radiation beams that were as much killers as cures.

I took my pipe, packed it full, and settled into the recliner. After lighting up and catching the first taste of No. 4, I turned to look out the window. The view showed me only an abandoned chemical factory and a cardboard box plant. I stoked my pipe to the clatter of Ally's knife and fork.

At last she tiptoed into the room and said, "Joe wants you to call him."

"About what?" I asked.

"He didn't say."

"When I get around to it," I told her and sent a cloud to the ceiling.

16 ♣ ♥

I CALLED JOE THE NEXT MORNING because, contrary to my feigned indifference, I was not a procrastinator. If Joe had something to say, I wanted to hear it sooner rather than later. Besides, anything that displaced thoughts of Diane's trouble was a good thing.

"This isn't something for the phone," he said conspiratorially. "You going to be at the bar this afternoon?"

"Yeah," I said, since the only thing I had to do was scrub toilets and act like I was a victim.

"See you around two," Joe said and rang off.

I'd paid Sergei, and Factor Associates wasn't expecting any money until the end of the month. The other bills, including the utilities and Marty, were paid in full. The balance sheet for Bonk's Bar never looked so healthy. As I pondered when my father might return, I heard someone knocking on the door to the street. My father had a key, Ally knew how to break in, and Sergei only called during business hours. So, it had to be a stranger down there.

Greg Dooling turned out to be on the other side of the door.

"Yo, Tom," he said. "You got a couple minutes? I want to show you something."

Being a good customer, he deserved some of my time. We headed down Tioga Street, toward his shop, and then crossed to the lot where he stored the giant tires that weren't in the building.

"Here's the thing," he began. "You got lots of people coming to the bar now. They're parking like fools and blocking the doors to my place. My man almost missed a service call the other night."

"Sorry, Greg," I said. "I didn't know."

"I got some signs coming," he continued. "NO PARKING. YOU WILL BE TOWED. Shit like that."

"I'll tell Stacy to let the customers know."

"Good. I got another idea, too," Greg put in. "Matt's going to organize all the stuff in the yard, put it over there, on that side. Then, there'll be room for at least twenty-five, maybe thirty cars on this side."

Scanning the space, I calculated that he was right.

"Let's go over to the office and talk details."

"Sure," I said and walked with him. Seeing that big tire still hanging from the crane, I asked him why it was there.

"Foam fill," he explained. "We pump in liquid polyurethane, which takes the place of the air. It has to stay in that position until it cures or you get a flat spot. Once the stuff is cured, it's like a spongy donut in there. Never needs air."

"Looks heavy," I remarked.

"That one weighs four tons," he said. "Goes on a machine that carries twenty times that."

"And it still rolls?"

"All the way to the bank."

We took a seat in his office after he cleared a chair for me.

"I'm thinking of opening the lot this week — Thursday. Have it open for three nights in a row and see what happens."

"Sounds good," I agreed.

"I'm going to put a guy there, like a rent-a-cop, who will collect five dollars a car."

"Nobody's going to pay five bucks to park when the street is free."

"If Larsen starts giving out tickets they will."

I eyed Greg cautiously, wondering if he would prompt the cop to do such a thing or if he knew intuitively that Larsen would do it on his own. Since the truth of the matter was less important than my sharing in the bounty, I said boldly, "I want a cut."

Greg smirked. "Doesn't everybody? How about fifty cents a car?"

"How about a dollar?"

"Deal," he declared, sticking out his hand.

"You pay the rent-a-cop and whatever Larsen wants for his favorite charities," I said.

"No problem."

I shook his hand and stood up.

"Keep the place going, Tom, and we'll have to open the lot five or six days a week. It may seem like chump change, but it adds up."

"Yes, it does," I remarked and found my way out.

On the walk to the bar, a truck bearing the official seal of the City of Philadelphia passed me. From the top of the stairs, I saw the crew bail out with their tools. They unloaded a stack of narrow metal poles, the kind for traffic signs. I didn't wait to see them finish the job. I knew that when I opened the bar for the night there would be official "NO PARKING" signs lining both sides of the street.

Lottery Joe wore his black T-shirt/sport jacket combo and didn't forget the oversized gold watch either. His pockets bulged with his cell phone, sunglasses, and a wallet that held nothing but his driver's license and that picture of himself in Harrisburg holding a giant lottery check. He showed the photo to people who doubted his story about hitting it. Today, he didn't look so much sleazy as he did slimy, but then again, I probably looked like a kid dressed up as an old man. Clothes were a low-priority budget item. As for photos, the only one I cared about was the one of John that resided in the cash register. The one above the bar mattered, too, but not as much.

Joe and I stood in the basement, where he insisted we go as soon as he came in the door. I had the place mostly cleaned out, except for the leftovers from the score at the firehouse. He picked up a length of molding and ran his hand over it.

"Nice stuff," he said as if he'd recently graduated from a school of interior design. "You going to refinish it and put it up?"

"Someday," I answered.

"This room is great. It's as big as upstairs."

"Almost," I informed him. It ran beyond the end of the bar to about half the length of the dining room.

"It's great," he repeated. "Those supports McNally put up

don't take no space, neither."

"Not much at all," I said, agreeing with his deformed grammar and sensing that he had a proposal for the basement. It was a wheeler-dealer day, so I was all ears.

"You play poker?" he asked suddenly.

"No."

"It's all over TV now. ESPN, Travel Channel, they all have tournaments. Fools line up fifty deep to pay ten grand to enter."

Knowing that Joe was as much a gambler as my father, I believed his account and nodded my head.

"Not everyone likes that scene," he went on. "They prefer private games."

"Oh, yeah?"

"Yeah," he said, looking at me for the first time since entering the building.

"What's in it for me?" I asked without ever thinking that it might be illegal to host poker games or that the Russian Mob might take offense.

■　　■　　■

Two days later, my father showed up, and not alone. He and Craig drifted into the bar, looking particularly smug, like guys who won for a change, instead of the usual close but not close enough type. I treated them differently, too, assuming an upbeat tone when I told them there was another project in the works.

"Like what?" my father asked.

"The basement. It has to be finished in three weeks," I informed him.

"Finished how?"

"Like a brand new room."

"What kind of room?"

"A swanky club," I told him. "A couple of tables, some chairs, a bar. Nice and classy."

His eyes squinted as he attempted to figure out what I was up to.

"I have a tenant who wants to have private parties one day a week, sometimes two."

"That's a lot of work for once a week. Why doesn't he use the restaurant?"

"I don't ask cash customers stupid questions," I replied, adding, "Diane won't be in to work for a while. She has cancer."

This news doused their smiles.

"She in the hospital?" my father asked quietly.

"Not yet. She's going to have surgery but it hasn't been scheduled."

"Damn shame," Craig lamented.

To this my father added nothing. It was like someone knocked the wind out of him. He worked his jaws but no words came out. It made me wonder if my previous assessment had been wrong, that maybe he and Diane once had something going on.

"Shitty luck," he said at last, joining her fate, and sometimes his, to the same master. The difference was that a blackjack table didn't sneak up on him the way cancer found its way to Diane's uterus.

"Yeah, should have happened to someone else," I agreed and turned away.

■　　■　　■

My father and Craig made way for McNally and his gang. Things that might have been sold on Tasker Street flew into Masgai's dumpster. McNally himself worked around them, taking measurements, making sketches, and giving me a running commentary on how he would transform the basement into a poker room, although I hadn't told him what the ultimate use was going to be.

"What's in there?" McNally asked pointing at the doors that led to the tunnel.

"A big closet," I answered. Inside, I had stacked a mountain of empty beer cases to the point where they stood four deep, wall to wall, floor to ceiling. If my father knew I was lying he didn't say so.

"You want me to do anything with it?" McNally wanted to know.

"Let it go. It's good enough for storage the way it is."

Due to the uneven nature of the floor, walls, and ceiling, McNally would be unable to employ many of his prefab techniques. Just the same, he said he could easily finish four walls, install a bar, a few lights overhead, and have the place ready to go before school started. Having seen him in action, I believed every word he said.

I joined Kyle and The Executives on stage both Friday and Saturday nights. The crowd was a little lighter than previous weekends. I attributed the decline in attendance to the fair weather, which gave people a big incentive to head to the Jersey Shore instead of the local bar. There were only a few weeks left to the season, about the same number as there were before the fall semester began.

Greg's parking lot netted me forty-two dollars, and a

roving meter maid handed out at least two-dozen parking tickets. Stacy did her best to warn the clientele, but they mostly ignored her. That was their problem. I was too busy banging out the hits on stage (and Tina upstairs) to provide any sympathy.

I did visit Diane on Sunday afternoon. She looked more worried than sick. Without providing details, I told her the basement was getting a makeover and that I was looking forward to going back to school. She had nothing to say about the future, either hers or mine. Larry gave a few depressed sighs that made me feel more inadequate than unhelpful. It pained me to be enjoying my hectic success without Diane. I wanted her there, patting me on the back, reveling in it, too.

However, I found my legs and stood up on them and rounded the kitchen table to her side. She looked up, and I bent down to kiss her on the cheek.

"You're going to get better, Diane," I told her, hoping my voice sounded as confident as my brother's had when he told me boot camp would be like a week at the beach, which for him, it had been.

She twisted her mouth but didn't reply. I suspected there was more to the story than she was telling me. When I looked at Larry, he glanced away, which furthered the notion that Diane's health was in greater danger than I knew. Like always, I focused on the future, on the good things that were going to happen now that the tide of money was flowing in rather than out. There would be cash to pay Diane's medical bills. Like my father's debt, I would find a way to make her trouble go away. Still moving forward, I decided to locate an insurance agent who could sell me a few policies. The bar was worth at least double what it had been at the beginning of my tenure.

Similarly, I'd like to have a health policy for myself in case Sergei did something worse than punch me in the face or I got cancer, whichever came first. Given that Sergei liked to box and I liked to smoke, I was bound to enjoy both sooner or later.

Back in the apartment, I was pouring over the phonebook, noting insurance brokers' addresses, when Ally slipped into the room. She was quiet without being sneaky. Her face betrayed her intentions, which at that moment seemed to be the desire for a conversation with me.

"What's up?" I asked.

She looked at the floor, around the room, out the window, everywhere but in my direction.

"Let's hear it, Ally," I prompted her. "I got things to do."

"Can I borrow your car?" she blurted.

Although I heard her clearly, I replied, "What?"

"I need a car for about three or four weeks. Just for a couple hours in the morning."

"Where are you going?"

"To school."

"School?" I questioned.

She zeroed in on me, hardened her eyes, and let out a puff of frustration. "I'm not the genius you think you are, but I'm not stupid."

"I didn't say you were."

"You didn't have to. I know that's what you think."

"No I don't," I retorted, even though she was right on the money. I figured her to be smart enough to avoid pregnancy but not much more. That was my own arrogance and it was also true, so it didn't matter.

"I'm not looking for a fight, Tom. I have morning classes,

and I can be back here by noon."

"You have a license?" I asked, getting technical and hoping she didn't.

"Yeah."

"Do you know how to drive?"

"Rotten bastard," she muttered and turned away.

I launched myself off the chair and caught her arm before she made it to the hallway. "Let's go," I said. "Show me how well you can drive, and I'll let you use the car for the price of the gas." It was a rushed decision, one that I hoped didn't come back to haunt me. After all, who was I to hold her back just when she was showing signs of self-improvement? Besides, I wanted to do something nice in the midst of the misery that currently surrounded the corner of Richmond and Tioga. Maybe good karma cured cancer.

Ally knew how to drive. She had confidence, good judgment, and sharp reflexes. She hauled me to the insurance agencies in style. Like any important executive, I made her wait in the car while I dealt with the broker I finally selected. It took forty-five minutes to hear his spiel, decide that his price was within a few percent of the others, and plunk down my deposit. He said he would stop by for an inspection and photos later in the week but that coverage was effective at midnight. As for health insurance, he didn't sell that.

"Is that your wife in the car?" he asked.

"My driver," I said and scooped my paperwork off his desk. My status as a neighborhood big shot was growing.

Ally returned us to the bar, where we found Craig and my father stripping the molding from the firehouse. Even in the open air, the chemicals made me gag. I gave them an encouraging word and turned to go inside.

"You screwing him, too?" Craig said to Ally, who lingered behind for a few sharp exchanges with him.

I played deaf. What did her love life have to do with me?

17 ♣ ♥

THE BURSAR AT MY COLLEGE, like everyone else in my life, wanted the money up front. I counted out my tuition dollars on my bed, all twelve thousand four hundred thirty-two of them. It lie on my sheets, looking better than Tina naked, better than the crowd that packed the bar on the previous two nights, but not as good as Diane on the first day we sold crabs. No matter, I was happy to have it in greenbacks instead of in the form of a check from a bank that had loaned it to me. Those days were over. I had means, as in the means to pay for things now instead of later.

Thanks to some breezy, rainy weather, it had been another profitable weekend. The bar played host to people who may have otherwise headed to the beaches for one last dip in the ocean before Labor Day. Greg settled my weekly cut of the parking with an envelope containing one hundred twenty dollars, McNally's crew put the finishing touches on my poker room, and Ally motored to school without dinging the Cadillac.

A guy in my spot should have been celebrating his good fortune with a trip to his haberdasher for a couple of new suits, a stop by the barbershop for a haircut and shave, and finally a big dinner with multiple bottles of overpriced wine. But I was a cheap bastard with other people's bills to pay. Diane's surgery had been scheduled, and I had yet to wrangle out of her how much that would cost. If nothing else, I intended to put a lump against the debt held by Factor Associates. Thus, there would be no candle-lit dinners, not yet.

I slid the next semester's payment into a pair of shoes for safekeeping. It wasn't due until the following Monday, the day when all of us students scrambled to pick classes, the same day Diane had to be at the hospital for her surgery. I grabbed an envelope off the kitchen table and slipped downstairs to check on McNally who awaited Dirkus and his final inspection.

This time Dirkus bore a smile and spoke with no sarcasm. He made a show of scoping out the room, flipping a few circuit breakers, and running his hand over the largest of the tables that my father and Craig had refinished.

"What do you have planned for here?" he asked as he signed off on the paperwork.

"I don't know," I lied.

"You paid McNally a lot of money to do all this and you don't know?" Dirkus replied.

"It was the only unfinished room in the building. I figured as well as things are going, why not get it done?" At that moment I was about to hold out the envelope containing my next contribution to the Kerry Outreach. Instead, I said,

"How's your kid?"

"Doing okay," Dirkus answered.

"I'll be sure to give this to Mr. Kern when I see him," I said, tapping the envelope with my free hand.

"Much appreciated."

What was most appreciated was the fact that he left without busting my balls. I was free to open my gambling den, collect the host fee, and make a few more bucks on the liquor and food the players decided to eat.

McNally heard the gears grinding in my head. "You want me to fix those windows in your apartment upstairs?" he asked.

"Maybe in the spring," I told him.

"You sure? It's going to be a cold winter."

I had no idea how cold it was going to be because working in the bar made me sweat like a blacksmith. That week I jacked more cases of beer, boxes of crabs, and bags of trash than ever before. People grumpy about the end of summer spent big on crab dinners and booze. They lingered as if they could stave off the inevitable, as if time would stand still for them so long as they remained in the building.

The weekend propelled me to new heights as well. It might have been Persey's doing or maybe someone else's, but there was a blind article in Friday's *Inquirer* about places to go for music and Bonk's was listed. By the time The Executives wrapped the first set the place was crammed beyond capacity. About ten people stood outside, bullshitting with beers in their hands, waiting for someone to leave so they could get in. I only played a few songs because Stacy, Magda, and Ally could hardly keep up. I decided to ask Craig if he wanted to work in a supporting role.

By the time Sunday morning dawned, I was sleeping atop

another fifteen thousand dollars, and that did not include the twelve five of tuition money. Tina was also there. An uneasy truce had been struck between her and Ally, which was acknowledged with formal greetings only.

I considered that Monday was D-Day in terms of paying tuition and Diane going to the hospital for surgery. To that point, I hadn't come up with a smooth way of helping with her medical bills. However, I insisted on taking her to the hospital, a trip scheduled for six o'clock in the morning. My plan was to get her settled in, and then return to clean up before heading out to pay the piper at my school. After selecting my classes, I would stop in to see how Diane came through the procedure. She knew how much college meant to me and insisted I get registered on time, that there was nothing I could do for her while she was under the knife.

Tina woke up, showered, and left in a pout after I told her I had work to do. Joe was coming by for a look at the basement, the catalog of classes lie on the kitchen table with only a few dog-eared pages, and frankly, Tina was starting to get on my nerves.

Joe loved the room, especially the heavy-duty tables and chairs from the firehouse. He pounded his fist on them a few times, proclaiming, "Real wood! Yeah!" as if he was an expert on furniture. Like the big shot he was, he suggested some special food items, "like shrimp cocktail-type stuff," and reminded me not to forget the top-shelf booze. "Grey Goose Vodka, Booker's Bourbon, and that shit they drink in Greece."

"Ouzo?" I asked.

"Yeah, whatever. Just have it."

"I'll have it," I said, "but someone is paying downtown

prices. No discounts."

"They'll pay, Tom, believe me they will."

The first game was scheduled for Tuesday at nine o'clock. My fee of one thousand dollars was due before the game started, and the cost of the extras was due at the time of service.

Satisfied, Joe left, and I headed over to Diane's. She had a small suitcase waiting by the door. Larry pranced around the parlor like a caged tiger. When she told him I would be stopping over to feed him, he gave me a dubious look.

"I'll bring some tuna," I said brightly, more for Diane's benefit than his.

We sat in the kitchen where on the table she had a few sheets of paper covered with her pretty handwriting. She folded the pages and stuffed them into an envelope. After putting the envelope on top of the refrigerator she turned to me with a sallow look.

"I'm putting this up here so you'll know where to find it," she said.

"What is it?" I asked.

"Some things I wrote, you know, in case it doesn't go so good tomorrow," she replied.

I paused a second to see if she had more to say. When she squeezed her lips tight and wouldn't look away, I got up and took the envelope from its spot.

"You won't need this," I assured her and tore it into pieces.

She was in my arms a second later, hanging on for dear life, which was the one thing I didn't know how to buy.

I returned to the bar only to find my father making one of his rare appearances. His bright eyes and tricky smile should have been recognized as a bad omen, but I had my mind on the course catalog and Diane's health. Anyway, my old man, the guy who knew how to scowl better than a Soviet Premier, was cheerful for a change, and I had to admit that it was a welcome emotion. The mistake I made was to think that it had something to do with me, which it did, but not in the way that I thought.

"I'm taking Diane to the hospital tomorrow," I told him as I packed my pipe with No. 4.

He came out of the kitchen with his usual sandwich on a plate. "Yeah? She'll be fine."

"I don't know," I said. "This is major surgery."

"Best hospitals in the world are here in Philadelphia," he reminded me authoritatively, "and she has better luck than any of us. Although I have been on a streak lately."

Good luck and cancer hardly went together.

"Here's the thing," I went on, striking a match. "I'll be registering for classes and then going to see her later in the afternoon."

"Good timing," he acknowledged.

"So someone has to pay Sergei."

"Let him wait," he said, his mouth full of sandwich. "I saw him the other day and the prick had the nuts to ask me for money."

"What did you tell him?"

"That he was getting plenty from you. He shouldn't be trying to double dip."

With a fist as powerful as a bear trap, Sergei wasn't about to take that kind of guff from the likes of my father.

"Are you going to be here to pay him or not?" I asked.

"No chance," he answered. There might have been a smile

in there. It was hard to tell given the way he was chewing.

"I don't want him giving Stacy trouble," I warned and thumbed through the courses.

"He took his time paying me whenever I won," my father informed me. "Let him see how it feels."

This from a guy who somehow avoided the kind of introduction Sergei gave me and someone else gave Ally. I suppose it was easy to be brave at the dining room table where nothing was more frightening than slipping in spilled milk. Elsewhere, meaning in the bar, on the street, or the opposite side of the world, things could be more dangerous. Out there, survival demanded less talk and more action.

Sunday night's trade was modest but profitable. Stacy, Magda, and Ally put up with the letches who liked to stare at them from behind shots, beers, and broken crab legs. I fretted over how I was going to study, run the bar, and take care of Diane. However, none of the aforementioned troubles got in the way of a good night's sleep. Lugging cases of booze, switching barrels of beer, and counting money wore me out.

The next morning I was at Diane's door at quarter past five. She looked like she hadn't had the rest I enjoyed. I put on my brave face, the one my brother showed me when he strutted off to boot camp, and took her suitcase to the Cadillac.

At the hospital, she wanted me to simply drop her off and continue down the block.

"No way," I insisted and wheeled into a garage.

I hung with her through registration, up to her room, to the point where a nurse said she had to change into a gown and get "prepped," whatever that meant.

"Thanks, Tom," Diane said. "I hope you get the classes you want."

Behind a thumbs-up, I said, "See you this afternoon."

Leaving her was the closest thing to heartbreak I'd ever felt. It was worse than that afternoon when the call came about John's death. In my brother's case the worst was over. For Diane, it had just begun. Riding down the elevator, it occurred to me that any particular goodbye might be the last one. This being the first time I'd had that thought, I have to say it's like falling off a ladder, eventually you hit the ground but not before you bounce off a few rungs on the way down.

In a hurry now, I rushed back to the bar for my own prep before going to school. The catalog, my notes, and Ally waited at the kitchen table. In record time, I showered, dressed, and declined her offer to make me something to eat. The last thing I retrieved were the pair of old shoes containing my money.

The first pair was empty, even of foot stink, and I truly thought I'd grabbed the wrong ones. After all, I had been in and out of there several times. It was possible I mixed them up. But when every shoe came up sans cash, I knew I had a problem. It only got worse when I rifled the kitchen cabinets, broke the crock-pot, and nearly destroyed everything in my father's room, the place where more than likely I had been conceived.

Ally dodged flying garments, pottery shards, and curses. She knew better than to enter the fray. I hit the recliner like a sack of bricks only to spy a folded piece of paper beside my pipe.

I.O.U. my father had written along with the total amount he'd taken, which included the five grand he'd given me under better circumstances.

Finally burned out, I asked Ally weakly, "Did you see my father when he left?"

"No," she answered, visibly shaken at the havoc I'd wreaked on the apartment.

"If you see him," I whispered, "kill him."

18 ♣ ♥

TO HER CREDIT, ALLY WAS SMART ENOUGH to figure out what was wrong as there were only two things that drove me bat shit: money or the lack thereof. She also gave me a clue, telling me that Craig liked to hang out around the old power plant at the end of Lewis Street.

"He and your dad have been together a lot lately," she added. "Maybe he can tell you something."

I bounded down the stairs, hopped into the Cadillac, and drove like a fool to the power plant. Philadelphia Electric knew how to make a statement back in the day. Once a coal-fired temple of high voltage output, the place had since become a weed strewn pile of columns, domes, and broken cathedral windows. A quick survey of the fence revealed enough holes through which a battalion could have marched. I took the one closest to my car without thinking twice that someone might jump me on the other side. Given my state of mind, any would-be attacker was in for some acute physical therapy.

The number of bottles smashed around the vacant spaces of the building indicated that the place could have doubled for an abandoned barroom. There were literally piles of them everywhere. There was also the sticky scent of stoking marijuana. It didn't matter to me that a couple of potheads might be floating on cloud nine. Who else got high at ten in the morning? Determined to find out, I followed the wafting odor of Jamaican Gold until I heard giggles, the true sign of the critically stoned.

Using slightly more caution, I peeked around a corner into a hallway that must have contained the facility's offices. Smoke hung in the streaming sunlight. At the end of the hall was the boss's office in which sat Craig and two other morons. They had their feet on the desks, joints in their hands, and were stunned to see Tom Bonk standing in the doorway looking meaner than an unfed lion.

"Yo, Tom," Craig managed to squeak. "I didn't think you toked."

"I don't," I told him. "You see my father?"

Behind a smirk, he replied, "Big daddy Bonk?"

In no mood for stoner bullshit, I reached across the desk, smacked the joint out of his hand, and took him by the shirt. He started to slide off the chair, pulling me over with him, so that we ended up in a heap on his side of the desk. To the sound of his pals barely suppressed chuckling, we got to our feet, squared off, and started shouting.

"What the hell!" he began.

"Tell me where he is!"

"I don't know!"

"The hell you don't!"

"Don't act tough with me, Tommy boy. You ain't your brother."

I charged. He nimbly dodged right. I caught him in my left hand and cocked my right to strike. He came in low, landed a shot to my gut, and immediately retreated around the desk. My stomach flared with pain, just enough to bring me back to reality.

"Tell me, Craig," I snarled.

"I got no beef with you, Tom. I mean, aside of Ally, that freaking whore, we got no reason to be sideways."

"You and my father were gone for a couple of weeks. What did you do?"

"We went to the track. He played the horses. When he won, we ate fancy food. When he didn't, we ate shit."

"He doesn't bet on horses."

"He did that time. Said something about how none of the casinos would give him a marker."

"What else?"

"We drove around, looked at the sluts on Aramingo Avenue then over on Pickwick Street where Larsen busted Ally that time."

One of his pals said, "Man, you're really bringing us down. Why don't you, like, head out? Okay?"

There happened to be an ashtray on the desk. I tossed that at him and zeroed in on Craig. This time he maneuvered too slowly. I tripped him, followed his bulk to the floor, and drove my knee into his chest. In the split second that passed while I twisted his greasy hair, it occurred to me that if Craig wasn't stoned he could have clubbed the shit out of me. But up close I saw every bloodshot vein in the whites of his eyes. He was beyond cloud nine on his way to the stratosphere.

"OWWWW!" he shouted.

"You God damn KNOW where he is!" I bellowed, twisting more pot-stinking strands.

"I swear I don't!" This was followed by the one phrase that even in my rage I knew was true. "He owes me two hundred bucks."

At that I let go of his mane and stood up. He took his time doing the same. We both caught our breath, and the whole time the other stoners never put down their joints.

Smoothing out his hair, Craig said, "Really, man, you should take a hit of this prime weed we have. It would mellow you out."

"You see my old man, you tell him to find me at the bar."

"You can kick his ass all you want, just get my two Bennies, okay?"

"I'll get them. Until I do, you want a job?"

"What?"

"A job," I repeated. "I need a guy to switch the barrels, stock the coolers, and do whatever else has to be done. Can you handle that?"

"You serious?"

With nothing more verbal than a flexing of my left fist Craig understood that I was beyond serious. To make sure things were sparkling clear, I said, "For the record, I don't screw Ally. She pays rent, drives my car sensibly, pays for her own gas, and that's all there is to it."

It took a few seconds for his brain to process that. Then he stuck out his hand. I shook it in a gentlemanly way, which was as much of an apology as I could muster.

"Two more things about the job," I said evenly. "You can't be high and you have to be clean."

"No problem," he said.

A guy lacking funds should not have been hiring anyone. But the stolen tuition money had nothing to do with the bar. If recent history were any indication, the place would be as busy as ever. No one cared whether or not I went to school. They wanted their crabs and their ice-cold Yuengling and a look at the hot Polack chicks who bent over to serve them. In other words, what little optimism remained in me said that I should plow on. Thus, Craig got a job, and I rolled to school to see if I could beg for the time to wrangle a student loan.

I should have known better. The days of sympathy for late-comers were over. Everyone knew the deadlines, including me, and my school's administration was notoriously strict about them. I did my best, telling the lady who handled such matters everything but the truth. She took three phone calls during our ten minutes together, which was a sure sign that I was free to see myself out.

On the way through the lobby, I ran into Barry, a guy with whom I had shared some classes and a couple group projects.

"This isn't getting any cheaper," he complained.

"Tell me about it," I said. "I'm taking a semester off."

"Sorry to hear that."

"No big deal," I lied. "My business is as busy as the gates of hell on Halloween."

He gave me a laugh and a clap on the shoulder. "I need to stop up there and check it out."

"Bring some friends," I urged him.

"Yeah, right."

Having accepted that school was on hold, I walked all the way to Jefferson Hospital. Diane was still in surgery and wasn't expected out for another couple of hours. The last thing I wanted to do was face Sergei empty-handed. He would want his five hundred or to give me a beating if I didn't have it. Taking Craig was one thing. Sergei, on the other hand, probably learned to fight during his stint as a Russian commando. At the same time, I couldn't let Stacy face him with nothing but her cute face and tight ass.

On the street in front of the hospital I called Joe.

"I need the thousand today," I said when he came on the line.

"That wasn't the deal," he replied.

"I know it wasn't the deal, Joe, but I got some extra expenses this week and I'm asking you to help out. What's the difference?"

He sighed. "I thought you could handle things," he said as if I was twelve and he had graduated from the Wharton School of Business.

Furious and wishing that I was close enough to give him a right hook, I said, "Look, you want to use the room tomorrow night, I need the money today, in the next hour. Drop it off at the bar. Give it to Stacy. If you don't deliver, I'll know the game is off."

To reinforce the point, I hung up. Screw him, I thought, him and his one-point-three-five-million lottery check. I was in the trenches, doing the best I could with what little I had. This was an all or nothing moment in more ways than one when I considered that Diane was still under the knife.

My phone rang exactly an hour later. It was Stacy calling to let me know Joe had left an envelope. I instructed her to open it, stick five hundred in her pocket and leave the other five hundred for Sergei.

"That pig," she muttered.

"I know," I said, "I'm sorry I can't be there, but I'm here at the hospital with Diane."

"I'll deal with him."

"Be careful, Stacy," I warned.

"You watch out for Diane. I watch bar. No worries."

I was worried, about the bar, about Diane, about missing a semester of college. And truth be told, I was more than a little worried about my father. Sooner or later he would run afoul of someone more willing to kill him than I was.

Back in the hospital, I thumbed through magazines, walked halls, and risked a meal of vending machine goodies. I dozed off with half a dozen other patient relatives. Every one of us had the harried look of people who didn't understand what was happening on the other side of the swinging doors and yet hoped for the best.

Finally, a nurse fetched me. She didn't have a word to say as we rode the elevator. I wondered how many times a day she escorted dazed, confused, and emotionally wrecked souls like me to see their loved ones. It was one job this money-loving schmuck wouldn't do for all the shekels in King Solomon's palace.

Diane lay in the intensive care ward, in a line with five other people surrounded by enough equipment to occupy an equal number of medical professionals.

"She's awake," my guide informed me. "You can talk to her for a few minutes, and then it's best if you go. Given her status, I would say you should stop in tomorrow morning."

"Okay," I croaked.

Several moments passed while I stood beside Diane's bed. The heart monitor's screen mesmerized me, as did the dripping, bubbling, and softly beeping devices around it. Glancing down at her face, I saw that her eyes were open in a blank stare. If she hadn't closed them and started to cry, I would have thought she was dead.

DIANE SLEPT THROUGH THE REMAINDER of my visit. I waited three hours for her to wake up, until the nurse forced me to leave. Although the machines indicated she was alive, I would have felt better if she had at least twitched.

Exhausted from lack of sleep and wringing my hands over Diane, I struggled up the stairs to my apartment, not minding the smell of the bar or even contemplating a minute at the piano. My bed swallowed me like a tidal wave.

"Hey, Tom," a sweet voice called me.

I cracked an eyelid to find Ally standing in my doorway.

"Yeah?"

"Marty's guy is here. Everything is inside but he wants to get paid."

The clock beside my bed indicated I had been sleeping two hours. I think it lied. I was fully clothed and my shoes were tied.

"You want to talk to him?" Ally prodded.

Not really, I almost said, getting up.

Downstairs, Marty's guy appraised my bedraggled self and couldn't help but wince. "You go on a bender or what?"

"Something else," I told him, adding, "Tell Marty I'll catch up with him next week."

"You're a COD account. I can't leave here with nothing."

"The account is paid up. He can cut me some slack."

He unholstered his cell phone, got Marty on the line, and handed the unit to me.

"What's the problem?" Marty asked.

"There isn't any," I answered, rallying my confidence. "I'll pay you next week."

"Next week is this week. That's what COD means."

"And if I call Bonner's Wholesale I can get the same shit you sell, probably a few percent cheaper."

"After a summer of no hassles you're going to jerk me around?" Marty huffed.

"I'm not jerking anybody around. I paid you off, and I'm telling you I'll pay you next week. If you can't live with that, tell your guy to hump the cases back in the truck and get the hell out of here." I gave the phone to the driver and went for a glass of water. When I came back, the guy was still there.

"Marty wants to know if you're having your period?" he asked.

"It's not due until Friday," I said. "Are you taking the shit back or what?"

"No, no. Marty said to tell you that he can match Bonner's prices."

"Great. So now he's admitting that he's been ripping me off."

"Come on, Tom. Business is business."

"You're right, and this is my business so tell Marty I want his new prices, in writing, before I'm wearing the rag or it's Bonner's for everything."

Overcome by lockjaw, the poor bastard stood there with his eyeballs drying out. I guess he wasn't used to people giving him both barrels like that. Just then Stacy came in, which was enough beauty to cheer me up and prompt him into leaving.

"I paid that dog," Stacy said, which I took to mean Sergei had received his weekly tribute. She also gave me the other five hundred from her pants pocket.

"Can you handle things tonight?"

"Sure. Magda come soon and Ally, too."

"Good. I need some sleep."

Like a complete asshole, I slept through the afternoon, the night, and part of the morning. When I awoke, the newspaper had just hit the steps. On my way through the kitchen, I spotted a sheet of paper on the table. It was a note from Ally, one more thing for me to fix.

"Get someone to cover for me tonight."

I had planned to work the poker game myself, hustling the food and booze down the stairs as required. If I was busy doing that, Stacy and Magda would be alone in the bar. Tuesdays weren't the busiest of days, and I figured they could handle it without Ally but I didn't like her taking unscheduled leave.

Peeking in my brother's old room, I saw the bed had not been touched, which indicated alternative sleeping arrangements. In the bar I made another discovery, this one in the form of a full cash register. Six hundred twenty eight dollars shared the space with my brother's picture. I left a hundred for change, John's picture as guard, and slipped out through the side door.

Propped up on a couple pillows, Diane looked no better than a corpse with a pulse. She was still unconscious, although I was told she had been awake earlier. Her face resembled an old candle and there was a new set of hoses draining ghastly fluids from her.

"She has a fever," the nurse told me. "The infection is causing it."

"Infection?"

"It happens," the nurse said.

I lacked the courage to bitch about her matter-of-fact way of talking about the only person I cared for at the moment. Frankly, I was scared. Maybe I shouldn't have torn up those pages Diane had written. Like so many other people, I expected miracles from doctors, especially the ones in this city.

"Does she have any other family?" the nurse wanted to know.

"Why?"

"Depends what happens. We may need authorization for various procedures." She flipped through the charts then corrected herself. "Wait a minute. She left a signed 'Do Not Resuscitate' order. That's covered."

"Let me give you my number."

"Who exactly are you?" she asked pedantically.

"The guy who cares and is paying for this," I said. "Is that understood?"

"Maybe you're not familiar with the ..."

I cut her off. "Spare me. Write this number down wherever you have to, and when Diane is well enough to speak, she'll tell you I'm the right person to call."

My demand was met with a harsh glare followed by the rapid departure of both the nurse and myself. I bolted north, pushing the Cadillac harder than it deserved. Larry greeted me with a growl. I filled his bowl, rubbed his head, and rushed out.

At the bar a few minutes later, I was just in time to secure a delivery of crabs and fresh shrimp, the kind of food Larry might have preferred. Lizzie and her crew showed up spot on time to start cooking. They wanted to know how Diane was doing.

"She needs your prayers," I said.

There was a moment of silence during which the three of them bowed their heads. Although not much of a believer, I shared a moment with the Almighty, asking Him to deliver Diane from illness, to keep an eye out for my brother if he had not yet arrived at the pearly gates, and to let my first poker game come off without a hitch. As for my father, he was on his own.

Game time bore down on me harder than my father's debt. I made the mistake of calling the hospital, which was met with the standard reply about not being able to give information over the phone. I made another mistake trying to shave, only to scrape my face into a ruddy carcass. However, I pulled myself together under my best white shirt and black pants, the ones I wore to John's funeral. After a final look in the mirror, I vowed to buy some clothes when next I made a few extra bucks.

No sooner had I entered the bar when Craig appeared. He was clean, sober, and decently attired as well as quite excited to be part of the scene. It took me a couple of seconds to process this reality, but I found my voice.

"Thanks for coming in," I said. "I appreciate it."

"You're paying cash, man, so I'm here."

After a quick review of the way things went behind the bar and an introduction to the rest of the crew, I headed to the basement. Lizzie's helpers had covered the tables with cloths borrowed from the church, which was another sin on my growing list. I loaded the ice chests, double-checked the fancy bottles, and peeked to make sure that if anyone stumbled through the doors to the tunnel they would be met by nothing but empty boxes.

"You down there already?" Lottery Joe called from the top of the stairs.

"Yeah!" I returned.

He strutted down like a peacock in heat. Two guys and a lady were behind him. They took their time appraising the room and me.

"This is Susan, George, and Billy," Joe said.

"Pleased to meet you," I replied. "Would you like a drink?"

They looked down their noses at the small bar, no doubt searching for their favorite brands. I got the sense they were used to playing in more opulent surroundings.

"Grey Goose, rocks," Susan dared to say.

"Gentlemen?" I asked the others.

"Come on guys," Joe said. "Relax. Tom's cool."

They decided to have nothing stronger than Coca-Cola, which put my total sale at ten dollars. If the night continued like that I was destined for a bullet to the brain from Sergei after Factor Associates foreclosed and Diane was abandoned in the hospital. But that's not how it went. It lit off like a refinery on fire, and the countdown began with Ally descending the stairs in a dress that cost as much as two payments to the Russian Mob, maybe more.

I'd never seen Ally in a dress, let alone an expensive one. She caught me staring, shot me a nervous look, and crossed the room to the biggest table. As she took her seat at the dealer's position, Billy, George, and even Susan checked her out. Using a lacquered fingernail, she slit the wrapper off a brand new deck of cards and fanned them out with style.

"Get me a Booker's and ditch this Coke," George said over his shoulder as he moved toward a seat opposite Ally.

"Sure," I heard myself say. After I served the drink, Joe went upstairs and returned with two more players.

The new guys wasted no time ordering hardy booze and taking seats at the table. They knew the other three, greeting each of them with handshakes, jokes about taking each other's money, and nods to Ally that it was about time she start dealing the cards.

And she dealt them like a pro. The hands played out for over an hour and a half before a piss break was finally declared. Joe minded the money on the table while everyone dashed to the bathrooms. I wanted a word with Ally, but Joe diverted me with a request for the shrimp cocktail and, "whatever else you can come up with."

On my way to the kitchen, I saw the bar was doing a fair trade. I pressed Craig into service, and together we carried a tray of food below. Joe poked his nose at it, decided it was "okay," and ordered it set out by the bar.

"They can help themselves," he said. "Losers followed by winners."

Billy was the first guy to bust out. He hung around long enough to have company at the shrimp platter, commiserating with another loser between mouthfuls. They paid their tab and departed only to be replaced by two more recent arrivals.

Susan liked her drinks brought to the table and for good reason. She was the biggest winner. At the same time, she put her hand on my leg with enough frequency for me to take the hint that I should make a pass. She did have a full chest and wasn't bad-looking either, but I resisted the temptation to mix business with pleasure. The other guys noticed her move and smirked, which gave me the feeling that I wasn't the first strong lad to feel her claws.

New players stopped coming around midnight. Vulgar taunts and profane retorts flew back and forth. The betting went out of control, spiraling into pots of several thousand dollars. At one point, a guy tossed his cards at Ally and accused her of dealing from the bottom of the deck. Joe hoisted him out of his seat by the back of his shirt. Immediately the guy turned docile, apologized, and begged to get back in the game.

"Next month," Joe said, ushering him toward the stairs.

Susan was the one to beat. The pile of money in front of her grew like a Chicago snowdrift. Her opponents peered over their cards at it, and I heard the calculator in Joe's head doing the math.

"If you boys would stop staring at my tits and that pretty girl over there, you might win a few," Susan said.

She did have nice tits and Ally, even after five hours of tension-laced gambling, was the kind of distraction that caused ten-car demolition derbies on Interstate 95. However, neither of those things held my attention like that mountain of dough. I estimated it at ten thousand dollars, which made me feel like a first-class chump. In all, ten players had participated. It cost Joe a hundred dollars a head to provide them with a nice location, a dealer, and a clean toilet. I wondered two things: 1) How much Joe charged them; and 2) what kind of jobs these people had, no doubt the kind that came after an uninterrupted four years of higher education.

Susan traded fire with the last two players, slowly grinding down their stakes. To their credit, the other guys played well, they just didn't get the cards. Susan, on the other hand, often drew a high pair to start then added to it as the rest of the cards came out.

"Let's make this interesting," she said. "How about best of three hands, winner takes all."

The other guys looked at each other. They had nothing to lose but their paltry stacks of tens and twenties.

"You're on," one of them said.

"Tom," Susan said to me, "bring me one more vodka, would you?"

As I set it down, she got my full attention by placing her hand on mine. Her eyes hid none of her lust, nor the crafty wiles of an experienced gambler. I felt sorry for the others, certain victims of this temptress.

Susan lost the first hand, cutting her odds to one third. Then she won the second round, which left the guys sweating. They grinned with false confidence that her luck was about to run out. Then Ally dealt the first two cards of the last hand, and I saw that Susan held a pair of queens. The community cards hit the table with a pair of eights showing and one ace. A two came next. The last card was a deathblow, another queen. When all the cards were on the table, Susan had a full house, queens over eights, which beat the guys who had two pair each.

Susan won graciously. She tossed Ally a hundred-dollar bill and offered to pay the other guys' bar tabs. They wouldn't give her that satisfaction, so she gathered up her money. She made a joke of stuffing it in her bra and then said, "I guess there's no more room in here, is there?"

We all went upstairs where the bar was vacant except for Craig who was mopping the floor.

"I'll finish up," I told him.

He stole a glance at Ally and continued to swab the deck. "I'm almost done," he said.

There was no way Ally was staying in John's room or going home with Craig. Joe had her by the arm. Since he'd paid my bill yesterday, he had no reason to linger. He didn't so much as tell me thanks on his way out the door behind the others.

From the top of the stoop I watched Joe help Ally into his BMW. The door behind me opened, and Craig stepped out. We both kept our mouths shut until the car turned down Richmond Street, no doubt bound for Joe's lottery-winner pad.

"I really don't know where your dad is," Craig said.

"He'll turn up," I replied.

"Yeah, see you tomorrow," he said and walked up the block.

I stood there until he was out of sight, and then a while longer. It was quiet enough to hear the streetlights change. I pondered where a guy like my father put his head down on a night like this. In the back of his car? In some whore's bed? At the moment I considered myself lucky to have the old recliner upstairs and the bed down the hall from it.

As things turned out, I wouldn't be alone. A car rolled up Tioga Street and parked near the side entrance to the bar. I stayed in position, watching Susan get out, lock her door, and amble up to me.

She put her hand at the base of my neck and pulled me into a kiss. Pulling back she searched my eyes.

"I love that sad look of yours," she said.

AN AILING FRIEND AND A HUNGRY CAT waited on me, so I didn't dither with my seductress. On my feet just after six, I rushed a shower, skipped a shave, and dressed in my hospital-visitor best.

"This place opens early," Susan said from my bed.

"How do you win like that?" I asked, ignoring her comment.

"I cheat," she said on her way to the bathroom.

The remark forced me to review the night. Although I was no expert, I had watched the game closely, as did Joe. No one was cheating, unless they had x-ray glasses or a magic decoder ring.

She saw my confusion, planted a kiss on my cheek, and explained. "It's all about distraction," she said, hooking her bra. "I give them every opportunity to look at my chest or my fingers stroking a glass, things like that. It only takes a little edge, something that gives away their hand or knocks them off track."

I found that hard to believe.

"Show me a man who doesn't have sex on his brain every thirty-five seconds, and I'll show you a dead body," she reflected.

I let her have that small victory and followed her to the street.

Larry met me at the door, which was a needed comfort. He seemed to appreciate my presence beyond the filling of his bowl. I sat with him a few minutes, petting his head, thinking about what I might face at the hospital. On the tables and walls of Diane's house there were no framed photos. No construction paper creations hung from the fridge. It reminded me of my place above the bar where there wasn't one picture of my mother, and aside from the one of John, no others of family or friends.

"See you later," I said to Larry.

The hospital was empty at that early hour. It seemed to be between the crush of overnight emergencies and regularly scheduled mayhem. I took advantage of the lull, sneaking into the intensive care unit before official visiting hours began.

Diane was awake, looking no better, and not in the mood to talk.

"Larry misses you," I said.

Her lips formed a smile but there was no real joy behind it.

"Have you talked to the doctor?" I asked.

She nodded.

"And?"

"A week, as long as the infection goes away."

I didn't ask her what happened if the infection didn't go

away. Instead, I said, "Then what?"

"Radiation."

Radiation, surgery, cancer, they were all words of impending doom, death sentences delayed. I couldn't help but feel that a bullet from Sergei's gun had to be the way to go. Of course, everyone says that until they're looking down the barrel. Having recently had that pleasure, I admitted there was nothing great about it. It left me sick to my stomach and angry at being helpless. I thought about my brother and wondered if he felt powerful at having the upper hand being a trained soldier. The trouble was, fighting Sergei or enemies on the battlefield was nothing like a rumble with cancer. At least it seemed that way to me.

"You want me to bring you something?" I asked Diane. "How about one of those spicy crabs?"

"No," she answered and then put out a question of her own. "When do your classes start?"

She caught me before a lie could pass my lips. I couldn't look her in the face and tell her my father stole the money that I was too stupid (or rather, greedy for want of the taxes) to put in the bank. I turned away and muttered that something came up, that I was off for the semester.

"Your dad?" she queried, revealing that her intuition was undiminished by her recent illness.

"Yeah," I said, wishing I had learned to lie, cheat, and steal, instead of all of the useless things my first two years of college had taught me.

"I'm sorry," she said and started crying the way she had the first day out of surgery.

I left the hospital with a full head of steam. If my father had been home I would have beat him senseless, if Sergei showed up I would have smashed a bottle of vodka over his head, and if Lottery Joe stuck his nose up at my food and booze I would have kicked him in the nuts. But there was no one in sight who deserved a beat down. I sat in my sagging chair, smoked my pipe until my throat was sore, and then drove over to see Larry, whom I was starting to like more and more since he kept his mouth shut and was happy with fresh water and a rub between the ears.

Stacy and Magda helped me open the bar, and then left me at the piano, where I stumbled through some songs just to pass the time. When Tony and some other regulars showed up, I spared them my misery, giving them free reign of the television as well as the view of two pert Polish asses.

I walked down to Masgai's place. Half a dozen of his roll-off containers sat in the yard, all of them full of rubble. It reminded me of that day when I came there with Ally. Looking down the block, I saw Craig walking up the sidewalk toward me.

"Doing some discount shopping?" he asked.

"Just getting some air," I said.

He stood there for three awkward seconds then told me that he didn't smoke any pot today.

"So long as you don't smoke it on the job, I don't care," I said.

"I'm just saying I'm not a total eight ball, Tom. I can, you know, handle life. I wish Ally would figure that out. She gets herself mixed up with people who have sick ideas about how to have a party."

He caught me off guard with that comment, forcing me to re-evaluate all my gripes. Except for my father, good people surrounded me, including in his own way, Craig. I suspected that if he wanted to, he could have kicked my ass when I confronted him at the power plant. More to the point, Stacy and Magda worked hard for their pay, as did Lizzie and her crew. Diane had been a source of inspiration. McNally put the bar into good shape, and Greg Dooling split his parking lot revenue, no questions asked. Whether I admitted it or not, they were a major part of the solution to my problems.

"I think Ally's on the right track now," I said to Craig. This I truly believed. She played her part at the poker game, didn't so much as ding the Caddy, and kept her quarters neat and clean.

"I hope so," Craig put in. "Back a while, she was mixed up with the K Street Klub."

He saw that I didn't know what he was talking about and explained.

"Hardcore drugs, stickups, stuff like that."

They sounded like the type of people who might give a girl a beating, too.

"Larsen busted a bunch of them. It was in the paper."

One more time, Craig surprised me. I hadn't figured him for a guy who read the newspaper.

"I begged her to get away from them because those things always blow up in a raid. Sure enough it did. She skated, though. Maybe she was already at Joe's pad by then. I don't know."

Telling him that Ally was better off with Joe than with a gang would have been insult to his injury. Therefore, I changed the subject.

"Let's go sell some beer," I said.

We fell into step, an unlikely pair but perfectly matched for the corner of Richmond and Tioga Streets.

Ally came home that night. Actually it was the next morning. I was awake, smoking in my chair, scribbling notes on a pad.

She flopped onto the couch, occupying my father's usual spot. "I'm sorry, Tom," she began, "I know I missed work but Joe kept me out. He ..."

"Forget it," I interrupted. My tone was unusually forgiving compared to the hard-ass routine she was used to.

She processed my forgiveness and smiled, which made me that much happier. At that moment she exposed a feminine side that was almost girly, something I hadn't seen before in her. The innocence of her expression soaked in, giving my otherwise hardening countenance a brief respite.

"You were driving to casino dealer school last month," I said.

"Yeah. Joe paid for it." Then her eyes swelled and she said, "Did you see the money those people bet?"

"I saw it. You were great, by the way."

She bounced on the couch a few times. "You think so?"

"That dress didn't hurt either." Seeing a street-tough chick like her blush was a thrill, and I took a few seconds to enjoy it. My brother probably felt the same way about me when I showed him my college acceptance letter. He put a hand on my shoulder, telling me that I better live up to his achievements in boot camp. I upped the ante, offering him a ride in the brand new Cadillac I would surely buy less than two years after graduation. At present, it didn't look like things were going to end up that way, but there was still time on the clock.

"Joe took me to this place where they sell clothes like that," Ally was saying. "They're used but who can tell? Joe said rich people only wear their clothes once and throw them away."

Joe this; Joe that. I held my jealousy in check the way Craig seemed to do and stuck to the matters at hand. "Listen," I began, "I need you to be here, Ally. I know you and Joe have something going on and that's fine, but I'm taking a semester off from school ..."

"What?" she interrupted.

"You heard me. This place can't be a flash in the pan. I need to make some serious money, and I need reliable people to work when they're supposed to. I have Craig ..."

"That's so cool that you gave him a job," she cut in.

"Right, well, you were here first. I'm counting on you."

"I got it, Tom. I do."

"You can have off the nights when you're dealing cards. I hope Joe is paying you for that. It's his gig anyway. The other nights you're either going to be here or I have to find someone else."

"No, don't do that. I'll be here."

"Just so we're clear," I emphasized. It was the most even conversation I'd had in months. I knew she was infatuated with Joe, his wealth, and her new station in life at the head of a poker table. I also knew that she would inevitably miss the odd night of work, which would perturb me; however, I was happy to have someone living in the same set of rooms as me, especially this version of Ally that was more sweet than tart. If it came to the point where I had to throw her out, I was planning to kidnap Larry just so I would have company.

"There's going to be some more changes next week," I went on.

"Sure, you know what you're doing. I can't wait."

"And I have to take care of Diane, too. She's having a rough time and needs every bit of help we can give."

That turned out to be the prophecy of the evening. Diane's infection lingered. I cried over the Cadillac's steering wheel two nights later after her doctor told me if the fever went any higher she would have brain damage. The Executives played without me both Friday and Saturday nights as I sat in the waiting room to which I had been banished by the nurses who tired of my vigil. In between these adversities, I fed Larry, collected the bar's money, and checked in with my employees.

Then, as Sunday night turned into Monday morning, Diane's fever dropped from the red zone into the yellow. It was only two degrees, but it was in the right direction. For the first time, I left the hospital feeling something close to salvation.

I arrived at home to find my father's room empty, Ally asleep in my brother's bed, and the poster of that ideal Marine staring out at me.

"Semper fi," I said one more time and picked my way down the hall in the dark.

21

THE NEXT MORNING, I TALLIED UP the week's receipts. The total proved that everyone was replaceable, including me. I spent more time at the hospital than the bar, and yet the money was there, as much as any week when I'd watched every penny. Even so, I intended to make my presence felt again.

I also motored to three different banks where I opened accounts using small amounts of cash. Whether or not this avoided IRS scrutiny was not the point. Dodging my father's sticky fingers was my prime concern. That piece of business out of the way, I returned to the bar to await Sergei's visit.

Despite the cold weather, he wore only his sport coat and that smug grin of the friendly neighborhood extortionist. This time I didn't let him get under my skin, not even when he remarked that I was smart to let my "Polish whores" do the dirty work.

"Strong back, strong hips," he said, thrusting his pelvis

into an imaginary sex partner.

I put his five hundred dollars on the bar without acknowledging his sordid gesture.

He left the money there for a few seconds, giving me a hard stare to which I refused to yield. I wasn't provoking him; I was standing my ground, which began at the edge of the bar. It was his choice to cross the line, not mine. He decided to stay where he belonged.

"I think this bar successful now. You do good things," he said.

"Thanks," I replied.

"Is my job to protect a place. Understand?"

I did but didn't say it.

"Other people see this, they want for themselves. No?"

"I don't know."

"Is true, you just boy in world of man. I explain. More success require more protection. Next week you pay two hundred fifty dollars for service I provide."

And to think I was worried about the IRS. I wondered if they would allow me to deduct Sergei's payments from my taxable income.

He took his money off the bar and made one more comment. "Your father, I not see him."

"Me either," I said.

"I see you next week."

Unless you get hit with a bus, I wanted to say, but kept my mouth shut. If I'd learned anything, it was that Sergei liked a fight. After all, he won them easily, thereby reinforcing his self-image as the man in charge. I would find out later that he had a boss of his own. In the interim I had a bar to run, poker games to host, and a cat to feed.

Joe pushed for weekend games but I told him the only open night was Sunday. The Executives drew a crowd that drank like camels after a desert trek, which earned more revenue than a grand plus the sales of swanky booze that otherwise would go stale in a joint like Bonk's Bar.

"And you gotta do better with the food," he said as we conversed in the dining room that afternoon. "Put some bacon around the shrimp. Get some fancy chips and dips. I can't have Ally dressed like a movie star and then you serve refried crap."

"I'll consult my chef," I promised. It occurred to me that Joe was striving for the ideal version of a private gambling den. He liked playing the big shot, the magnanimous provider of the good life, a sort of mirror image of Sergei. To cast Bonk's Bar in that role stretched the imagination. It was more roadhouse than nightclub, more working man's entertainment than high-class retreat.

"I got people coming Tuesday and Thursday. Saturday would be perfect, too, but you ain't giving me nothing except Sunday. I'll have to see what I can set up."

"And work on your grammar," I said, unable to resist the jibe. I got up to indicate there was nothing more for us to talk about.

More good news greeted me at the hospital. Diane was awake, still feverish, but appeared to be through the worst. I gave her the good news: Larry and I were getting along great, and the bar was undergoing another facelift.

"I can't wait to leave here," she said solemnly.

"It won't be long," I assured her. "I'll stock the fridge for you. Get some books. Make sure the cable TV is working."

She squeezed my hand. "Thanks," she said, adding, "I wish your brother was here to see what you've done with the bar."

"He sees my every move," I said, the recruiting poster in my mind's eye. If I kept it up, a new Cadillac might be in my future, too.

The hospital held Diane for six more days and nights. During that time, I served better food at the poker games thanks to Lizzie's interpretation of the cookbook I'd bought that day with Diane. I also played four sets with The Executives on two different nights. Despite not seeing Susan, I denied Tina the pleasure of my bed. She didn't take it well.

"You're turning queer," she spat at me after the last set on Saturday night. "Or else that teenage bitch found her way into your pants."

"I need to sleep, Tina. Let's leave it at that," I said and practically shoved her out the door.

The fact was that I did need the sleep. Running the bar into the early morning hours drained me. There was the added stress of the poker games, which required my personal attention. On top of that, I spent innumerable hours driving back and forth to see Diane, checking in on Larry, and brainstorming about how to keep minting money.

On Monday morning, after I made the rounds at my banks, I double-parked in front of the hospital and hustled to the automatic doors where Diane waited in a wheelchair. The orderly rolled her curbside; she had to make the last few steps on her own. She was strong enough to fasten her own seatbelt and do little else.

Larry almost leapt out of his skin as she came through the door. I scooped him off the floor so he wouldn't trip her, but he wiggled free and clung to her like fresh lint.

"I walked all of ten feet, and God, I'm tired," Diane said, easing herself onto the couch. "This kind of life isn't worth living."

"You want something to eat?" I asked trying to lighten the mood.

"No."

"How about a Coke?" I suggested.

"Don't try too hard, Tom. I'll be okay."

She was right. Before I left, I put a new cell phone on the arm of the couch.

"Use that to call me if you need anything," I said.

She looked at the phone and then waved me out.

I never expected to see Sy Kranick at the bar. Each month, I paid Factor Associates a little more than what was owed by rounding up the payments to even hundreds. He walked through the door and took his time appraising the place in a manner reminiscent of the one used by the insurance company's inspector.

"Big changes," he said coming back to the bar.

"You should see this place on Friday night," Tony chimed in. "Band playing, Tommy there on the keys, me fighting to get a drink."

"Is that right?" Kranick asked.

"Yeah," Tony went on, "I remember when this place was like my living room. I could watch whatever I wanted on TV. Now I gotta get in line for a Yuengling."

Kranick focused on Stacy and Magda who were at a loss as to whether or not he wanted a drink. I stepped up to the plate.

"Can I get you something?" I asked.

"No," he answered. "I'm just checking on our investment."

It was my investment, not his, and I didn't appreciate his self-inclusion on the board of directors. However, just as I avoided a battle with Sergei, I did so with Kranick. The best thing was to give him what he wanted, which I determined to be a tour.

"Let me show you the basement," I said waving him toward the stairs.

He followed like a good tourist, asking a question here and there, nodding at McNally's carpentry. When we were upstairs again, I offered him one for the road, but he declined.

"Keep those payments coming," he reminded me and ended his visit.

I kept them coming, to him, to Sergei, to Marty, to everyone other than myself. I lived on leftovers out of the kitchen and the smoke of Special Blend No. 4. In the months leading up to Christmas, I lost five pounds of fat and put on ten pounds of muscle.

Part of my transformation had to do with watching Diane suffer through radiation treatment. Her visits were scheduled over the course of two months. The day after was the worst, when she was puking over the bowl like a hopeless lush. The rest of that week she would hardly eat. Then, just as she got her appetite back, the next appointment came due and the cycle repeated.

I reacted like any pansy who was afraid of what he didn't understand. Aside from the exercise I got stacking beer cases and barrels, and frolicking with Tina or Susan, I did pushups, sit-ups, and chin-ups at every opportunity. The monotony of counting the reps distracted my worried mind. There was something else, too, maybe a bit of the fighter in me preparing for the next showdown. Being a physical wimp had a downside; people thought they could screw with you at will. Thus, I exercised to improve my odds.

My anticipated confrontation didn't come as quickly as it could have. Christmas and New Year's passed without incident. Only Sergeant Larsen came looking for a contribution. I bought fifty tickets for his Santa Raffle and contributed another five hundred to the Kerry Outreach as insurance against a visit from Dirkus.

"You're a good man, Tom," Larsen said, slapping my back.

He was right. I dusted the photo of my dead brother, held what was left of Diane's hair away from her face as she retched, and paid fair wages to everyone who worked for me. Although I hadn't seen my father in more than three months, I worried about him, which was a powerful testament to my character given what he'd done to me. It was the piano. Whenever I played it, I remembered the day it had been delivered and that my father thought enough of me to present such a gift.

My reward for all this discipline and diligence was more than fifty grand, spread over three bank accounts, the hiding place in the floor of the tunnel, and my own pocket. It was enough to get Sergei off my back or pay my last two years of college. The choice was mine.

For more than one night, I pondered the idea of skipping out on the bar, getting a regular job, and hitting the books. The spring semester began the second week of January, so it was the perfect time for such a stunt. However, whether I wanted to admit it or not, I was as much a gambler as my father.

I made up my mind on the third day of the new year. I fooled around on the piano, trying to improvise melodies of songs that were getting stale. When that failed to distract me, I looked around the empty bar and decided that one more semester away from school wouldn't kill me; I wouldn't turn into a blithering idiot; I might learn something that formal education didn't teach; and if I could net fifty thousand in three months, then I could triple it in the nine months until the fall semester.

I was a good man all right. I had the power of prophecy, too. Yet, there were a few things absent from my revelations. Things that, had I known what they were in advance, would have led me down an easier path. Luckily, I had done my exercise along with my homework. There was heavy lifting to be done.

22

DIANE WAS FURIOUS. I'd never seen her angry, let alone spit fire. She smacked her hand on the kitchen table, and Larry bolted under the couch. I sat there dumbfounded, hoping it would blow over before anything was broken.

"You should have registered," she was saying. "Every semester you delay only puts you that much farther from graduation."

"I know," I said, "but I have to pay bills at the bar."

"Don't tell me about bills!" she hollered. "They only started sending me the ones from my surgery. I can't imagine what the radiation costs. I'll be lucky to be out of hock before I die."

"I'll help you with some of those," I put in.

"I hope to live to see you graduate," she murmured.

Exhausted, she leaned against her chair. Her last treatment session was behind her, but she hadn't returned to full strength. "Promise me you'll go in the fall," she whispered.

"I will."

"Let me hear you say it."

"I promise," I said.

A punch from Sergei was less painful than an argument with Diane. Like a good mother, she expected more of me than I expected of myself. In the end, I knew she would see it my way, especially when I was a full-time student with nothing to worry about but getting to class on time.

I retreated to the bar, where unbeknownst to Sergei, he was about to receive the entire principal of my father's debt. A shoebox held the fifty grand, all of it in hundred-dollar bills. I had it with me at Diane's, and as I climbed the stairs to the bar, I couldn't help but feel triumphant. Sure, Sergei would get his two fifty a week from me, but that was all. Five hundred more would be where it belonged, in my pocket.

Yeah, I had another thing coming.

Sergei strolled in looking awfully good for a guy with the stress of collecting from people like me.

"Bonk!" he announced today as he put his hands on the bar. "Is new year!"

"It is," I said and reached for two shot glasses. For this occasion I had purchased a bottle of Stolichnaya Elit (the Russians left off the last e at the factory), and it was that oily liquid that I poured.

"Oh, is special," Sergei said.

I picked up my shot, downed it, and smacked it on the bar. His hit a second later. "Another?" I asked.

"Is for pleasure or business?" he wanted to know.

"Both," I answered and refilled the glasses.

The ceremony completed, I placed the shoebox next to the bottle. "Here is the fifty thousand dollars my father owed you," and then I put another five hundred on top of the box. "That's the last of the interest."

The smug prick couldn't help himself. He actually gawked at the box, at me, and back at the box. If I'd had the old shoes that came out of the box I could have shoved one down his throat, the other up his ass. He closed his jaw and opened the box. The money sat in there, neatly bundled in ten packs of fifty, one hundred-dollar bills.

"Count it," I said. "I don't want any misunderstandings."

"You would cheat me?"

"Count it and you'll know for sure," I cracked. "You want another shot?"

He didn't reply. Instead he took out one of the packs and fanned the bills.

"Satisfied?"

"Is everything your father owe from before," he said.

"From before and forever," I stated for the record.

Sergei corrected me. "For new year, we have new contract. Business arrangement. Yes?"

I neither accepted nor denied his declaration, choosing to issue my own terms, all the way to the fine print before so much as blinking. After all, this guy liked to change the deal when he felt like it.

"Let's be clear," I explained. "If my father bets on a game or the numbers, that's your arrangement with him. I have nothing to do with that."

"You separate now from father. You pay for bar. He pay sports book, number, whatever. This what you tell me?"

"Yes."

He sat back. "Please. Is stupid for me to do this. You and him have business here. Him, you, no difference."

"Big difference," I countered. "This is my place now. I paid for it."

By the expression on his face, Sergei was caught off guard. Of course, I was lying but it was worth a try. Given that he was a loan shark I felt no compunction about deceiving him. How else was I going to escape my father's habit?

"Your father say nothing of this to me," Sergei said next.

"You spoke to him?" I blurted.

"Three days ago."

"Where?"

"Please, I not baby sitter. He take small loan, one thousand four hundred dollars. He make special point tell me not for gambling."

"Then for what?" I asked.

"Maybe you not listen. I tell again, not for gambling. Personal loan. His words not mine."

Capitalizing on this revelation I said quickly, "See, he doesn't want to mix things together anymore. He's got his gambling, his personal loans, and neither one is about the bar. Our business is settled."

"Is just begun, Bonk," Sergei retorted. "You show me you know things. How to make money. How to operate bar establishment. We like partners. I protect. You serve."

This was another moment when I wished I'd had those old shoes.

"Next week, I collect five hundred for bar," he said.

"Five hundred?"

"Now you complain like woman? You have good business. Five hundred is small price for my security. Besides, your father, he must be on lucky streak. I not see him for long time. Then, he borrow fourteen hundred but want not to make bet on sports. Not Eagles, not nothing. This confusion, no?"

It was very confusing. By paying off my father's debt, I expected to reduce my expenses by five hundred dollars a week. All I'd done was prove that the payment could be made. Hence, it was to continue. As for my father's fourteen hundred dollar loan, how could I decode the meaning of that?

"Okay," I said in pursuit of a minor rebuttal. "Give me a number I can call when I need you."

He thought I was kidding. When I tossed a pen and pad at him, he let it flop on the bar. I watched his eyes as he tried to figure out if I was insulting him or not. I was taunting him, treating him like Marty's driver, or a salesman trying to sell me napkins. Fortunately, he didn't get it. Carefully, he wrote his ten digits on the pad.

"Is cell phone. Leave message."

"Thanks," I said. "You going to count the money?"

He didn't count it. He tucked the box under his arm and left the bar like one of my take-out customers. If only he tripped down the stairs and broke his neck, then I would have had a reason to celebrate. My luck wasn't that strong. Not yet.

It might have been that my father siphoned off some of my good fortune. He had no way of knowing that I was going to pay off Sergei, and yet he had the nerve to take out a personal loan from the thug. Only a guy rolling in four-leaf clover would have the nerve to do that. In a way, my father was — I provided the clover and he rolled the dice.

For the exercise and psychotherapeutic effects, I began stealing old bricks from Masgai's dumpsters. These I piled in neat stacks on either side of the tunnel. Sooner or later, the Doolings might discover that passageway and follow it to my poker den. While they were good neighbors, I didn't want any surprises. Nor did I care to have anyone go through from my side. No one but me.

Ally caught me one night. She had an eye for detail and noticed where my coat had caught on the bottom of Masgai's fence.

"You were dumpster diving, weren't you?" she said after we'd closed the bar and retreated upstairs for the night.

Always a lousy liar, I said, "Yeah," and tried to sneak away to my room.

"I could have helped you," she said. "What'd you get?"

"Just some bricks," I said, sticking with the truth.

"Bricks? What for?"

"This building is made of bricks," I said. "I'll need them sooner or later."

She accepted that then put forth a better idea. "Why don't we fix this place up?"

I looked around the apartment. It was vintage 1963 décor, a perfect location to film a Hitchcock movie.

"Don't pay McNally to do it. We can paint; we can put some tile in the bathroom. What's the worst that can happen?"

Considering that my brother was dead, my old man had stolen my college savings, and Diane had won a round with cancer, I thought it only fitting to brighten the mood.

Each day we made a little progress and had a lot of fun. I made her listen to The Doors and she retaliated by singing badly. I wished Diane were there, if only for me to prove that I wasn't wasting my time between semesters.

We started in the front bedroom, which was my father's and a spot I wouldn't care about if the work turned out sloppy.

Together we scrubbed the walls, patched the plaster, and applied fresh coats of primer and paint. It wasn't brain surgery. We did a good job, going so far as to pry off the molding, strip it, and put it back in place after applying a nice stain.

"Curtains," Ally said on the afternoon when we finished. "A set of curtains over that big window would make this perfect."

"And some new furniture," I added.

"Let's give Craig those end-tables to refinish. He doesn't have enough to do in the bar."

She was right. I noticed that since the new year turned, the bar was not as busy as it had been. The weather wasn't all that cold, the economy was chugging along, and The Executives played their hearts out, but my receipts had slipped a little. I wasn't complaining; I was still accumulating money, putting it into the banks and hiding places, even if it wasn't as much as I had hoped.

Ally and I continued to work on the apartment. In between we visited Diane, who was looking better every day. We begged her to come visit our refurbished digs and to hang out at the bar. She insisted on staying home. Her new medication caused various forms of unpredictable and embarrassing intestinal distress.

Proud of what we'd done in my father's room, we tackled the living room next. Ally insisted I get rid of my old chair and spring for a new one. I stood my ground on that issue, getting a couch from the discount place on Aramingo Avenue instead.

By March we were in the kitchen. Craig joined in full-time to help with the cabinets. They were solid wood, and beneath the coats of crappy paint, showed a beautiful grain. In preparation for sanding the frames, I removed the doors for Craig to strip, while Ally scraped the old paper from the shelves.

"There's some stuff back here," she said. "A couple of big envelopes."

I put down my screwdriver and crossed the room. Ally put the envelopes on the tarp that covered the kitchen table and waited for me to open them. The yellowed tape on the flaps practically fell off. I slid the contents out of the first one. There were original birth certificates for John and me. There was a photo of John in the arms of a woman I assumed to be our mother. I knew it was him because she died before I was an hour old. Next were several elementary school report cards and a copy of the church program for the Mass said to propel my mother's soul to heaven.

Then I came upon a group photo that included my brother, my father, Diane, and me. We stood in a line in front of my piano. Instantly I remembered the occasion. It was my twelfth birthday, which was held in the dining room. Among my gifts: songbooks, a bicycle, some clothes, and a digital watch.

The inexpensive timepiece came from my brother who already had one like it. I put it on my wrist, held it next to his, and thought that we were two of a kind. Less than a year later, John smashed his watch while playing a game of dirt-lot base-ball. I took mine off and put it in my desk drawer, where it sat until the battery went dead. Was this fate knocking on the door? Maybe.

"You were a cute kid," Ally said, looking at the photo. "Who'd you take to the prom?"

"Didn't go," I replied. "Too expensive."

She blew out a frustrated sigh then prodded me to open the other envelope.

This one contained a copy of the deed to the bar. It gave

the legal description, a summary of the premises, and showed that the transfer tax had been paid when my grandfather bought the place.

"You better put that stuff in a safe or something," Ally advised.

I placed both envelopes on my bed. When next I went to the bank, I would rent a safe deposit box to hold them.

By the time winter ended, the kitchen was finished. Ally started to spend more nights with Joe after the poker games, returning just in time to clean up before working at the bar. Susan and Tina both wanted to know why I hadn't updated my own room. I lied about being too busy. The truth was that without Ally making jokes, humming songs, and lending a hand, the work was boring. I enjoyed having a pal, someone who jumped in on the dirty work, who didn't complain, which was more than I could say for most of the people I'd worked with on college projects. I liked her, not in the sense of a girl-friend, but certainly as a favorite sister. In light of that first night when I kicked her out of the bar, this was nothing short of a miracle.

Which is why I was out of my mind on the Second of April when I heard her crying in the bathroom.

It was a Monday, and there had been a Sunday night poker game. Ally had gone home with Joe. Susan hadn't been a player so I'd slept alone. When I came back from a run to the bank, I noticed Ally's dress lying on her bed. I waited in the living room for half an hour before deciding to knock on the bath-room door to see if she'd fallen in.

At the sound of my knock, I heard her flip the latch. How-ever, she didn't respond to my query.

"You want something for breakfast?" I asked.

"No," she said.

I barely heard her, but couldn't miss the sobs that came behind that reply. I paced down the hallway, around the living room, and headed back. She must have slipped out of the bathroom when I'd had my back turned because the door now hung open. I checked to make sure, found nothing but water in the sink, and hurried to my brother's room.

There was no lock on that door. I barged in to find her standing at the end of the bed, flat footed, wearing nothing but her panties and a rash of bruises from her rib cage to her thighs.

"Jesus Christ!" I breathed.

She sat down hard, rolled onto her side, and started to wail. I saw more bruises on her back, small ones, the kind made by two sharp knuckles.

"I'm calling the cops," I said.

"No!" she screeched.

"Whoever is doing this is going to kill you," I said.

"I'm hurt, Tom. Really hurt."

"I know, that's why you have to tell the cops what happened," I urged.

"I'm peeing blood."

"Jesus Christ," I repeated, knowing that she had to go to the hospital before anywhere else.

TO THEIR CREDIT, THE PEOPLE at the hospital worked like pros. They dealt with Ally's health issues first and then assigned a social worker to sort out her domestic problems. This dedicated soul made no more progress than I had because Ally clammed up. The social worker surrendered and released her to my custody. A handful of pamphlets were shoved into my hand, all of them on the subject of abuse and how to deal with it.

During Diane's worst week, I sat with my mouth shut, and I managed to do the same during the ride home with Ally. She lived with me, off and on, for more than six months. We worked together upstairs and in the bar. She was the closest thing I had to a living relative given that my father had yet to show his face, and Diane and I had never dwelled under the same roof.

Ally's pain reminded me just how helpless I was. Guiding

her up the stairs, I realized that my brother had made the right choice by joining the Marines. They were all for one, one for all. When someone screwed with them it meant war. Sure, the politicians were holding back on a full-scale retaliation for what had happened to my brother and his men. At the same time, I knew that behind the scenes a FORCE RECON platoon would parachute into some patch of sand and settle the score. No one may be the wiser, no one but the fools on the receiving end of a visit like that.

I entertained myself with violent adolescent fantasies, the kind of comic book escapism that fueled a generation of video game experts who now pushed the buttons of the world. It did nothing to assuage my anger. If anything, it fired me up that much more. At last, I decided to do something.

"You going to be okay?" I asked Ally from my brother's doorway.

"Can we find another place to live?" was her reply.

Not understanding the question, I told her what I thought she wanted to hear. "Soon," I said.

She turned her head away, leaving me to burn a pile of No. 4 and mull the possible identity of her tormentor.

Joe wasn't the type of guy to smack a chick around. He had his money, his clothes, his BMW coupe, and a bachelor pad that probably did the trick with his female company. If they didn't want to play, he could show them to the elevator and call another.

My Russian nemesis was as much a likely candidate as not. Without hesitation he'd laid a hand on Stacy. He also let me have it. However, in both cases he had been provoked, which demonstrated some sense of control in normal circumstances. Had Ally mouthed off to him? It wasn't likely.

She played her part with Joe, acting like the sidekick to a game-show host, not a cocky debutant. I saw no reason why she would aggravate Sergei.

The other person who knew Ally was Craig. I didn't know where he lived, and since he started working at the bar, he seemed to be on the straight and narrow. For the fun of it I cruised by the power plant for a look. He wasn't there, not in the old office, nor any of the other rooms.

I was clueless and still reaching.

At Diane's I lost my nerve. She didn't need this kind of bullshit to ruin what appeared to be a solid recovery. I managed to get caught in a lie about nothing bothering me, but made a quick escape with the excuse of having to meet Kyle and the rest of the band.

"I'm thinking about changing up the repertoire," I said to Diane as I made for the door.

"How?"

"I don't know. Those Doors songs are getting old. The place needs something new."

"Nostalgia sells in this neighborhood," she informed me. "The past is cheap. We can afford it."

She was right. Everyone lived in the past. Tony and the regulars liked the bar when it was their place, before the new crowd made it loud and sweaty. There were people who stared at the river and dreamed of the shipyards. Others missed the crowds at church on Sunday. Some complained about the lack of English spoken on the streets, as if their parents' first language had been the Queen of England's.

I parked in one of the few curbside spots beside the bar. Stacy and Magda had the place open for the several patrons who started their drinking immediately after lunch.

I wasn't in the building five minutes when Sergeant Larsen and Mr. Kerr showed up. It was the perfect opportunity for me to enlist their help. The words were on the tip of my tongue, ready to spill out, when that pack of raffle tickets came out of Larsen's pocket.

"Who knows?" the big cop said. "This may be your lucky year, Tom. Your new chum Joe picked the winning numbers, didn't he? You should be able to win a Caribbean vacation for two."

The way he said new chum Joe made me rethink my approach. Was he hinting about the poker games? Before I answered my own question he went on.

"What's Joe up to these days?" he wanted to know.

"Living the good life in his penthouse," I said.

The sergeant fired again. "You think he won enough to afford all that? How much did that BMW cost? What's the insurance on that race car?"

Feeling the floor fall out from under me, I said. "I have no idea. Tell me about this Caribbean vacation?"

Mr. Kerr said, "A trip to the island of Aruba. Direct flight from Philadelphia International, one week hotel, a sunset cruise, fifty dollar voucher at the casino, and a candlelight dinner as well."

"If you win, maybe you'd be a good sport and show Diane some real sunshine. Five dollars a chance," Larsen added. "You're in for twenty tickets, aren't you, Tom?"

"For a trip like that? Sure." I gave him money from my pocket while Kerr solicited Stacy, Magda, and the patrons.

"Your support is greatly appreciated," Larsen said after I had my stubs.

The hairs on the back of my neck couldn't stand up. They

were drowned in the sweat that sprung from my pores. The captain knew something about my basement activities. He was having fun taunting me. It took a second to find my spine, the one that gave me the strength to stay beside Diane when she was down for the count. I told myself I wasn't doing anything but paying bills, making a living. What difference did it make if people threw money away gambling in Atlantic City or in my basement?

"By the way, where is Ally?" Larsen asked. "She still work here?"

"Ally's a great employee," I said, looking directly at the cop to reinforce my conviction.

"Good to see you employing locals. They need the same opportunities strangers take in this country," was his final word to me on the subject.

"Speaking of which," Mr. Kerr said, "Have you thought about the University of Pennsylvania?"

Having done so, I nodded.

"Just let me know when you're ready. My friends over there are always looking for good students," he informed me. "I pass a name on to them once in a while."

"See that, Tom?" Larsen put in. "You have to be sure you have the right friends. Eh?"

I remained where I was until he and Mr. Kerr had gone.

Though I'd made a stand, I wasn't an idiot. I knew I had to take precautions. I dialed Joe and told him to expect me in a few minutes and that it was important we spoke immediately. I couldn't wait to see that pad of his.

The apartment Joe picked sat near the top of a new building on Front Street. Thanks to ten-year abatements he paid no taxes while Bonk's Bar and others less fortunate carried the load. His decorator styled the place like an over-priced IKEA. Everything was blond wood, stainless steel, and plate glass. He had the plasma televisions, the high-powered but hidden stereo, and unintelligible art that made him seem like a sophisticate.

"Yo, Tom, we got a problem or what?" he greeted me, revealing that he was nothing but a lucky prick with poor grammar. This also proved that the right people never won the big jackpots.

"You tell me," I answered. "Sergeant Larsen of the Philadelphia Police Department asked about you today."

"Yeah, what'd he want?"

"He wanted to know how you were, if I ever saw your place. Great view by the way." The view was spectacular, even if it was of Camden. The *Battleship New Jersey* was over there and the Delaware River in between was a handsome sight.

"That means nothing."

"I could tell he was fishing," I said. "He wanted to know how much you paid for your car, what the insurance was. He was hinting how you might not have won enough to support your lifestyle. He also asked about Ally."

"Her too?"

"If she worked at the bar," I explained. "By the way, what happened with you guys last night?"

"If you're going to get possessive, Tom ..."

I cut him off. "I'm looking out for me, Joe. What you and Ally do between the sheets doesn't concern me so long as it doesn't get violent."

He played at indignation, which didn't impress me. "This sounds like some chicken-shit game you're playing," he said. "After all the money you got, you're wetting your pants over some off-the-wall questions by a cop who couldn't find his way to a doughnut shop."

"The only one pissing her pants is Ally, with blood, too," I fired back.

That didn't compute for him.

"Yeah, Joe, she showed up this morning, black and blue, and won't tell me what happened. Maybe you can shed some light on the subject?"

Stunned, Joe took a second to check my poker face for a tell. Satisfied that I wasn't bluffing he said, "She came back here for a drink, and before things got intimate, her cell phone rang. She told me she had to leave. I told her that if she wanted to turn tricks instead of make an honest buck with me, she was free to go."

"Then what?"

"She gave me the finger and left."

This sounded like the truth, the old Ally poking through the princess veneer. I wanted the details. "You didn't see who picked her up?"

He snorted. "Like I care. You know I paid for the school that taught her how to deal cards. I paid for everything: her swanky dresses, shoes, slutty underwear, the whole rig. I got a list of broads who would have jumped at that offer." He looked at me, showed the same dissatisfaction, and continued. "And you, turning into a sissy. What the hell happened to you in college?"

"I found out I wasn't the smartest guy in the room," I said, "and neither are you, Joe."

A tougher guy might have punched me at this point. Joe took it because he knew I was right. There was another reason, too, one that we both shared.

"I make a grand a night," he muttered. "Two, three grand a week on average. Cash. Same as you, which by the way is very generous on my part."

"Thanks be to God," I said with a slight bow. "We're going to have to cut in a new partner if we want to avoid the cops."

"Let's get something straight," Joe protested. "You and me ain't partners."

"As if the Russian Mob gives a shit."

 24 ♣ ♥

NO MATTER WHAT JOE SAID, he no longer thought of me as a sissy. I told him I had paid off my father's debt to Sergei and shelled out five hundred a week for protection. This dose of reality muddied up his penthouse view of the world. He dabbled in the criminal fringe with his poker games, while I was up to my neck in my father's mistakes, Sergeant Larsen's impositions, and Sergei's street tax. Unlike me, he could have dropped the ball and gone home, collected his interest, and dallied with chicks he fished out of classier bars than mine. As mentioned earlier, he wasn't the smartest guy in the room.

Neither was I.

My brilliant idea was to bring Sergei in on the games. The logic went like this: Sergei was already a loan shark, extortionist, and probably worse. In the event of a bust, I'd plead ignorance. My story would be that I only rented the room to him. What he did down there had nothing to do with me.

"We're not going to get away with that. The players know me; they know you."

"So what? We're peons. He's the boss. We can get a plea bargain if it comes to that."

"We won't get shit," Joe huffed. "This sucks. I should have bought a bunch of condos down in Florida. I could have resold them for double."

"It's too late for that," I said. "I'll work out the host fee with Sergei and live with our cut."

"I need at least five hundred a game. Less than that and I'm throwing in the towel. There's other things out there for me."

The real sissy had revealed himself.

In my surreal world, it was better to tell the truth to a gangster than to the cops. Despite this certainty, I plunged in, thinking that I was actually making progress. And it was because the only measurement I used was the amount of money I owed, or rather didn't owe.

Back at the bar, I cornered Craig and asked him point blank if he ever laid a hand on Ally. He was livid, which was understandable given that I jumped him with that kind of question.

"I gave up on her when she came to live with you," he said. "No offense, 'cause I'm not saying you're the reason, but she doesn't show her face in this part of town anymore unless Larsen is giving her a ride. She doesn't know who her real friends are."

"You may be right," I said, trying to placate him. "Anyway, someone worked her over, Craig. Who do you think it was?"

"It could be anybody, man. She's your problem."

I was stunned that he could let her go so easily.

"I didn't see your dad either," he added and moved behind the bar to restock the coolers.

Upstairs, Ally sat on the new couch, eating cereal and watching television. I told her the poker games were delayed for a couple weeks. She acknowledged what I said with barely a glance away from the TV. Her lack of spoken words gave me the hint that she didn't feel like chatting.

As much as I wanted to get this mess under control, I resisted the urge to call Sergei. Besides, the poker games were only one facet of the business. I needed to keep the bar full of paying customers and the musical portion of the entertainment was a significant part of the draw, especially on weekends.

Kyle arrived after supper. We sat in the basement, across the table where I'd seen thousands of dollars change hands.

"The crowds aren't as thick as they were," I began.

"It's still pretty good," he countered.

"I need something fresh."

He eyed me sideways. "Like what?"

"I think The Executives should play a couple sets Saturday nights, like a house band. For Friday, it should be two new acts, and if one of them brings a crowd, let them do another couple sets on Saturday."

He lost it. "Man, I fixed your broken-string relic of a piano up there! It was my idea to build that stage, too. Shit, without me, you would never have landed that groupie ..."

"Take it easy," I cut in. "She's more of a pain in the ass than anything."

"You're still giving me the shaft."

"How about this?" I offered. "You become a sort of musical director. You book the bands; you deal with the schedule."

"Now you're going to make me a lackey?"

I held my anger in check. It was good practice for what I anticipated with Sergei. "I don't expect you to do it for free," I said.

"Oh, that's different."

"Look, you know the scene. You know other bands like yours. You know that this place already has a reputation."

"Which I built."

"Which you got paid for, including the new string in my piano. So let's stop beating our chests. You want your name in lights then buy me out and put up your own sign." I took a breath and let him see that he'd pushed enough of my buttons to get close to the one that went BANG.

"Alright," he said. "Suppose I put some other bands in here. What are you offering for that?"

"Same as me," I replied. "A cut of the door."

We hammered out a deal, one that gave him plenty of incentive to make sure the bands he booked would bring a crowd. I also agreed to do some advertising to support the effort.

I took a night to sleep on my pending confab with Sergei. No divine revelations were forthcoming, not even a bad dream. I slept, drooled on my pillow, and awoke to Ally making breakfast in the kitchen. She told me she wasn't peeing blood anymore, which was an awkward moment. I told her not to miss the next appointment at the doctor no matter how well she felt.

Then I showered and put on my best underwear. If Sergei put a bullet in me, I wanted to look good for the undertaker.

No bullets flew, nor fists, nor foul language. We sipped tea, which I had read Russians preferred to coffee. Stacy poured the steaming liquid, offering Sergei another chance to do something vile, but he kept his hands to himself. He was too intrigued by my request for a powwow to be distracted by female flesh.

"A friend and I have an idea," I began. "Something we think you would be interested in."

He was all smiles, like the alpha male who ruled the pack and got laid whenever he wanted to. "Is business, no?"

"Business," I said with care. "Gambling."

"Gambling? Please, is illegal."

I paused for him to sip his tea and then led with my chin. "So is fifty percent interest," I said, "but that doesn't stop certain transactions."

He rolled his head in agreement. "I listen, like nice grand-father, without making promise."

"Fair enough," I said and proceeded to make my proposal. He listened attentively without neglecting his tea. I expected him to have questions or comments or to laugh in my face. However, he sat there, smiling at me patiently and showing a mild side that was almost likeable.

With my plan revealed, he said, "Is good idea, Bonk. Good luck. I come visit."

What that meant I didn't know. I figured he was wary of a police trap. Therefore, any incriminating words would not be forthcoming.

"I see you," he said and left his empty cup for me to wash.

I cleared the table, put the tea service in the kitchen sink, and returned to the bar. Stacy and Magda had watched our meeting with furtive glances, and as I walked up to the register, I felt that their opinion of me had changed. They seemed to be afraid or worried or both.

"Mind the bear that smells honey," Stacy said.

That Polish proverb in mind, I climbed the stairs to meditate on what I'd done.

Joe called twice a day for more than a week. All I could tell him was that during his recent Monday visit, Sergei asked if, "Games are played?"

"This is killing me," Joe said, as if he might miss a meal or a trip to the spa.

He didn't bother to ask about Ally so I said, "Our dealer needs to earn some money. Let's set a game up for Sunday night and see what happens."

"Can you upgrade the chow again?"

Yes, I did something about the food. Lizzie filled the fridge and pantry with what she needed to make a decent spread. There were riblets and baby egg rolls, bacon pinwheels and miniature steak kabobs. She tossed in some veggies and dip just to keep things nutritionally balanced.

Joe blessed Lizzie's offering after a few sniffs. He showed up with six players, three of whom promptly busted out only to be replaced by new ones. Around eleven the room came to a dead stop when Sergei strutted down the stairs. This meant that he checked his cell-phone messages because I'd left one with no specifics, just a single clue.

I poured him a vodka before he asked. He held the drink, perused the table, the players, and my elegant finger food.

"Is nice," he said and took a sip. "Pretty girl," he added with a nod to Ally. "Good in bed?"

"I keep my hands off the help," I said.

He nodded. "Is good business practice. Still, sometimes passion is strong."

Not for me, at least when it came to Ally, Stacy, or Magda. If Diane ever gave me the look of love, I might tear my pants on the way to the bedroom. But I doubted that would ever happen. Our relationship transcended sex.

After one last look at the money on the table, he waved me up the stairs. I followed him through the bar and out into the street. He didn't stop until we stood in front of Dooling's roll-up garage door.

"Impressive, Bonk, this place you make into real business. You come to me with opportunity. I appreciate. Is sign you understand way of world."

"Thanks," I said.

"Now, gambling is dangerous. People talk, other people try to steal. No? Police make big deal when should be worried about other things. Keep children safe, things of this nature."

"Of course."

"No one steal from you because I protect. Police have other troubles. Naturally, fee must be paid. These people who play with cards, they can afford."

"They can," I agreed. "But how much?"

"One thousand dollars each game," he said. "Is easy number to remember."

Once again, my take had been cut. Having no choice, I took his deal with a handshake. He gave me his glass, which still held some vodka.

I might have been more depressed, or maybe angry, or just plain frustrated over the money. However, when I entered the bar, Tony said, "Look who it is!"

There stood Diane, smiling at me the way I remembered from my childhood. Sergei was right. Sometimes passion was strong. I gave her the hug of her life to show it.

25 ♣ ♥

DIANE HELD COURT LIKE A VISITING PRINCESS with Tony serving as court jester. The other regulars wanted to hear about her surgery, gory details and all. I laid on a round of free food, mostly bites that hadn't been consumed at the poker table. I was about to strike up a tune in her honor when she announced she was leaving.

"We miss you," Tony said.

"I'll be on the job tomorrow," Diane assured him.

I insisted on taking her home, right to the door, where I told her how great it was to see her in the bar. New paint, clean bathrooms, and fancy bottles were nothing compared to her presence. It made me feel as if every decision had been the right one and that nothing could ever go wrong.

"You're doing good, Tom," she said. "Don't forget about school. You promised me."

Her smiling face and encouraging words propelled me to

the next level. There were three, sometimes four, poker games a week. Kevin booked three bands a weekend in addition to The Executives regular Saturday night gig. I banged out The Doors for loyal fans and added a rollicking, honky-tonk version of the old Loggins and Messina standard, *Your Mama Don't Dance*. Greg Dooling grinned every time he dropped that envelope of cash on the bar, and I gave him a free beer to show I was a good sport.

There was money like never before. After Sergei and Joe got their respective cuts, I still possessed sufficient funds to make double and triple payments to Factor Associates. There was so much cash that I rented a safe deposit box to contain it. And because I thought my people were doing a great job I gave them much-appreciated raises. It was time to start thinking about operating the place like a real business. I scoured the yellow pages looking for an accountant who could show me how to keep the books and therefore take advantage of all the tax breaks of being a business owner.

Then at the height of the summer, just as I was dreaming about my return to academia, things began to unravel. It started with Tina. I should have ditched her long ago, but the sex was fun, if a bit physical. Getting the milk for free spoiled me for buying a cow of my own. I figured sooner or later she would get into a fight with Ally and that would be that.

It didn't work out that way.

It was a long Saturday night, one during which the first band ran late and The Executives and I played so well we actually thought our next stop was a concert at Lincoln Financial Field. We took a break before our final set, each of us enjoying the adoration of the crowd and a round of drinks.

I slipped behind the bar for a look at the register and to

check in with my crew. With Diane on the scene, the place ran like a jet-fueled cuckoo clock. Satisfied with my quick inspection I tapped a glass of ice water and turned for the door in search of fresh air.

A guy wearing a three-day beard stopped me at the edge of the bar. "Are you Tom Bonk?" he wanted to know.

"Yeah," I said. Before I could drop my glass he fired a right jab that hit me squarely in the solar plexus. It lacked Sergei's power, but it was enough to send me reeling and the water glass into the back bar where it smashed two bottles of booze. He reached over to me with both hands, grabbed my shirt, and dragged me forward. I lashed out with a foot and ended up tripping myself. He came down on top of me, practically knocking all the air out of my lungs.

People gave us room to brawl. They started shouting and cheering and calling out names as if this were a title fight. Given that I had suffered a cheap shot, was out two bottles of liquor, and looked like an idiot rolling around on the floor, I decided to go berserk. No idiot was going to come in my bar, kick my ass, and make a fool of me.

I slipped away from my assailant when he got tangled up in one of the barstools. Back on our feet, we sized each other up. He was a little bigger than me but at least twenty years older. I knew I could take him if I landed a few well-placed blows.

"Open the door!" I hollered.

Tony obliged and I took my chance. I rushed forward, caught my attacker in a bear hug, and continued to push him toward the street. Locked together, he could do nothing but stumble along.

Outside, I took a step away but held his shirt with my

left hand. Not letting go, I drove my right fist into his gut at least four times before realizing he wasn't hitting back. Confused, I released him and surveyed the damage. He made the mistake of swinging a right hook. I ducked under it, delivered a left-right combination to his face, and down he went.

"What's your problem?" I asked, glaring at him with my foot ready to kick his ribs.

"You're the one fucking my wife," he replied.

Before I could deny it, Tina scampered over. She checked out her old man and then hit me with an open palm slap that echoed down the block.

"You almost killed him!" she shrieked.

Reflexively, I returned the slap, shouting, "You never told me you were married."

She staggered a few steps as I took a look around me. There were people along the sidewalk, in the doorway to the bar, and in the street, all waiting to see what happened next.

I'd had enough fighting and adultery for one night. The way my hands hurt, I wouldn't be playing that last set either. Still, I got a round of applause from the crowd on my way inside.

Only Diane wasn't impressed. She shook her head and avoided me. Truth be told, I was as disappointed in myself as she was. Had I known Tina was married I wouldn't have bedded her. As far as kicking her old man's ass, I was proud of having held my own but felt sad for him. He didn't deserve the insult to his injury. Returning Tina's slap was automatic and therefore forgivable.

The fallout came to a head the following afternoon when Sergeant Larsen made a personal appearance. He was solo, without Kern or so much as a patrolman. A wave of his hand drew me out to the sidewalk, the same spot where I played Rocky the night before.

"There's been a complaint about you," he began. "Don't deny it because it's true and you know it."

"A guy hits me in my own bar. What am I supposed to do?" I retorted.

"You're supposed to call the cops," Larsen informed me. "We hand out the beatings."

"There wasn't time."

"Maybe not, but there may be a chance to divert this before any ink hits the paper."

"You're telling me this guy starts a fight and wants to file charges against me?"

Larsen shifted his heavy cop belt. "He and his wife."

I almost laughed in his face, which would have been the wrong thing to do. I kept my mouth shut and let the Sergeant have his say.

"He has a battered face, some scrapes, and the testimony of his wife that you're responsible. I told him I would come talk to you, that you were a reasonable guy. Tom, I think we can work this out."

"Work it out?" I said evenly.

"Sort of a gentlemen's agreement. You stay away from his wife, he stays away from your bar, and maybe a few dollars changes hands to salve a bruised ego. That could be the end of it."

This had to be the most incredible moment of my life to date. There would be a few more in the near future, but there and then, it was far and above any other. "I'm going to pay a guy to drop charges against me, the same guy who started the fight? His wife practically tore my clothes off whenever I let her. I'm going to stay away from her? How about her staying away from me?"

"Don't get yourself confused," Larsen advised. "You're just getting up on your feet with your business. You've done well with the place. You don't need bad publicity or an assistant district attorney coming here to ruin the whole thing. Think of it as a cost of doing business."

There were plenty of costs of doing business, real ones like Marty's weekly invoice, the electric bill, and the price of fresh crabs. Paying some schlub whose wife had hot pants didn't count.

However, I saw in Sergeant Larsen's puffy face the reality that the guy had me by the balls, and he was squeezing. It made me wonder if it was a set up from the very beginning. Who was the idiot now?

"How much?" I asked.

"I think two grand would do it," Larsen said.

"Tell him a thousand," I replied. "For two thousand I can probably buy five hours of top-notch legal advice."

Larsen held my gaze, weighing the counter offer to see if I was bluffing. I'd watched enough poker to know bluffing was for people who didn't have the cards. I had the cards, and the strongest suits were truth and courage, both of which I'd learned from my brother.

"Let me talk to him," Larsen finally said.

The cop worked his magic. He sent Mr. Kern to collect the settlement along with another batch of tickets for some raffle to support dead-cops' wives. Kern wore an apologetic face, as if he was on my side and just doing what had to be done.

There was a peaceful lull in my life. Several days of regular business passed with quiet nights spent sitting in my chair smoking Special No. 4. I put Tina and her old man out of my mind and went back to staring at the latest course catalog. Majoring in business seemed like the right choice. The bar had given me some practical experience that could only be improved upon with educational endeavors. It wasn't the biggest business, but lessons learned there could certainly be scaled up. Hadn't I managed my people well? Hadn't I learned creative financing techniques? Hadn't I dealt with regulations and bureaucrats? I certainly had. I thought to myself that if I could take Bonk's Bar from a debt-laden dead end and turn it into a popular venue that delivered steady cash to its main shareholder, then why couldn't I do the same for some other business?

The short answer was that I could have been a turn around artist, a sort of bottom-feeding asset converter, and I probably would have been after completing two years of logical coursework, a stint at a reputable firm, and a divorce from a first wife who couldn't stand the hours I worked.

However, the next morning's mail brought a certified letter. It wasn't from Tina's husband or the district attorney. It was a piece of heavy stationary from Factor Associates notifying me that they had "confessed judgment," whatever that meant. The rest of it was easy to understand.

I had thirty days to deliver the balance of $52,320 or vacate the premises, which would be promptly foreclosed to recover the above-mentioned sum.

CONFESSION OF JUDGMENT, I CAME TO LEARN, was
a legal maneuver used by creditors to take possession of collateral when said creditor woke up with a bad case of gas
and came to the conclusion that the debtor couldn't make
the payments. The fact that I was making on-time and extra
payments had nothing to do with it. If for some reason the
creditor thought the debtor couldn't pay, they were free to
take measures to secure their interest. For this advice I paid
two hundred dollars to a store-front lawyer who would also
handle my slip and fall case if I needed him to. He would help
me fight, too, if I wanted to go that way.

"What's the point?" I asked.

"It would show them you're not afraid," my counselor
replied.

I was afraid of Sergei's gun and Sergeant Larsen's vice
squad, not of Sy Kranick and Factor Associates. I found their

foreclosure decision perplexing. After all, they were getting their money. Why did they pull this shit when things were going well.

"Simple," my lawyer explained. "The place is worth more than the balance due. They cream you, take possession, sell it to the highest bidder and walk out with a bundle for very little work."

Vultures, I thought, and then asked, "What are my choices?"

"Pay them, take them to court, or get out."

Between a safe deposit box, various bank accounts, and my right pocket, I had fifteen-something thousand dollars. This left me thirty-five short. Immediate payment wasn't an option and another four weeks would hardly bring in the balance. This was the summer. People were at the shore, listening to bands and spending cash on drinks within sight of the ocean. In the best case, I might raise another fifteen, which counted for nothing because as I now knew, this was an all or nothing situation.

I actually wasted my time talking to the banks that held my accounts. Loan officers proffered paperwork and bullshit. Lead times on commercial mortgages exceeded my available days. One perky chick in a stylish pants suit said she heard of my place. Just the same, someone else would handle my lending needs once she passed the paperwork to the next bureaucrat.

No matter what happened, my sabbatical seemed on the verge of extension. The delay itself bothered me less than how Diane would view it. I'd rather face the terrorists that killed my brother than let her down.

For another week, I mulled my options. Of course I hid

my irritation poorly, which put everyone on edge. Stacy and Magda mumbled in Polish. Ally found reasons to take her meals elsewhere. Diane played mother-hen, offering to do things that didn't need to be done.

It was a Thursday, the one before my glass slipper was due to shatter, when Sy Kranick himself walked through the door. A couple of guys in fancy suits shadowed him. I thought about smashing a whiskey bottle across his teeth, but that would have been a waste of good liquor. I let them walk around, take in the scenery, and appraise what they were sure to own in a matter of days. I caught Kranick looking over his shoulder at me. He didn't have the brass to catch my eye. In fact, he seemed a bit apprehensive, but at the same time, thrilled to be in the lion's den. Maybe this was how he got his kicks.

Since I wasn't a coward, I met them in the dining room and asked if they wanted something to eat or drink. The least I could do was make a few bucks off them.

"You know," Kranick replied, "how about a round of Coca-Cola?"

"Right away," I said and headed for the bar.

"Who are those guys?" Diane queried as I filled three glasses with ice.

"A bunch of vampires," I answered.

At Kranick's table, I was offered a seat on a chair I still owned.

"I've been thinking about you, Tom," Kranick began.

I cast a wary smile at him, and then winked at the others.

"Seriously," my tormentor continued. "You shouldn't take this judgment personally. This is how the business works. It's a concept some business schools don't teach."

But life certainly does, I wanted to put in. Instead I said,

"I thought I'd missed something."

He ignored my crack and went on. "I was telling my associates what a great job you've done with this place, how it was a dump, not worth a quarter of what was owed against it until you came along."

"You *were* thinking about me," I said looking him square in the eye.

"I was thinking that you know your way around distressed assets like this bar here. You know the people, the neighborhoods, how things work. You would do very well working for us."

"Are you offering me a job?"

"An internship is more what I had in mind — a summer, maybe two, learning our side. Then, when you finish school, you could take a nice position with nothing more to worry about except what color you want that new Mercedes to be."

In other words, I could work for free, rolling the dice that out of his grand benevolence, Mr. Kranick would grant me a position at the firm. Given that he showed no remorse for shoving a crafty legality up my ass this round, who was to say he wouldn't do it again?

"That's a fantastic offer," I said gleefully. "Exactly what type of Mercedes are we talking about?"

"Take your pick."

The suits chuckled over their Cokes.

"I'll let you know on Monday," I said finally and got up.

As they made their way out, I heard one suit tell the other, "That's one mature young man."

They had no idea that I'd bet my brother a Cadillac and had also figured out how they played their game. Making payments had nothing to do with the score, either. I could have been early or late, a hundred dollars over or fifty dollars under. It wouldn't have made a dime's worth of difference. This was about grabbing the cookies when they were hot out of the oven, and I had baked a tasty batch for them the way a naïve dolt is supposed to. The time had come for them to enjoy dessert.

That afternoon I double-checked the paperwork regarding Factor Associates. The deadline for full payment was Monday at 5 PM. If certified funds were delivered before that hour, I was off the hook. If not, I had to vacate the premises peacefully or face eviction by the sheriff.

A phone call interrupted my musings. It was Marty, inquiring about my order for next week.

"The way you been ordering kegs I'd think your taps never close," Marty said. "You want to try another one of those micro brews or what?"

At that moment, I made my decision, the only one that could give me everything I wanted. It wasn't as difficult as it was debilitating. It left me feeling like the rabbit that had been beaten by the turtle. Just the same, the rabbit had learned his lesson. Now that I understood my adversaries, I was free to demonstrate that this brother of a Marine was also no better friend and no worse enemy.

Diane insisted on Sunday dinner at her house. It was the two of us presided over by Larry, who seemed more like an anxious father than an overfed feline. My hostess pushed small talk mixed with a few unsuccessful forays into my sullenness.

"I picked my classes," I told her as she scooped a heap of chocolate ice cream into a bowl for me. I'd kept this news in reserve, saving it in case she dug deep into what was bothering me and I needed a distraction.

"That's where you belong," she said stoically. "You're doing great things with the bar, Tom. The whole neighborhood talks about it. I know you can go a lot farther. You could have a string of bars or nightclubs from Philadelphia to L.A. if you wanted."

Normally, a kind word from Diane weakened my knees. This night, however, I was already numb. I managed a grateful smile and lapped a spoonful of calories.

The comfort of Diane's company held me there for another five hours. Only during two of those were we awake, having dozed one more time in front of a movie. When next I opened my eyes it was after midnight, Diane was snoring softly, and Larry was minding the front window.

I crept to the door where I noticed a stack of opened envelopes on a thin table. Seeing that they were from Jefferson Hospital, I took a peek. Naturally they were invoices, one for more than twelve grand. If I wanted to make a dent in her debt I'd have to start shelling out larger bonuses.

27 ♣ ♥

"I GOT THINGS TO DO," ALLY HEARD ME SAY in a rush. She deserved a more pleasant landlord since she hadn't missed paying the rent, which meant she'd been at work without exception for as long as I could remember. She also seemed fully recovered from her last beating. That mystery was not at the fore of my mind since this business with Kranick used up every bit of my brainpower. She might have gained a few pounds, which was another good sign as she had always been on the scrawny side. This was no surprise given the way she cooked and ate.

After a few stops along the way, I parked in the garage below Factor Associates' office in the sky. Of all the things that were on my mind, it was my father's absence that bothered me most. I hadn't heard from him in nine months and was wondering if it was time to file a missing person's report. Sure, I resented having to pay his debts and was outraged that he would disappear without so much as a phone call to let me know he was among the living. That said, he was the only blood relative I knew, the others having been smart enough to get out of town or die.

Then the elevator door opened and I was walking toward an etched glass door behind which sat one crafty son of a bitch. The secretary took me straight to his office, as if he had been waiting for me.

"Come to talk about that internship?" Kranick asked waving at the dwarf-legged chair.

"I came to give you this," I replied reaching into my pocket.

His eyes pegged for a second. I smelled his fear and dragged that delicious moment into three, four, and five more, until I had one thin envelope between my fingers. This I dropped on his desk like a plate of dog shit. He looked at it and then at me.

"Don't set foot in my bar again," I deadpanned.

The envelope on his desk contained a certified check for the total amount due. I should have sent it via an attorney or registered mail, but I wanted the satisfaction of seeing the look on Kranick's face. It was worth it. He expected me to roll over, to take it in the ass from him and his clever pals. Well, I swore on my brother's ashes that if they did that then I was a no-good sissy of a human being, unworthy to be the brother of a dead Marine.

I knew that as much as Kranick was to blame so was my father. It was my father who gambled the money away, who took the marker, who signed the note. Still, they led me down the lane, let me fix up the bar, and took my extra payments with smiles and handshakes. All the while, they were planning to drop the ax when the time was right, as in when it seemed like I might pay them off before they could grab the bar, which was now worth seven times what was owed. At least that's what the insurance appraiser said after his last inspection. The premium had been adjusted accordingly, too.

Of course, Sergei rejoiced at the prospect of collecting another round of weekly interest. "I trust you, Bonk," he'd said after placing the money I requested on the table between us. "With you, no risk. Your father, he is different story, but he not come to me in recent days."

I'd taken fifty thousand dollars from this Russian, probably the same bundles of cash I handed him in January.

"I curious. What you do with money? Eh? Buy building beside? Construct big stage for bands? What?"

"Get rid of someone I don't like," I'd answered.

He let that sink in, not sure if I was talking about buying out a partner or paying a hit man.

"The fewer partners the better," had been my final comment. Once again, a cloud of prophecy hung in the air.

I swam with my anvil of debt, spending the last third of it to register for the fall semester. A computer printout of my classes graced the refrigerator door. The next morning I looked at it and smiled. It was official. I was a student again, on my way to that magical place where I wasn't in hock for fifty grand to the Russian Mob, contributing to vague charities on behalf of Licenses and Inspections, or buying raffle tickets for dubious causes. I hefted that anvil on my shoulders and got on with life.

Everyone in the bar noticed, especially Diane. The first week of classes she asked enough questions to qualify as a student herself. I gave her the answers, pleased with having someone who genuinely cared. She insisted I go upstairs early to study. And I did, because I trusted her and the rest of the crew to run the show. She took my place at the poker games, giving me the evil eye when I popped my head in to see how things were going. She wore herself out to the point where other nights she was the one going home before the six o'clock news.

Fridays and Saturdays were different. I slung booze to the crowd, played with the band, and let my eyes wander over the girls. Susan rolled me in the hay a few times, noting that my style had mellowed a little.

"Comes with experience," I said.

"Don't get old before your time," she warned.

It was too late for that. I was paying Sergei his interest, Joe his cut, and a few of Diane's bills, too. I gave the Kerry Outreach a donation and purchased a book of tickets for another of Larsen's drawings. Below the grate in the tunnel was a growing stash of money that would soon set me free for the last time. Then there were papers to write, exams to take, and a group project to crank out. I told myself I didn't deserve a medal for working hard. Plenty of people juggled things like this. Who was I to expect an easy ride? Besides, I volunteered for it, every single assignment, including knight-errant on one particular Wednesday evening.

It started over the silliest of things, an exchange of bawdy comments by a couple of guys at a back table. On my way into the dining room with a platter of crabs I heard them say:

"You see the tits on that chick?"

"The dark-haired one?"

"Yeah. If it wasn't for that belly she'd be an eight or better."

"Good enough for me the way it is."

I saw that they were talking about Ally who was mopping a table on the other side of the room.

"Watch your mouths," I remarked after delivering the crabs to a regular customer.

"She your woman?" the first guy asked.

"She's not yours," I growled.

The guy looked me up and down like a schoolyard bully. It might have been that look, or the fact that it was the end of a tough month, or maybe I was simply looking to relieve some stress. Whatever it was, I dropped the tray and grabbed the guy by his shirt and hauled him out of his seat. Before he could say, "What the fu...," I dragged him to the door where I shoved him down the stairs.

His pal made the mistake of jumping me from behind. He was no match for a hyped-up, indebted college student turned tavern keeper. He rode me down the stairs to the sidewalk where I rolled him off with a quick snap of my shoulders and one-two punched him into the concrete.

"I'm calling the cops!" the first guy hollered.

"Better make it an ambulance!" I shouted back and moved forward for the next round. I wasn't a step closer to him when Ally appeared in front of me.

"Hurry, Tom!" she said, taking my arm.

"Get out of the way," I told her.

"Forget them," she blurted, "It's Diane."

"What?"

Diane had blacked out. I found her lying on the floor in the kitchen with Lizzie mouthing the Rosary over her. I reached for the first aid kit, the one that McNally told me had to be there if I wanted to pass a Dirkus inspection. The smelling salts were below everything else. I opened one under her nose the way I saw my high school gym teacher do for a kid that smacked his head on the floor during a basketball scrimmage.

After a wincing sneeze, Diane's eyes opened. "I'm going to be sick," she said and started gagging.

I eased her onto her side just in time for a stream of vomit to splash out.

"I'll call an ambulance," Ally said.

"No," I ordered. "I'm taking her myself."

At the emergency room a quick-witted physician promptly called the office of her oncologist after I told him that she'd had surgery for cancer. He then transferred her to Jefferson. I didn't have the details of her condition until the next morning.

The oncologist was a young man, maybe mid-thirties. He ushered me into a conference room for a briefing and wasted no time getting to the point.

"Diane's cancer has spread," he began. "It's everywhere, especially in her lymphatic system and her lungs. This is typical of uterine cancer."

"How can that be?" I asked. "I thought everything had been cut out. She had radiation for Christ's sake."

His next comment floored me. He said, "The spread might have been detected sooner, but she hasn't been keeping her appointments. The last time I saw her was more than eight months ago."

Four semesters and two months of college taught me nothing about medicine nor much about human nature. I should have known Diane was skipping out on her doctor visits. For one thing, there were no new bills on the little table in her house. For another, she went home early on non-poker nights and came in later and later each month, neither of which I ever dared to question for all the right but now wrong reasons. Did she look a little tired? Yes. Was she eating right? Some of the time.

The mystery of why she stopped going to the doctor would never be solved. It was up there with my father's gambling, the conflict in the Middle East, and the origin of the universe. Her radiation treatments left her wrecked, as had her post-surgery fever. Just the same, I never saw Diane as a quitter. It appalled me to think that she'd taken her chances or given up when talented people like the MD on the other side of the table might have given her another forty years at the price of some miserable treatments along the way.

As much as I wanted Diane to give me an explanation, I didn't have the nerve to ask the question. I never inquired of my brother why he joined the Marines. It fit him to be one of them the way it fit me to go to college. Yet, Diane ignoring a cancerous relapse collated with no logical parallel. It might have been that she would rather be dead than live like Frankenstein.

"So what can we do?" I asked the doctor.

"Mr. Bonk, her condition is terminal."

I bristled at his verdict. "If this is a question of money," I said, "I can pay whatever it costs to get her what she needs to ..."

His hands went up and he shook his head. "Mr. Bonk, money is not the issue."

I delivered the bad news to my crew that afternoon. Lizzie promised to have a special Mass said for Diane. Stacy and

Magda crossed themselves and exchanged a knowing look, one their grandmothers probably shared when the Russians and Germans invaded. Ally retreated to my brother's room where she sobbed until I checked on her.

"What are we going to do, Tom?" she asked.

WE DID WHAT WE HAD TO DO, none of which was easy. Ally stuck with me through it all. She brought Tony and some of the other regulars to the hospital for visits. Taking orders from Diane, she dropped me off for classes and picked me up when they were over. She double-checked the deliveries from Marty, kept an eye on the register, and made sure I ate breakfast.

Despite her support, my coursework slipped. I couldn't keep the balls in the air when I knew one of them was going flat. The other members of the group project carried me through it, but I knew they wouldn't have me for the next one. Failing one of my midterms was a signal that I should start thinking about giving it up until the storm passed.

Business slowed at the bar, too. Kyle hired decent bands and the crowds spent a fair amount on booze. However, the mood wasn't the same and the customers picked up on it. Joe bickered with Ally and I about the reduction in poker games, which had been cut to one a week. He threatened to hire another dealer, but Ally went home with him a couple of nights to appease him.

Sergei was more circumspect and every bit as unaccommodating.

"When is over, is over," he said. Until that time the interest was due and payable as was the payment for each poker game, which I was reminded to notify him of so there would be no misunderstandings or uninvited guests. This I accepted. Then he told me the rest of the story.

"Your father, he still owe me one thousand four hundred."

"Too bad," I reflected.

"Bad for you, son of this man. You pay interest until I collect principal when next he and I meet."

The word "no" must have left my mouth because Sergei recoiled a few inches and squinted.

"No? You say, no? Wrong answer. Now not good time to start argument. Is football season. Maybe your father bet on Eagles like before."

All I could do was hope that the Eagles winning streak continued.

Sergeant Larsen, the one man who should have been above it all, managed to raise my ire to a new level. He showed up looking for suckers to buy chances for a Thanksgiving Day feast at a fancy restaurant. Given that Diane had been transferred to a hospice, it didn't look like she was going to enjoy the cranberry sauce.

"The whole precinct is sorry to hear about Diane," he said. "I'm proud to see you doing the right thing by her."

It would have cost him nothing to make a visit but his

ruddy cheeks had yet to grace her bedside. I was about to remind him of this when he brought up another of my push-button subjects.

"Hopefully your father will turn up soon," he said.

I took my left hand out of my pocket. This was the hand I led with, the one that jabbed Tina's husband, that cracked that knucklehead leering at Ally's tits, and was now balling into a fist.

"Where do I go to file a missing person report?" I asked.

The bastard actually chuckled at the question. "Come on, Tom, you know him better than anyone. He's probably had a good run at the blackjack table, or maybe he took the points on last Sunday's game."

"Ten months is a long run," I noted.

"He'll turn up. Now, how about a handful of chances at this fancy turkey dinner?"

I took them only as a distraction. If not, I might have punched him and that would have disappointed Diane more than my failing grades had she known about them. I kept this secret from her, figuring no harm would be done.

Two nights after Larsen's visit, I was sitting beside Diane's bed with one of my textbooks folded open on my lap. She was pumped full of drugs, barely lucid, and struggling to tell me something. I put the book in my satchel and moved close to her.

"I promise I'll finish college," I said. "I'll get a graduate degree, an MBA from Wharton."

Her eyes rolled and she smiled. I wiped her face with my sleeve.

"Hope you don't mind that I've been giving Larry tuna every Friday."

She slipped between the pillows and drew a full breath. For a moment I thought she'd fallen asleep. Then her eyes creaked open. Even as I watched her lips move, I couldn't believe what I heard.

"Did Ally keep the baby?" she asked.

This question I could not answer. I didn't know Ally had been, or was still, pregnant. Thankfully, Diane had passed out, leaving me free to sprint home to inquire with my tenant. I waited until one o'clock, at which time Ally was delivered to the front stoop in Joe's BMW.

I found my seat, left the pipe in the ashtray, and took deep breaths until the door opened.

"How's Diane?" she asked, removing her coat.

"Worse," I remarked.

"We'll go tomorrow for lunch," she said.

"Good. You can tell her what you decided about the baby."

She held her breath, no doubt in anticipation of a few questions. I held back, giving her the chance to say what she wanted to. It was a Mexican stand off for a long moment. Then she blinked.

"It's too late," she said.

"Too late to have an abortion or too late to stop it?"

"You must be blind," she replied. "My tits have always been nice, but I've never been this fat."

"I've had a lot on my mind lately," I reflected.

"It's okay. I can handle it."

"Who's the father?" I asked.

"You know it's not yours," she spat.

She could have found a better way to dodge the question, and I could have found a nicer way to offer advice. We ended up in a shouting match that probably sounded like two seagulls fighting over the same perch.

I started it with, "You're screwing up your whole life."

"This from the guy who's about to flunk out of college."

"I've been taking care of Diane and running this bar and ..."

"And being a big pussy!" Ally yelled. "You were smart enough to get into college and get your old man's bar going. Now you're letting it all turn to shit. Don't start telling me about priorities."

"Nothing is turning to shit," I fired back.

"I've been counting the money, Tom. It ain't as much as it was. People see you moping around the bar. They don't hear you on the piano. They walk out muttering what an ass you are. How you're letting the place go."

"Thanks for the memo. What else have you been doing but banging Joe and who knows how many others?"

"You're only mad because you aren't on the list."

Instantly, it occurred to me that Ally's mouth brought on the beatings. I wanted to give her one myself. She didn't give me the chance.

"I'm out of here," she blurted and departed coatless.

I let her go. Although I had nothing more to say to her, I did have words for Joe, who I figured was the father of Ally's yet to be born child.

He agreed to see me at ten the next morning, though I hadn't given him the topic of discussion. We skipped the small talk about Diane, and after I was sure Ally wasn't in the apartment, asked him point blank if he knocked her up.

"Yo, Tom, I lay these chicks left and right, Ally too, but

there's no way I knock them up."

"Joe, if that kid is yours ..."

"It ain't my kid. I know it ain't. I got my nuts cut right after I hit the number."

"Nuts cut?"

"A vasectomy, man. I would appreciate it if you wouldn't mention this, you know, around the bar. Some people think you're not quite a man if you have the plumbing disconnected."

"She talk about anyone else?" I asked.

"Chick like her? Could be anybody. That's why I double down and use rubbers all the time. Who knows what they got? Disease-wise is what I mean."

A comment like that deserved a broken nose but I was too frazzled to give him one.

"Forget her," Joe said. "I got this other one, Carla, fresh off the farm. She can deal cards, doesn't touch drugs, and ain't bad in the sack. She's been to the doctor and came back with flying colors. She comes clean two more months in a row I might stop wrapping the rascal."

I'd had enough of his pimping. I returned to the bar where I found Marty's guy waiting for me. We lugged cases and barrels to the taproom, hung a few girlie posters, and exchanged words about Diane.

I lurked in the basement until it was too late to go to class. The tunnel contained enough bricks to build half a wall. I decided the monotony of carrying and stacking bricks would keep my mind off Diane, Ally, and my poor academic performance. My timing couldn't have been better. Three nights in a row, Masgai's dumpsters overflowed with demolition debris. I wore myself out lugging bricks first to the fence, and then in the wee hours of the morning, to the tunnel. Carrying six at a time in a makeshift sling for a hundred yards was good exercise.

Carla dealt the cards for Sunday night's poker match. Sergei himself watched most of the game, helping himself to free vodka shots and letting me know that the new dealer could make an extra two hundred if she wanted to go home with him or some other guys he knew. It made me wonder about Ally, if she really did turn tricks or if that was all bullshit spread around by guys she wouldn't screw. I hadn't seen her in almost a week. As far as I could tell she hadn't returned to my brother's room. Her coat remained over the chair in the kitchen.

After packing up the basement I headed over to Diane's house. I'd resisted the urge to move Larry to my place. Keeping him there gave me a small measure of hope that she might come home. Of course I was kidding myself, but I was no stranger to delusion.

Delusions or not, I was getting more familiar with surprises. The latest one came when I unlocked the door and spotted Ally seated in the kitchen at the back of the house. Larry was on the table, enjoying the remnants of whatever Ally had been eating.

She watched me refill Larry's dishes. My responsibility fulfilled, I took a seat from which I admired the cat's ability to clean a plate.

"What are we, Tom?" Ally asked. "Are we brother and sister or something else?"

During the good times, I certainly thought of her as my sister. When we were fixing up the apartment or selling booze and crabs across the bar, then she was a proud member of my entourage. The first time she showed up with bruises, I felt the kind of genuine pain and anger a real brother might have felt. However, I'd been an asshole about the rent, about her sex life, and about most everything else. I played ambulance driver and left her to her own devices. I never offered as little as a friendly talk or a kind word or a night out with nothing more expected than a casual kiss goodnight. What if my brother had treated me the same way?

My brother was dead. Diane was dying. My father had disappeared. Who was left? No one but the three of us in the room. One of that trio walked on four legs.

"Give me a hand with Larry," I said. "It's time he came to live with us."

THE DAY BEFORE DIANE'S FUNERAL, I sat in my recliner, smoking, hating the world, and thinking that justice was nothing but a word in the dictionary. This was more than a pity party; it was a reflection on the state of my life through an obscenely objective lens. The worst stuck out like black hairs in a facial wart. While certain aspects were beyond my control, like Diane's cancer, Ally's beatings, and the price of beer, the rest had been my own creation. As my pipe went cold, I decided that the end of Diane's life was a signal to begin again. Sure, the past had to be wrapped up before I could untie the future. This was something I'd done before and would do again.

And then the phone rang. It could have been the priest at Diane's church, or Lizzie, or Marty, or even Enright's Seafood with a special deal for me. It was no one but my father. Luckily my pipe was leaning on the ashtray or it would have fallen from my mouth, spilling ash into my lap.

"You there, Tom?" he was asking.

"I'm here."

He sucked in a deep breath and said, "I just heard about Diane."

As the good people at the hospice had said, so I repeated, "She's not suffering anymore."

"Yeah, terrible," my father noted. "The service is tomorrow afternoon, right?"

It was, and I gave him the time and place.

"Okay, I'll be there," he said. "I'm getting out for the day."

"Getting out?" I asked.

He stuttered a few times then spilled it in one long burst. "I've been in a program, Tom, like Gambler's Anonymous, but different. It's upstate, away from the casinos and bookies and all that. You have to live on the compound. They get you a job locally, too. Nothing great, just so you can make a few bucks on your own. Gives you some dignity, integrates you with normal life."

Working definitely does that, I thought, impressed by the thoroughness of the curriculum. "Why didn't you tell me where you were?"

"In case it didn't work out, Tom. You gotta understand this addiction is powerful. There were times when I slipped back a few steps, but I got it beat now."

I knew all too well how powerful it was, gambling as I did in my own way with the crabs, remodeling the bar, featuring bands, and hosting block parties. All the while I failed to pay proper attention to Diane and others around me, but I did satisfy the urge to hit the big time.

"So I'll see you tomorrow," he said. "I'm going to check in with Sergei and then ..."

"Don't ..." I interrupted.

"I'm not betting on the Eagles. No way. Part of this program is you have to confront your demons. You have to be able to walk by the casino without going in. Well, I'm gonna tell Sergei he'll get his fourteen hundred from me when I finish the program."

"When's that?" I inquired hopefully.

"Another month."

"I'm glad to hear it," I said meaning every single word. For one thing, he could manage the bar while I went back to school. For another, I missed the guy who bought me that piano. The one who threw a party for his pals when he won. The man who, whether I admitted it or not, instilled in me the ability to look forward more often than backward, each time with the kind of confidence that only a true gambler possesses.

I hung up thinking that maybe triumph does come from tragedy.

Dozens of people attended Diane's funeral. Lizzie arranged everything at her church, where Diane had also been a member. Ally and I sat through the entire Mass. There were no family members to receive condolences but us. I shared handshakes and hugs with most of the bar's regulars as well as many people I didn't know from Adam.

The only person absent was my father. He might have been stuck in traffic, or maybe he got into a car wreck, or maybe he got cold feet and didn't want to get within a tollbooth of the casinos. Whatever the case, Diane's casket was lowered into the ground without sight nor sound of him. People departed quietly, last of all, Ally and myself.

Did I really expect him to show up? Yes, I did. He sounded like the guy who drove with me to Parris Island, like the guy Diane talked about, like someone who was putting his life in order. Therefore, I drew no conclusions about his lack of attendance.

Since it was Thanksgiving week, I left the bar closed. Using Diane's oncologist as a reference, I landed Ally an appointment with an obstetrician. We sat through his exam and lecture like a regular couple, not bothering to explain who was who. Instead of catching up with my schoolwork, I took Ally to the movies, which provided a welcome respite from the stress. I blew money on a nice suit so that we could spend more money on a couple of nice dinners, including one at Two Rainbows. Crabs weren't on the menu, but what we ordered was fantastic. Ally minded her manners, as did I. There were no arguments, no fistfights, no profanity. She didn't ask about my father. I didn't ask about her mother.

The Monday after Thanksgiving, Ally waited in the car while I formally withdrew from classes. I figured it was better to withdraw than to flunk. I promised Diane's ghost and myself that after the New Year I would make things right.

The following week it was back to regular business. Just as they had when my brother passed, people attempted to exchange kind words in pursuit of free drinks. Stacy and Magda gave nothing away, not even to Tony who deserved at least one Yuengling on the house now and then.

I was in the dining room, scribbling ideas to revive my flagging sales, when Sergei walked in. He scanned the bar then took a seat opposite me.

"You close for whole week," he informed me. "Is bad for business."

"I didn't see you at Diane's funeral," I said.

"She not my family."

Yeah, I thought, but she had been part of mine. If for no other reason, he should have made an appearance to show one of his reliable earners a measure of support. Surely any self-respecting member of the Italian Mafia would have done this as a matter of course. These upstarts lacked that level of class and insight into what mattered to people.

Despite his poor etiquette, I knew I owed him five hundred in interest plus the payment for the bar. The money lay under the tablet between us. There was also an envelope containing twenty-five hundred for Marty's guy. I decided to make him ask for his money like everyone else who presented an invoice at Bonk's Bar.

"You writing book?" Sergei asked indignantly after I failed to deliver.

"No," I answered. "I'm making a list of my mistakes. That way I won't make the same one twice."

His eyes turned hard, and he said, "Okay, Bonk. You pay now."

He stood over the table, a man strong enough to break me in half regardless of my recent exercise regimen. I didn't feel the least bit afraid. After all, he was a new arrival to my country, the one in which I'd been born. It was my brother who died for it, too. And Diane took a short ride through the land of the free while this scumbag got to enjoy the home of the brave, all the while lording his viciousness over the likes of me and countless others who made his life possible. He could barely speak the language, yet, I was the one answering to him.

I might have taken a different course, one that would have made sense to a real businessman or someone more mature than I was. A smarter guy would have put Sergei down as a cost of doing business, raised the price of beer a quarter to cover it, and left it at that. However, I was still young, arrogant, and tired of being dragged around on a leash by people who weren't my betters.

If all that wasn't enough, there was Ally peering in from the kitchen doorway. She was more than four months pregnant and had suffered at the hands of someone just like Sergei, an abuser whose name I still didn't have. She might have had a sharp tongue but that was no cause for a clubbing. I perceived more than her fear. I sensed that she was judging me, evaluating whether or not I was worthy enough to play at being her brother and/or her father. If I let her down, she would be out the door in search of whatever might be better. It was my turn to stand up for that last measure of what was supposed to be mine.

My eyes met Sergei's. "Fuck you," I said in classic American slang.

In a flash, the table disappeared and I felt Sergei's foot land on my chest. I went over backward, chair and all, landing on my head. Although barely conscious, I heard something snap. A second later, I felt blinding pain shoot from my hand all the way to my shoulder. Then there were three well-placed jabs to the center of my chest. As the air left my lungs I realized I wasn't a tough guy like my brother, who never would have let Sergei get the drop on him. However, I was a calculating, motherless, temporary college dropout to whom money had meant nearly everything. The sliver of importance between love and money now stood taller than the Berlin Wall.

"You stupid boy," Sergei said as he looked down at the mess I'd suddenly become. "Stupid boy of stupid father." He spotted his cash next to my notebook, that and the envelope for Marty. He wasn't above stooping to pick it up. Through blurred vision, I watched him count the hundred-dollar bills. Then he tore open the envelope and thumbed the contents. Suddenly enraged, he kicked me in the ribs. Twice.

Rolling with the blows, I saw that Ally had not moved from the doorway.

"Stupid fucking father not pay so now you pay. Understand? Write big letters so not forget. You pay for bar, for loans, for poker game. I ask, you pay. Yes?"

Sergei need not be concerned about my reliability. He would get his payments and a huge bonus. Like the professional that he sometimes was, he would go on to forgive my transgression and invest his trust in me. That was his mistake, not mine.

First, however, I had to get my hand fixed. There would be no honky-tonk riffs for some time to come. His commando karate chop had broken some bones in my right hand. My ribs, on the other hand, were only bruised. No stranger to the emergency room, I waited my turn, accepted a painkiller, and let the doctor put the pieces in place.

Ally noticed my almost pleasant air through the whole ordeal. Driving me back to the bar, she looked across the Cadillac and smiled. Knowing that I had passed her test gave me a sense of joy that I hadn't felt since Diane and I sold that first batch of crabs. I patted her leg with my good hand just to share the sentiment. Having a sister who liked me was more than an inspiration; it was a source of pride.

Sergei made a terrible mistake that day. He assumed he had the upper hand, that he could milk the blood from a stone. He opened his mouth to inform me he was a fool when he could have kept it shut and left me wondering, and he did it for fourteen hundred dollars, chump change in a big dollar world.

And for want of that, I never expected to see my father again.

Having turned the corner to my future, I ramped up to full power. Ally replaced Diane; Carla dealt cards. Stacy, Magda, and Craig manned the bar. Kyle booked the bands and asked me every time he saw me if I was exercising my hand.

"If not," he warned, "you'll never be able to play the way you used to."

"I'll play," I assured him. On odd mornings and late evenings I practiced scales for an hour at a clip.

Three months after he busted me up, Sergei had the nerve to ask me how my recovery was going, as though he wasn't the source of the problem.

"Better than new," I told him over an envelope full of greenbacks.

The imbecile was thrilled to be getting more money than ever before. I pushed Joe for three poker games a week, and Monday and Wednesday became open mike nights for people who wanted to try their hand at comedy. Most of them were pathetic, but they dragged their friends along, and they needed booze to drown the bad jokes.

Not even Sergeant Larsen could piss on my parade. I

ponied up for his holiday toy drive and his New Year's extravaganza.

"Where's Ally been hiding?" he asked after I bought two hundred dollars worth of chances for his Polar Bear Prize Patrol on a February afternoon. "Seems like she's never around when I come in."

"Taking a nap," I informed him.

"That kid has to be due any day now."

"A couple of weeks," I said.

"Wasn't the smartest thing for her to do," he remarked. "I thought it might be Joe's."

He expected me to fill him in on the baby's parentage. All I gave him was, "She knows who the father is."

Larsen squinted at me for a second then left without another word.

Over the winter months, Ally and I had discussed what she should do once her baby was born. The topic of adoption came up on numerous occasions. At first, she felt guilty at mention of the word, as if she were taking the easy way out. I was no one to judge another person's wisdom. I told her I would support her whatever she decided. If she wanted to keep the baby and raise him in the apartment we shared, she was more than welcome. If she thought it was better to give the child up, then so be it. I found her a counseling service through my college. Some of the sessions were hokey bullshit. Others featured nuts and bolts details of the social service system, including adoption, neonatal care, and how to collect child support. With two weeks to go, she had yet to come down on one side or the other.

It was during that week that I finally had enough money to pay off Sergei. I counted it three times to be certain. Just as before, I bundled it into ten packs of five thousand each. These I slipped into a shoebox, which fit perfectly beneath the grate in the tunnel. For extra assurance, I set a raft of bricks atop the grate.

The rest of my life was about to begin.

30 ♣ ♥

ALLY'S WATER BROKE FOUR DAYS EARLY. She was tallying kegs from Marty when she suddenly dropped the list. Thankfully Marty's guy was someone I trusted. He agreed to hump the last of the order into the bar and lock the door when he left.

As I pulled away from the curb I noticed Larry staring down at us from the only good window in the living room. Maybe Diane was up there too, and for all I knew, my brother might have been lurking in the shadows. My father's place in the firmament was uncertain, but I had an idea what had happened to him.

Ally's delivery came quickly but with complications. The baby was fine. Ally, on the other hand, had a tear, was bleeding, and required emergency surgery. This took a couple more hours, during which I solidified my plans for the next few days.

When Ally opened her eyes in the recovery room, I asked her how she felt.

"I don't want my baby to have to start over," she said. "I want him to get it right the first time."

Ally was still in the hospital that Sunday night when I was downstairs watching the poker game. Susan gave me a wrapped present for Ally and wanted to know if the baby had a name. I told her not yet. She also wanted to know if I would be available later, as she hadn't slept over in months.

"Not tonight," I said with some regret.

"I'm feeling rejected," Susan moaned.

"Just bad timing," I assured her.

Joe pulled me aside for a little chat. "Let's do the math," he began. "We're pulling fifteen hundred a week out of this action. That's like seventy-five grand a year, tax free which is the same as over a hundred if we had to pay the government their share."

"More or less," I reflected.

"I say we up the buy in. I'd like to clear the hundred mark this year. It has a ring to it."

"Let me talk to Sergei," I said.

"Man, if we didn't have him, we'd really be raking it in."

As if I had to be reminded of this reality. What Joe didn't know was that tonight was the night I intended to pay Sergei off. There were four hours of poker before my opportunity came. My Russian loan shark showed up late, catching only the last few games. I gave him his usual drinks and snacks. He made small talk with Susan when she took a break. He must have spoiled her luck because upon re-entering the game, she promptly busted out. I followed her up the stairs, letting her grope me as a cheap consolation prize.

Back downstairs I entered the tunnel as inconspicuously as possible. I shifted some bricks, lifted the grate, and pulled out my shoebox safe. Coming back in the room, I nodded for Sergei to join me at the bar. He recognized the box and wasted no time flipping open the lid. Only after he fingered a few of the bundles did he look over his shoulder to see if anyone was paying attention. Seeing that everyone's focus was elsewhere, he stuck out his hand.

I shook it, holding on for an extra second to pass the message that I was twice the man he dreamed of being. Then I poured us two vodka shots to seal our finished business.

The game was down to the last few players. There was a lot of cash on the table, too, at least ten thousand dollars, probably closer to twelve. Joe had his mouth stuffed with shrimp when Stacy shouted down the stairs. I bolted over to see what she wanted.

"The cops?" I asked, loud enough for everyone in the room to hear.

Joe spit his shrimp on the floor and the pandemonium began. Before he could repeat, "Cops?" a player grabbed his money and made a break for it. The others followed suit. They piled into each other at the bottom of the stairs.

I crossed the room, pulled open the doors to the tunnel and picked up my flashlight. Sergei saw what I was doing and let the others go up the stairs on their own. The shoebox under his arm, he hurried over to me, asking, "Where you going, Bonk?"

"This is another way out," I said.

"Smarter than father," he said as I pulled the doors closed behind us.

We squeezed past the piles of bricks I'd left in the tunnel. Together we climbed the short stairs and entered Dooling's shop at the other end. Red and blue lights danced across the high windows. I made my way to the big garage door that fronted Tioga Street. Peering through a crack I saw a cruiser parked at the bar.

Sergei went for the man-sized door, reaching out to push the panic bar that would open it.

"No!" I shouted. "You'll set off the alarm."

"Shit!" he hissed and backed away.

"This way," I urged, waving him to the other side of the building.

He took his time, scanning left and right like a soldier. I arrived at the other door ahead of him and checked the street using a window beside it.

"Stay there," I said without turning back. I heard his footsteps stop. After making sure there was no one outside, I reached for the chain that stretched up from the doorframe. Glancing over my shoulder I saw his eyes shining in the gloom.

"Is safe?" Sergei wanted to know.

"Perfectly," I told him and pulled the chain.

The police never went downstairs. They had responded to a report of a brawl, which was known to occur now and then at Bonk's Bar.

"False alarm," I told Patrolman Snyder. "I've been on good behavior all night."

He walked around the bar, asked a few patrons if there had been any fighting, and was satisfied by their shaking heads that there had been none. "Let's go," he said to his partner.

I cleaned up the mess downstairs. The food went in the trash, the stray hundred-dollar bills into an envelope, and the loose cards back in the pack. By the time the place was in order, Joe found the nerve to ring my cell phone.

"What happened?" he huffed.

"The cops looked around and left," I explained. "They ask you anything, especially Sergeant Larsen, tell them it was just you and me talking over a game of gin."

"This is going to put a lid on things for a while."

"I could use a vacation."

"That's a good idea. You want to run down to Myrtle Beach to play some golf?"

Not knowing which end of the club to hold, I said, "No, but thanks for the invitation. I'm going to check on Ally. Catch you later."

I drove to the hospital where I found Ally sitting in a chair beside her bed. She looked a little drained but generally in good condition.

"There were some people here today, a lady and a nice couple," she informed me.

"What did they want?"

"The lady is an adoption specialist I heard about during those counseling sessions we went to."

"And?"

"This couple, they've been trying to have a baby for ten years and nothing's worked. I felt terrible for them, especially the wife. She was strung out over it."

"I understand."

"The husband has a good job, too. He's a software engineer, whatever that is."

"It's a good job," I told her.

"My baby could start his life with them and never know the difference, Tom."

"He could," I agreed. I didn't tell her that he would never know his real mother. That might not matter, or it might make all the difference in the world.

"I have a good reason," she said and told me what it was.

31 ♣ ♥

THE SHIT HIT THE FAN THE NEXT MORNING around seven. The action was down the street, at Dooling Tire. I watched as best I could from my living room window. Larry joined me for the show.

The cops came first, followed by the heavy rescue unit from the fire department. Then the coroner's hearse arrived. I stayed where I was, noting that Sergeant Larsen looked particularly upset at the goings on. He argued with a few detectives, shouted at his patrolmen, and had no patience for the coroner.

It wasn't until mid-morning that anyone came to talk to me. I answered the door with a cup of coffee in my hand. A pair of police detectives, Taborn and Gale, stood on the other side. They asked for permission to enter and take a look around.

"Sure," I said. "You guys want coffee?"

"No thanks," they said in unison.

"You mind if we go downstairs?" Taborn wanted to know.

"Let me show you the way," I said, leading them to the stairs.

In the poker room they sniffed at the bar and the tables. They acted like they had no interest in the doors to the tunnel for several minutes. Gale tried the knob, seemed surprised that it turned, and pulled the doors open.

"There a light somewhere?" he called back.

"I can get you a flashlight."

Taborn swung both doors open wide. Enough illumination fell into the space that they could see the piles of bricks heaped to the ceiling.

"I keep some extra beer in there when I run out of room in the coolers," I said.

Taborn nudged a cardboard box with his foot. "Let's go upstairs," he ordered.

At a table in the dining room they went through their inquiry. Where was I last night? Who was I with? What time did I go to bed? Was I alone in bed? I gave them the unmodified truth. I was at the bar, bullshitting over cards with my pal Joe, the son of a bitch who won the lottery. We were talking about a trip to Myrtle Beach. Patrolman Snyder interrupted our soiree, something about a fight but there was none. Then I went to visit my friend Ally in the hospital. She just had a baby, a few problems, but was doing fine. I was back for last call, went to bed with no one but Larry the cat.

"You going to be around for the rest of the day?" Taborn asked finally.

"I have to be here," I replied. "There's a truckload of beer coming."

On their way down the street, a reporter shoved a microphone at them. I smirked and went back inside.

The story led the six o'clock news. There was a beautiful shot of Dooling's garage door. As the camera pulled back, the sign for Bonk's Bar was visible at the edge of the screen. Better than that, the same pretty reporter gave me a plug when she began with, "Just down the street from Bonk's Bar, a well-known venue for spicy crabs and local music ..." From that point on it was all wrong. She reported that a man was found dead inside the nearby tire shop. Police weren't saying exactly what happened, but the implication was that he might have been in the process of stealing tires when a massive tire accidentally fell on him and killed him.

There was nothing accidental about it. I led Sergei to slaughter like the Judas goat on a path I mapped out four months earlier. He couldn't have stood in a better place, although it was hard to miss with a tire that was over eight foot in diameter. I was no mechanic but it was easy to rig that crane. A tag on the winch read, "DO NOT DISABLE SAFETY FOR FASTER OPERATION." I disabled the safety and attached a thin chain to the pin that engaged the brake. Yanking the pin allowed the hook, and the four-ton tire hanging from it, to freefall. I dropped that tire three times: the first to make sure it worked, the second to kill Sergei, and the third to drop it on him again after I retrieved my fifty grand. It was only fitting that he met his fate in this manner. He was as much a terrorist as those idiots who killed my brother and the other men who were setting their country free.

I was bloodied now, a killer, a guy who exacted some justice. It was a powerful feeling. I wondered if my brother felt the same way earlier in his tour of duty.

Sergeant Larsen cut short my reverie. He was less pleasant than Detectives Taborn and Gale. Locking his arm in mine, he hauled me into the street for a verbal thrashing. He had Patrolman Snyder and his partner for backup in case I unleashed some of that Bonk feistiness.

"Congratulations," Larsen said when we were out of earshot. "You gave all the right answers."

I didn't rise to that prompt the way he probably wanted me to.

"You botched a very sophisticated investigation, one that's been in the works for almost three years."

I let my eyes get big, pointed at my chest, and said, "How could I possibly do that?"

"Too smart by half, college boy," he replied. "Or have you flunked out by now?"

"I'm on a leave of absence."

"The only place you'll be going is jail if you keep it up. I know all about your poker games and your payoffs to the guy who turned up dead down the street."

I risked a grin then said, "I only make legitimate contributions to approved charities as you well know."

"Now you're going to be cute?"

"I'm sure that guy, Persey, from *The Philadelphia Inquirer* would like to know how things work on the street."

"Reaching for the big time are you, Tommy?" he said after a deep breath. "I'll have you down to the Roundhouse for some real interrogation if you keep that up. Back on point, Sergei was known to this department as a hoodlum working protection and loan shark rackets."

I coughed at his assessment. "In other words, you're admitting that you let him strut around the neighborhood preying on people too weak or too stupid to fight back."

"In the name of a bigger fish, you idiot! He's small time,

what Bonk's Bar is to Yuengling Beer. You think taking out guys like him does anything but scratch the paint on the people he works for?"

I had no idea, but I did know that the Yuengling Brewery treated me pretty well. They sent free lights, girlie posters, and limited edition glasses etched with the American eagle. It was more than I could say for the cash I'd given to Sergeant Larsen. He got me a pass from Dirkus, one that I had to pay for several times over.

"We were ready to pinch Sergei to get his boss, a guy you'll probably be meeting soon."

"That has nothing to do with me," I said and started for the bar.

He pulled my shoulder around then lowered his tone when he said, "I put the pieces together, Tom. You cried wolf to 911 about a bar fight. When Snyder responded, you led Sergei through your little secret passage. You already had the crane rigged and you let him have it. Then you slipped back to the bar after stacking up your bricks."

"Only one problem," I reminded him. "I never touched the phone last night, and I was in the bar until I left to visit Ally in the hospital. I signed in, signed out, and smiled for the security camera in between."

"You're lying out your ass!"

"File charges or leave me the hell alone," I said. "I got the money to hire a real lawyer and the publicity will only be good for business."

"So smart, you little bastard. You better work with me on making a new bust or I'll beat you within an inch of your life."

I decided to reveal everything I knew in case he was only being sarcastic. "The way you beat Ally? Did you have to smack her around to get her to talk or was that foreplay?"

He made the mistake of reaching for me. I'd been beaten by experts. One more was nothing to fear. I could have cracked his jaw with the tension that remained in my left arm.

"She's the only one who could have given you all the information about what was happening in the bar. Who else had access to every corner of the property? And those chubby knuckles of yours would have matched her bruises perfectly. By the way, do you stick your dick in every hooker you bust or just the really young ones?"

His eyes flared only inches from mine.

"Ally out-foxed you but good," I continued. "Got herself pregnant as the only way to escape your fist. Managed to carry that kid to term despite a couple rounds with you in the ring."

"She's a stupid whore," he snorted. "All she had to do was answer the questions."

Ally, like me, knew that the questions would never stop the way Sergei's extortion would never stop. Larsen had her in a vice and squeezed when he wanted to. She confessed this the day she gave up the baby, admitting that she seduced Larsen and allowed herself to get pregnant to tie her irrefutably to him. He used her on all sorts of cases, including the K Street Klub, which was a convenient way for him to get all the reward with none of the risk. If ever she made a mistake, he could cut her loose. Who was going to believe she was working in an undercover capacity for him?

"You pimped her out," I said, thinking back to how I collated Ally's confession with Craig's comments about her mixing with the wrong people. "You set her up with drug dealers, burglars, all kinds of scum."

"She's not far off that kind herself," he reflected.

"But not stupid, huh?" I shot back. "She worked her way in with me, saw how life could be a little better, and started giving you the brush off."

This he took in silence, which indicated I had it exactly right.

"You increased the pain factor until she broke and dished on the poker games, Sergei, and the details you needed to outshine the detectives. Maybe you'd like to grow up and be a detective yourself some day."

Losing patience but wanting to hear it all, he shifted on his feet.

"That wasn't enough. You had to stick your own finger in the pot, take a taste of that body of hers. She offered her ass up to you instead of the drug dealers. Yeah, she did kinky shit with them but kept herself clean just the way you demanded. When she resisted, you worked her kidneys over just to let her know who's the big boss."

"The only one who's going to get a work over is you," he said. "You'll do fifteen to twenty for murder one in Graterford."

"I'll go just as soon as you take the paternity test," I informed him. "Ally trapped you like a love-struck high school prom king."

"You're on the wrong end of this trade and you know it," he threatened, taking hold of my shirt in preparation to beat me senseless.

Snyder and his partner rushed in to save the day. Each taking a side, they dragged me out of range.

"You want to put him in the tank?" Snyder asked.

"He'll get his," Larsen said. "Let's go."

■ ■ ■

I got mine alright. I got two weeks of peace and quiet.

Ally came home from the hospital. She convalesced in my apartment, attended counseling sessions, and cooked me numerous good meals by applying skills learned at Lizzie's elbow. When she wanted to cry about the baby, I let her do it. When she told me she thought it was the best choice, I agreed. And when she asked me to take her to the movies, I did that, too. People saw us coming and going. Surely they were guessing: Was it really Tom's baby? Are they going to get married? Do you think he killed that guy over at Dooling's? These questions hung in the air behind shifting eyes and under soggy coasters.

For her part, Ally never raised the subject of Sergeant Larsen again. What happened wasn't her fault. She was caught in the crossfire, collateral damage in a war with no sides. She made the best of a bad situation by delivering the baby. If Larsen ever pushed too hard, she could pull that card to trump any he might be holding, which were very few since it was Craig who dialed 911 from a Caster Avenue payphone on Seigei's final night.

Still, just as the cop predicted, the honeymoon ended. Sergei's boss showed up, and he wasn't alone.

32

TWO GUYS ENTERED THE BAR on Monday afternoon. Both of them were thin-lipped, broad-shouldered, and lily-white. One look from Stacy and I knew this pair came from the wrong side of the Volga River. I'd rehearsed my lines and wasted no time delivering them. The only surprise was that the man who thought he was in charge spoke English better than me.

"Two Yuengling Lagers, please," he said.

I tapped the beers and carried them to their table in the dining room.

"Have a seat, Tom," he continued. "I'd like to speak with you for a few minutes."

Like so many times before, I seated myself in the company of a scumbag disguised as a polite gentleman. As refined as his speech was, I might have taken him for an English professor.

"My name is Abelev," he informed me. "My associate is Mr. Komar."

Associate Komar put out his hand. I shook it to show him I wasn't afraid to get mine dirty.

"You remember Mr. Marinin, of course," Abelev went on.

Confused, I said, "Other than Gary Kasparov, I know no other Russian surnames."

"Sergei Marinin, the man who loaned you money."

"I knew Sergei," I said leveling my gaze.

"I assume what happened was a matter of honor between the two of you regarding your father," Abelev went on.

Not hesitating one heartbeat, I said, "I haven't seen my father in months."

"Exactly," my guest said and sipped his beer.

We waited for the second act to begin. Being the star of this show I should have gone first, but I let Abelev take the lead.

"Sergei had what you would call disciplinary issues. He was more aggressive in certain areas than say, Komar here."

"Your men are your problem," I said.

"Please, I'm not going to hold what you did against you," Abelev said, adding, "There is a lesson here for all of us."

"I must have missed the lesson, and for that matter, what I have to do with it."

His patience chafed, Abelev, tapped the table with his fingers. "Sergei spoke of your achievements here, how you turned this place into a fine business. Only a clever, hardworking, and ambitious young man would be capable of accomplishing that in a short period of time. Such a young man would be the only one capable of outwitting Sergei, who should have known better than to turn his back after what he did."

He was the second person to accuse me of murder, but the first one to give me a solid hint that Sergei had made my father disappear, not that I had any doubt.

"He got his fifty grand with interest. He should have taken my father's word about the fourteen hundred." It was the closest I was going to get to a confession.

"You show a good mind for these things," Abelev remarked. "We all bear some responsibility when things get out of hand. I chastised Sergei for his error because, as you say, it should have been worked out another way."

He was right. Just as Sergei could have let my father slide, I could have paid the fourteen hundred without a squawk. At the time, I was making more than that on the slowest nights. However, I stood on principle with Sergei, and for that matter, with myself. Did I feel guilty? No, I didn't. My father didn't deserve to die, but even if he'd lived, nothing would have changed. As for taking out Sergei, he drew first blood. I was only defending myself.

Which left me with Abelev and Komar.

"I'm not going to hold this against you," Abelev reminded me one more time. "We can both call it a lesson learned and move on. No one shows weakness. No one is dishonored. We can move forward with a clear understanding and better communication."

Such a generous offer would have been hard to refuse had that been all there was. Of course there was part two, and Abelev wasted no time letting me know how things were going to work for the foreseeable future.

"Komar replaces Sergei. He will look after my interests here, in a much more pleasant way, I might add. There's no need to live in the past, acting like hoodlums. All your activities continue as before. I believe this neighborhood is due for a transformation like the ones to the south. Who knows? You and I could work together on some new projects."

I appreciated his assessment of my business acumen. Just the same, I wasn't working for him or anyone else. The bar was mine, free and clear. I had fifty grand in bloodstained cash that I was going to plunk down for my final two years of undergraduate study.

My application to the University of Pennsylvania was in the works courtesy of Mr. Kern. He arrived as a messenger of peace, sent by Sergeant Larsen. Kern's olive branch underlined a spot at that Ivy League institution if only I took the time to fill out the paperwork and keep Ally as my silent ward. Cool heads needed to prevail, Mr. Kern noted. I couldn't have agreed more.

However, the matter of Mr. Abelev stood before me. He made his case without considering that Bonk's Bar would be my business with no partners, related or otherwise. I spoke respectfully, with no sarcasm and without raising my voice.

"Mr. Abelev, this is a barroom with a stage for live music. I have a liquor license, a cabaret permit, and a certificate of occupancy. My activities here fall within the bounds of the law, and the only taxes I'm paying are those due to the City of Philadelphia, the State of Pennsylvania, and the United States Government."

"Why would you give up the opportunity to make so much more?" he countered graciously.

"Because there's more to it than that, and you know it," I replied. "You're welcome to come here for a drink or to listen to the music, but don't stick your hand in my cookie jar."

Komar rolled his shoulders. No doubt he awaited his cue

to behave in a less gentlemanly fashion. I preempted him. "I don't care if Komar puts a gun to my head," I said calmly. "He might as well do it right now and pull the trigger, too, because I'm not paying you a nickel."

He saw that I was serious and took a few moments to weigh my position. He said, "That's very short-sighted."

"On the contrary," I snapped. At that point, I stood up to let him know that, as well-behaved as he was, he was no longer welcome.

Getting to his feet, he said, "Okay, Tom. Let me take a few days to think about what you've said. You'll have my answer soon."

To Komar's credit, he gave me no dirty looks, no wry smiles, nor obscene hand gestures. He was a well-trained soldier. I, on the other hand, was a guerilla fighter prepared to use whatever tactics achieved victory.

They had no idea what they were getting into.

Saturday night featured a band named Canadian Invasion. They brought a herd of groupies with them, all of whom stayed late for The Executives. None of the ladies caught my eye and not for lack of trying. My mind was on Ally. No one asked her what happened to the baby. I told the crew about her decision. How they felt about it went unexpressed. She was living with the boss and his reputation had changed. He was no longer a frazzled social climber. He was a comfortable dude, enjoying his current position on the ladder to success. No one wanted to offend him, especially since the rumor was that he had something to do with that tire falling on a guy who had given him a hard time.

Ally and I turned in at the same time but slept in separate

beds, in different rooms. So it was that I awoke with Larry on my chest. He was pawing my face and whining about something. Sliding him to the side I immediately recognized the smell of smoke.

Donning my pants a moment later, I rushed across the apartment. My bare feet felt a floor warmer than it should have been. I opened the door leading down to the bar only to be met by a plume of smoke and sparks.

"Ally!" I hollered on the way down the hall.

My presence of mind amazed me. I shook her awake, told her to get dressed, and added that the building was on fire. She took a second to process that before bolting past me to her closet. I remembered a time when the Philadelphia Fire Department paid a visit to my elementary school. They demonstrated how to escape a burning building by covering your head with a wet towel and crawling along the floor.

Since Larry was now in a full panic, I grabbed him by the scruff, ignored his claws on my arm, and stuffed him in my wet towel. Ally darted around the living room, alternately picking things up and then dropping them. Her purse hung over a kitchen chair. I threw it at her and headed for the door.

Then I remembered the fifty grand in the new crock-pot I'd bought.

33

THE PHILADELPHIA FIRE DEPARTMENT did the best they could. Someone mashed the threads on the two nearest fire hydrants, which meant the hoses wouldn't connect properly. The firemen were forced to set up a relay from several blocks away. By then, the building was fully engulfed. The brick walls soon buckled under the pressure of three separate nozzles. Minutes later, my home and business collapsed into the basement.

None of us felt brave enough to confront Diane's ghost in her row home, so we took up residence in a motel not far from the airport. I paid the extra ten dollars a night to have Larry there. I spent more money buying a week's worth of clothes, take-out food, and a new litter box.

I assisted the Fire Marshall with his investigation by answering every question, some truthfully, some not. Did I have known enemies? No. Was the competition angry at my success?

Maybe. Did I smoke in bed? No. Did I burn candles or incense? Not on a dare. What about the chick shacking up with me? Cleaner than me, no bad habits, a great cook. See any kids messing with the hydrants? No. Any new insurance policies? Yeah, about a year and a half old. Did I need money? Not one red cent.

The insurance company sent their own person who left no smoldering remains unturned. His outfit was on the hook for three hundred and fifty thousand dollars. This guy poked, sampled, tested, and took more notes than a class full of pre-med students. All involved knew this fire was no accident given the way the building went up. Proving arson was another matter. The minor wounds I suffered in the escape gave the investigator pause. No doubt he was wondering if it was a kooky suicide pyre or fraud gone haywire.

Had he asked along those lines he would have discovered that I had more to live for than Lottery Joe with his penthouse in the sky and his BMW in the basement garage. Of many other things, I was bound for the University of Pennsylvania. Dreams sometimes came true.

For a price.

At last the insurance guy gave me the okay to put my own nose in the pile. I picked my way through the debris, stumbling around busted wood, broken glass, and soggy memories. Not one charred key from my piano stuck out of the heap. Amazingly, my grandfather's cash register sat upright amidst a jumble of whiskey bottles. It opened at the push of the NO SALE button. My brother's picture was in there, not one speck of soot on it. I put it in my pocket and searched no further for his scattered ashes.

Greg Dooling invited me into his office. Like everything

else in the building, it reeked of fresh rubber.

"What'd the fire department say?" he asked.

"They're not sure," I answered, "but lots of old wood, flammable liquor, and vandalized hydrants were contributing factors."

He tilted his head hard to the right. "Nothing to do with what happened out there in the shop?"

"I have no idea," I said, knowing full well Abelev had issued a decree for my place to be leveled. What I found amusing was that this otherwise intelligent Cossack believed destroying a perfectly sound building and endangering the life of the owner was a path to victory. If he found a scorched hole in the ground a prize worth winning then I could only marvel at his ignorance. That hole would yield nothing of mine.

"Do you want to buy the land or not?" I asked Greg.

"No," he replied, "but McNally says that's a busy corner." This was a proven fact.

"He's on his way," Greg was saying, "He wants to talk to you about it. And there's a package here for you."

At first, I thought he was talking about the weekly envelope we exchanged with the parking money. Instead, he pointed to a tall, flat box leaning against the wall. The shipping label read, "JOHN BONK. BONK'S BAR."

"UPS couldn't deliver to your place this morning, so they left it here."

The box contained a bronze plaque. On it was an image of my brother, a version of his boot-camp graduation photo. Beneath his name was the year of his birth and death. Taped to the back was an invoice: $1,400. PAID IN FULL.

■ ■ ■

McNally showed up, shaking his head at how his good work had been wasted. We used Greg's office to make the deal. He wanted more than the real estate, which he rightly figured was the least of the business.

"I need the recipe for the crabs and the bar's name, too."

"You want to call it Bonk's Bar again?" I asked.

"People know your joint, Tom. Without the name, it's just another bar."

I couldn't help but grin at his affirmation of my efforts. "Okay," I said, "with one condition."

"Name it."

"You put that plaque on the wall, a memorial to my brother so people will know who he was and where he was from."

He stuck out his hand. It was a deal.

I may have sold the bar, but I hadn't abandoned my brother. I let him rest in peace, his ashes mixed with the bar that was supposed to be his. Any literate soul would know that the neighborhood begat a noble son, one who stood his ground so that they could bitch and moan about minor injustices.

On the way to the Cadillac, I ran into Sergeant Larsen. He got out of his cruiser and sidled up to my driver's door just as I pulled it closed.

"Now what?" he asked.

"I'm leaving," I said.

"Going where?"

I didn't tell him that I was bound for a rented house in a close suburb, from which I would drive back and forth to the University of Pennsylvania. I could have revealed that I was going with a nice girl, a spinster in the making who liked to cook, didn't mind cleaning, and tolerated pipe smoke. I might have added that the insurance company would probably send me a check for three hundred fifty grand to add to my blood-stained fifty. There was also the money due from McNally, a cat that liked tuna on Fridays, and a new piano in the works. These things I could have told him and had the satisfaction of watching him steam.

Instead, I heard myself say, "I never wanted to be a bartender."

AUTHOR'S NOTE

This story is fiction. Nonetheless, at the corner of Richmond and Tioga Streets in Philadelphia stands Bonk's Bar. There is a plaque on the wall memorializing John Bonk, Jr., who was killed when the Marine Barracks in Lebanon was destroyed by a terrorist attack in 1983.

ACKNOWLEDGMENTS

I would like to thank the early readers of this novel, those who helped make it a better story, including Diane, Tami, Linda, and Helen. My editors, Susan and April, know what they're doing and do it well. Everyone at Hawser, thank you. All my friends at P.J. Dooling Tire Co. deserve a story of their own, and I'm working on it. The entire Bonk family must be recognized for creating a Philadelphia institution and special mention should be made of Joe and Rich for maintaining the legacy. My parents took a chance bringing me into this world, and I'm grateful they did so I could have the opportunity to write. Of course, Heather is a constant source of guidance and support. Finally, Mr. Vernon Fletcher is not to be forgotten for his wary countenance.

Daniel Putkowski was born and raised in northeastern Pennsylvania. He is a graduate of New York University's Tisch School of the Arts and NYU's Stern School of Business. After nearly two decades of operating a marine business on the Philadelphia waterfront, he and his wife now divide their time between the city and the Dutch Caribbean isle of Aruba. In 2008, his first novel, *An Island Away*, became the #1 bestselling book in Aruba.

To learn more about the author, visit
danielputkowski.com

"As the story unfolds, Putkowski makes one thing clear ... he is a keen observer of the human condition." — ARUBA.COM

"Characters so finely drawn they leap off the page. A terrific read."
— PATTI WHEELER, WDXB 102.5 FM, BIRMINGHAM

"A no-holds-barred look at Aruba. A must-read." — LAGO-COLONY.COM

"Reveals aspects of island life that few visitors ever know."
— THE NEWS ARUBA SUNDAY EDITION

Paradise
but not for amateurs

In Aruba, far from the sparkling beaches and glamorous hotels, lies a waning refinery boomtown of barroom brothels, flexible morality, and one tourist trap known as Charlie's Bar. Luz, a young Colombian mother works as a prostitute to pay off her family's debt. She encounters Sam, an American expatriate looking to perpetuate his flamboyant youth. Together they find Captain Nathan Beck, washed ashore and barely alive after his tugboat sinks in a storm. For each of them, San Nicolaas provides hope amid desperation as they live dangerously in pursuit of their dreams. Through it all, Charlie's watchful eye sees the best and worst, knowing that on his desert island you have to improvise.

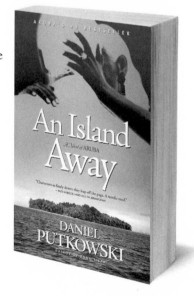

ARUBA'S
#1 BESTSELLER
Available wherever books are sold